Friends First

by

Angela Lam

Friends First

Cover Art by *Tina Lynn Stout*

The Wild Rose Press, Inc.
PO Box 708
Adams Basin, NY 14410-0708
Visit us at www.thewildrosepress.com

Publishing History
First Mainstream General Rose Edition, 2020
Print ISBN 978-1-5092-3080-8
Digital ISBN 978-1-5092-3081-5

Published in the United States of America

One glance at the overweight woman in her mid-thirties, and Greg shuddered. *Why do I get paired up with the walking body pillow and not the leggy blonde or the buxom brunette?*

Stepping closer, Maddy squinted. "Don't I know you?"

Frowning, Greg thought a moment. "Your voice sounds familiar." He rolled his shoulders at the possibility they'd met and had sex but he forgot. Was she one of those women he met online and chatted with before turning down an offer to meet in person?

She widened her gaze and pointed. "You're TheGeneral404Runner."

Oh, shit. She recognized him. Scanning the length of her shapeless body, he sighed. Was she the woman with several odd jobs who only dated on Wednesdays or the woman who couldn't leave the apartment until she potty trained her new puppy? He didn't recognize her face. Did she post an altered photograph online along with a misleading tagline of curvy woman seeking slender man?

He strained his memory for a few seconds, thinking over the many women he spoke to over the last couple of weeks before he finally placed her. "You're Maddy from PerfectFit.com." No wonder she ridiculed him for calling overweight women fatties.

She tilted back her head. "What a coincidence."

He cringed. Not only was he waking up early to drive across town to work out with a bunch of strangers, but he was paired up with Fatty Maddy, the gym owner's sister. Everywhere he turned, the walls collapsed around him. Why did he listen to that damn psychologist?

Dedication

For Renee Hoffman and Doug Greenberg

"I really wish people would see fat people as humans. Our bodies are vulnerable, our bodies are strong; they matter just like other bodies."

~*Roxane Gay*

****

"The brave men and women who serve their country and, as a result, live constantly with the war inside them exist in a world of chaos."

~*Robert Koger*

Chapter 1

"All I want to do is drink alcohol and eat." Maddy gripped the pen tighter as she wrote in her diary, unleashing the pent-up frustrations she wished she could confide in a friend. *"I've gained even more weight since the engagement, and Darren wants to know what's wrong. He calls me Porky. When I told Jane, she said he was only teasing, but when I told Peter, he said I'd better lose the weight quickly and for good. No yo-yoing. Peter is right because the night before Darren left for his latest business trip he said if I gain any more weight then he won't find me attractive, and the wedding will be off. I've always wanted to get married, so I don't understand why I can't lose the weight."*

Maddy broke off writing, grabbed a bottle of beer, and guzzled without tasting the bittersweet hops. She plunked the bottle against the kitchen table of the Emory Point luxury apartment in Atlanta, Georgia, she shared with Darren who would be returning home in two days, three hours, and forty-seven minutes. Early afternoon spring sunlight filtered through the white lace curtains but the powerful brightness could not expunge the darkness within her.

In the background, an infomercial played in the living room. The soothing sounds of a man and a woman convincing viewers to purchase a weight loss supplement lulled Maddy into the illusion of being in a house full of people. Maddy hated being alone, even for a few moments, ever since she was six years old and woke up from an after-dinner nap all alone in a dark house while her parents and siblings shopped at a last-minute sale. Sometimes, she didn't understand why she ended up with Darren, who often traveled two weeks out of every month for his sales job.

Wiping her mouth with the back of her hand, she picked up her pen and wrote. *"I haven't had sex in three weeks. Maybe he doesn't find me attractive anymore since I haven't lost weight."* She took another swallow of beer and continued writing. *"If only I could stop drinking maybe I could stop eating and then maybe I could lose weight."* Setting down her pen, she grabbed a handful of salty potato chips and shoved them into her mouth. The crispy crunch grinding between her teeth overpowered the nagging thoughts she just confessed in her diary. Ignoring the pang of guilt squeezing her chest, she walked across the tile floor, opened the refrigerator, popped off the top of another bottle of beer, and took a long swig.

A catchy tune played on her cell phone.

She wiped her hands on her jeans and punched accept. "Hello?"

"It's me," Darren said. "I'm at the airport. My last sales calls were canceled. I'm coming home."

Gasping, she swiveled. Chips and beer littered the kitchen table. A pen nestled between the pages of an unfinished diary entry. Thundering heartbeats galloped in her chest. How much time did she have to clean? "How soon is your flight?"

"I thought you'd be more excited than you sound."

"I am." She groaned. "I'm just tired." *Of being alone.*

"What have you been doing all weekend?"

She gripped the phone tighter. Heat flamed her face. *Oh, I'm so ashamed. I can't tell him the truth: drinking beer, eating junk food, and writing complaints in my diary.* She shifted from foot to foot. *Hurry. Think of something else to say.* She forced a smile. "I've been catching up with my sister."

"Did you shop for a wedding dress?"

"I never shop with Jane." Anger stiffened her back. Although she loved her little sister, she also hated her for being thin and wealthy. Whenever she stood beside Jane, frumpiness and poverty invaded her. "I can't afford the shops in Buckhead."

"You only buy a wedding dress once."

She laughed. How could he promise to be married forever when he threatened to cancel the wedding if she became too fat? Wasn't love supposed to be unconditional?

"Well, I've got to go." He heaved a sigh. "They're boarding the plane. See you in three hours. Maybe we can go for a walk. Okay, Porky?"

Irritation bristled across her shoulders. She hated that nickname, but she didn't have the courage to tell him. "Sure." She took another sip of bitter beer and slumped against the wall. "Love you."

"Love you more."

After the call ended, she finished her second beer and seized her diary off the kitchen table. She curled into the sofa and scribbled. *I hate him. I love him. I hate him. I love him.* Tears stung her eyes. With a heaving chest, she slammed shut the diary, stalked into the kitchen, and poured herself a shot of whiskey. She didn't want to clean the apartment. Darren lived meticulously with all the linens stacked by size and color in the hall closet. She preferred to clean by necessity, tossing her clothes on the floor until laundry day.

Maybe if I buy a wedding dress, he'll forgive the mess. Taking her laptop into the living room, she turned off the TV and browsed for wedding dresses online. She wanted something cheap and classy she could fold into a suitcase for the destination wedding Darren planned in Kauai in September. The ceremony was a vacation for her and her family, but a coming-home party for him and his family since he grew up in Hanalei Bay.

Maddy had met Darren at PerfectFit.com, an online dating site where she worked as a tech support manager. Darren was a sales representative at a pharmaceutical company who traveled around the country negotiating advertising space in both print and online media. His account with PerfectFit.com was one of the company's main sources of revenue on the free version of the website with a steady stream of pop-up ads about male enhancement drugs. Maddy preferred premium sites focused not on advertisement revenue but customer satisfaction. For that reason alone, she preferred to pay a monthly fee to suspend all advertisements.

But she refused to spend over one hundred dollars on a wedding dress. She could afford to spend more.

After all, the wedding cost only their round-trip plane tickets. Her brother, Peter, her sister, Jane, and Jane's family, would pay for their own airfare and hotel accommodations.

Since both of her parents died fifteen years ago, she didn't have to worry about shopping for a mother of the bride dress or renting a tuxedo for her father. Even the honeymoon was free since they would be staying at a vacation rental condo owned by Darren's cousin at Islander on the Beach in Kapaa. The actual wedding ceremony would be held in Darren's parents' backyard followed by a potluck. Money aside, she flinched at the concept of spending thousands of dollars on a dress she would only wear once.

Forever-frugal Maddy ended up on Today's Best Dresses, a website full of bridal gowns for one hundred dollars or less. She clicked on picture after picture of gowns made of ivory lace, white tulle, or creamy gossamer. Long dresses, short dresses, traditional dresses, and modern dresses filled the screen. As she gazed with envy at the happy-looking women beside their grooms, nervousness filled her. Was she content? Would she make a good wife? Did she have the stamina to withstand the day-to-day monotony of marriage? Could she get past the wedding without feeling like she was a drunk, horny, overweight mess?

As she clicked through the screens full of dresses, she blinked against the dizzying lightheadedness from drinking too much booze. Standing, she wobbled into the kitchen for a glass of water. The smell of sour beer and greasy chips mingled with the stale coffee grounds under the kitchen sink. She winced, knowing she should dump the trash into the compactor and run the dishwasher. She ran a hand over the counter. Something sticky rubbed against the pads of her fingers. Probably sauce from last night's barbecue rib take-out she purchased on the way home from watching a romantic movie.

After she turned on the faucet, she wetted a sponge with warm water and a dab of liquid soap. As she scrubbed the spill, memories of the movie's happily-ever-after ending floated through her mind. Grimacing, she dried the counter with a dish towel. *Why isn't my life perfect?*

Returning to the living room, she sank against the soft sofa cushions and placed the laptop on her thighs. She clicked through more pictures.

An image of a couple running hand in hand on the beach caught her attention. The bride wore a flowing white gown with a plunging neckline and a long slit above the knees.

Ah, yes, she found what she wanted—a dress symbolizing carefree romance. She didn't care Darren preferred she wear a more modest gown. She didn't care her body was shorter and boxier than the woman modeling the dress. She cared only how the image of the dress made her feel: beautiful, desirable, and loved. In her drunken haze, she fumbled in her purse for her wallet. Skimming over the fine print on the website, she selected a size, clicked buy, typed her credit card information and mailing address into the appropriate tabs, and waited for an order confirmation to be sent to her email address.

A rush of relief flooded through her body. She

poured another shot of whiskey to celebrate. The liquid burned her throat. She smacked her lips and whistled. Whoo-hoo. She was done shopping for her wedding dress. Done. No worries about Jane critiquing every style or the hassle of dressing and undressing in a cramped stall under fluorescent lighting or parading up and down the runway of the store for other customers to see. She purchased her dress online. The pain and worry were over.

Minutes later, a pounding headache knocked against her temples. Returning to the kitchen, she gulped two aspirin to stifle a hangover. Oh, why did she eat and drink so much? Yawning, she checked the time on the stove's clock. Two-thirty. She grabbed the diary off the kitchen table and wandered into the bedroom. After hiding the sacred book underneath a pile of unused lingerie in the top drawer of the night stand, she stalked into the living room and surveyed the pile of fast food wrappers on the coffee table. She sighed.

Should I take a half hour nap before cleaning or clean before taking a half hour nap? She wished she could discuss the options with someone. *I can't talk to my brother. He lives alone without a care in the world. I can't talk to my sister. She has a housekeeper who cleans and a nanny who cares for her children. She can nap whenever she pleases. Writing in my diary is one-sided. No perspective is here except my own.* She sank into the sofa cushions and buried her head into her arms. *I need a friend who understands me.*

****

In his dream, Captain Gregory Power wore night-vision goggles in the pre-dawn desert. Crawling on his hands and knees over dunes, he inched toward the Iraqi trenches to confirm the enemy soldiers were buried alive by the allied tanks. An explosion erupted in the dream, coinciding with the triggering sound of the answering machine, and he woke, propelled back into the present.

Beep-beep-beep.

Floundering in the tangled sheets of the queen-sized bed in his studio apartment in downtown Atlanta, he listened to the rapid gunfire in his chest. A trickle of sweat dripped from his forehead. Clutching his head with his hands, he considered dropping and crawling across the room to crush the answering machine with his bare hands.

One thousand one, he breathed in. *One thousand two*, he breathed out.

Blinking, he adjusted his vision to the harsh afternoon sunlight cutting through the dual pane window. Lowering his arms, he stared at his shaking hands against the soft gray sheets soaked with sweat. He was not lying in dry, coarse desert sand but against a damp satin sheet. No gritty granules seeped beneath his uniform and rubbed against his skin. Only silky softness slipped against his body.

He focused on the calendar of peach trees on the refrigerator across the room. *I'm in Atlanta, Georgia. Not Iraq. Not Saudi Arabia. Not anywhere in the Middle East.*

Beep-beep-beep.

Scrambling, he sat and swung his hips toward the side of the bed. His right foot landed on the cool hardwood floor while the residual limb of his left leg hugged the edge of the mattress. With both hands, he rubbed the sweat off his face and swept his damp hair off his forehead. As he sucked in a deep breath, desperate to feel normal, he concentrated on the air entering and leaving his lungs.

Across the room, the red light blinked on the answering machine. He groaned. The caller could only be one of three people: his mother in Long Island, his fiancée in New York, or a telemarketer. The third option he welcomed more than the first two. He didn't want to talk to his mother who worried about everything—from whether or not he ate enough protein to whether or not he would return to New York in time for his own wedding in September. He also didn't want to talk to his fiancée, Amy, who offered only sweet platitudes and constant prayers for his well-being, which always left him feeling a deep stab of guilt for his need for distance.

Maybe I'll go for a run.

He grabbed his phone off the night table and glanced at the time and temperature—two-thirty in the afternoon and sixty degrees Fahrenheit. Perfect running conditions. He strapped a running blade onto his residual limb and shoved his right foot into a trail shoe. Grabbing his keys off the kitchen counter, he headed for the door, leaving the blinking red light of the answering machine untouched.

After driving through the sparse Sunday afternoon traffic to Lullwater Preserve, he parked in the nearly vacant lot and laid his hands against the warm hood of his car to stretch out his hamstrings. He rocked back and forth on his heel, feeling the tug in his right

Achilles. Standing, he grabbed for his right foot with his left hand and tugged toward his hips until his quadriceps lengthened. After he released his leg, he swung his arms back and forth across his chest, breathing in the crisp, cool spring air. Overhead, the sky was blue with little cloud cover. Before him, the entrance to the preserve beckoned with lush green leaves and branches dotted with clusters of white, pink, and lavender blossoms.

Greg jogged along the dirt path next to a steep, wooded cliff that cradled the world in a warm pocket, keeping the air moist and fragrant with the scents of oak and magnolia. Sweat clung to his back. His breathing, deep and strong, matched the long, even strides of his legs. Keeping his balance along the uneven mulch was a skill he honed over years of physical therapy. As his foot and blade slapped against the dirt, one after the other, toward the historic Houston Mill House, the tightrope one-legged balance he struggled to master seemed effortless.

Bright laughter cascaded down the hill toward him, and he glanced up to witness a bride dancing with her groom on the terrace above the bridge. A pang of longing clutched his chest, and his breath caught in his throat. *Amy.* He imagined her sitting alone in their apartment, wondering when he would visit.

Since his father's funeral two days before Thanksgiving, he had not returned to New York. He assumed burying his father would destroy the anger and bitterness he clung to since returning from the Gulf War, but the feelings manifested in night terrors. Each time he fell asleep, he returned to the battlefield. Each time he woke, dread pummeled him again. *I'm a failure. I should have never enlisted.* The thoughts, like cobwebs, blew away with his conviction. *I'm proud to have served my country.* The war inside waged, although the battle he fought ended decades ago.

Staring up at the dancing newlyweds, he felt a fresh wave of guilt wash over him. *I should close my account on PerfectFit.com. I should stop seeing other women.*

Twenty years ago, he discontinued using drugs. Ten years ago, he quit drinking alcohol. Now, he needed to end the habit of abusing sex. Most of the time, he never acted on his thoughts, but since his father's death, the feelings he kept locked inside rushed out in a flood of lust he could not always contain. He succumbed to the comforting numbness of dating women who didn't know about his past and who wouldn't be part of his future.

He stared at the dancing couple, feeling the warm sun against his back.

I need to marry Amy.

Twice, they planned a wedding. Both times, he failed to say, "I do."

The first time, after his final surgery for his leg, they stood on a beach in Nantucket. He held Amy's hand. Hearing the reverend speak the vows, Greg couldn't avoid a gust of wind blowing sand in his eyes. He plunged from the wedding into the war zone. Terror seized his throat. He released Amy's hand and rubbed his eyes. The pain stung worse, and his eyes watered. "I can't," he said, when he heard the question if he would take Amy to be his lawfully wedded wife.

Family and friends gasped, and Amy burst into tears.

They broke up for two years.

Fourteen years later, they planned to get married again. But the indoor wedding happened on the hottest day of the year, and the church suffocated with heat as stifling as an oven. Sweat beaded against his palms, triggering the memory of blood on his hands as he crawled over a dead man's body.

"With this ring, I thee wed," Amy said, reaching for his hand.

Raw with panic, he tucked his arm close to his body and clenched his fingers into a fist.

For the second time, they broke up.

A week later, he flew to New Orleans for a temporary assignment as a paralegal contract worker for FEMA after Hurricane Katrina while Amy stayed in New York to work as a curator for a gallery. Eventually, after a year of phone calls, the tug of familiarity forced a reunion. Two years later, they bought an apartment in Manhattan. Six months after living together, he took another temporary assignment in Colorado. He needed his space almost as much as he needed Amy. The delicate dance between staying in Manhattan and running away to another state continued year after year after year.

When his father died, Greg believed he could finally marry Amy. They planned a fall wedding after his temporary assignment in Georgia ended. He hoped the cooler weather would not trigger a panic attack.

Alone, at night, and afraid of the nightmares that terrorized his sleep, he browsed the online profiles of single, attractive women. Sometimes, he winked at them. Other times, he asked them on a date. The majority of the time, he just daydreamed. The local dating website, PerfectFit.com, promised his romantic dreams would come true. But the site knew nothing of his dreams for a restful night's sleep or his prior commitment to Amy.

Dappled sunlight and loving laughter from the dancing newlyweds failed to scatter the shadows of depression haunting him. *I need help. I wish I had a friend to confide in who could offer a different perspective, someone close enough to care but far enough to respect my need for distance.* He glanced away from the noise. Deep inside him, dark clouds of hopelessness loomed. If he left now, he might outrun despair.

Chapter 2

"Wake up, Maddy. Wake up." Darren gently shook her shoulder.

Guilt knotted in Maddy's chest. She rolled onto her back from where she slept on the sofa, placed her arm over her forehead, and squinted. Memories surfaced like flotsam and jetsam. She decided to clean first then nap. She gathered the empty beer bottles into a cardboard box, bagged up the trash, started the dishwasher, ran the vacuum, and dusted the furniture before collapsing on the sofa.

Darren hovered, rattling the cardboard box full of empty beer bottles. "Were you drinking during the day?"

She shuddered from his glowering onyx eyes and deep frown creasing his wide brown face. Nudging her fatigued body into a sitting position, she bowed her head with her long hair shielding her face. Shame heated her cheeks. *Oh, why didn't I trek downstairs to dispose of the recycling and trash before vacuuming and dusting?*

"I take your silence as a yes." He handed her a water bottle before leaving. "Sober up. We're going for a walk."

Wincing from a dull throbbing headache, she unscrewed the water bottle and took a healthy sip. *I don't want to walk, but I don't want to fight either. Two years ago when I moved in we were happy. What happened?* Fogginess clouded her thoughts. Aches tightened her neck and lower back from falling asleep on the uncomfortable leather sofa. How could she be thirty-five and feel this bad? Between a poor diet and no exercise, she felt like she was fifty.

Her brother, on the other hand, owned a gym and led a healthy lifestyle. He was almost forty, but he could thrust a monster tire up a hill. Her thirty-three-year-old sister maintained her high school weight and figure, even after having two children. She also had enough energy to conquer the squirrely activeness of a four-year-old daughter and a three-year-old son.

If Maddy ate right and exercised, would she move around with energy and grace?

"Ready?" At six feet, Darren filled the doorway, blocking out the light from the setting sun. He was thirty-eight years old, of Samoan descent, with large bones made wider from the body-building routine he honed to a thirty-minute workout while on the road.

When they met, Maddy was attracted to Darren's logical, practical mind. He was a failed screenwriter who moved to Georgia to escape Los Angeles and returned to school to earn his master's degree in business. "Pivot toward success" was his motto, and within three years, he turned his failed career into a lucrative sales position at one of the world's largest pharmaceutical companies. Maddy presumed being with Darren would inspire her self-improvement, but their relationship only enhanced her low-grade depression and steady stream of self-reflective criticism ingrained from childhood teasing.

Darren tossed Maddy a jacket. Together, they strode out of their fourth floor apartment. As soon as they stepped outside the building, a blanket of cool spring air descended on their shoulders. The silence of early evening echoed in the parking lot.

Shoving her hands into her pockets, she kept up with his long stride but soon fell two steps behind.

Turning, he cupped his hands around his mouth. "Keep up, Porky!"

Grumbling, she picked up her pace.

At the park, they sat on a bench. The last rays of the sun set behind a bank of magnolia trees. The lamps along the boulevard lit up like birthday candles.

He groped for her hand.

Startled by the moment of tenderness, she leaned against his shoulder. "I'm sorry for not cleaning." She swallowed the pain in the back of her throat. "I'm sorry for drinking during the day and eating nothing but junk food while you're away."

"Why do you do it if you know it's wrong?" He tugged her closer, touching his head against hers.

"Because I'm lonely and I miss you." Grumbling anger percolated in her stomach. *I need some M & M's.* At work, she kept a glass bowl full of the sugar-coated chocolate candies on her desk. She would scoop out as many as she needed to quell any and all emotions. She didn't like to feel and didn't trust others to listen to her vent her frustrations.

He squeezed her hand once before letting go. "You should stay with your sister while I'm away."

She gritted her teeth. "I don't like my sister. She's

a spoiled, rich, and entitled woman who doesn't care for her kids."

He scooted away and raised his eyebrows. "She's family."

Shaking her head, she shifted to the far end of the bench. *He doesn't understand. If she wasn't family, I would never talk to her.*

"Listen." He narrowed his gaze. "I can't leave for work and come home to find you passed out on the sofa after binge eating and drinking on a Sunday afternoon. What am I supposed to do? Dance around and be happy?"

Heat prickled her face. Later, in her diary, she would write, *"I feel like a two-year-old when he talks to me."* Suppressing the unspoken words, she aligned her thoughts with his, hoping for the semblance of agreement. "I guess not."

Nudging closer, he wrapped an arm around her shoulders. "So, besides drinking yourself into oblivion, what else did you do after we ended our phone call?"

Tensing, she cringed like she was on trial, and he was the judge and the jury. Fishing her phone out of her pocket, she scrolled through a gallery of pictures. "I bought a wedding dress." She smiled and handed him the phone.

He stared at the picture of a happily married couple running on the beach and frowned. "Where did you find this dress?"

"Online." She squared her shoulders. "I bought the wedding gown for one hundred dollars."

His frown deepened. "The dress won't fit." Shaking his head, he offered the phone.

Embarrassment rushed to her face. Seizing the phone, she shoved it into her pocket. "If the dress doesn't fit, I can return it for a larger size."

He shook his head. "If it doesn't fit, you return the dress and go shopping with Jane."

Another tsunami of anger crashed through her. She clenched her fists. "I guarantee she will pick out something beyond our budget."

He lifted his eyebrows. "Do you care only about how cheap something is?"

"Not cheap. Frugal." After her parents died when she was twenty, she feared she might have to quit school and work if she spent more than what Peter budgeted. She raised her chin. "Don't you want a woman who lives within her means?"

Chuckling, he clasped his hands between his knees and wagged his head from side to side. "Maddy, Maddy, Maddy," he whispered. "What will I do with you?"

His lighthearted laughter eased the tension in her shoulders. Anger slowly dissipated from her chest, and a quick smile spread across her face. She scooted closer. "Make love to me," she whispered.

Scooting away, he pointed to their surroundings. "Not here."

"Of course, not here." A part of her hoped he would at least lean over and kiss her lips. Every nerve in her body tingled. "Later, at home."

He stared a moment longer. "Maybe after we clean the apartment."

Disappointment deflated her smile. "I *already* cleaned." Why did he have to go over her work, polishing and scrubbing until the house gleamed with perfection? By the time he finished, he would be too exhausted to even cuddle, and she would fall asleep feeling all alone. She would pull out her diary, festering with resentment, and unleash all the pent-up frustrations in a jagged scrawl in an endless effort to keep the peace.

****

When Greg returned home an hour later, he glowered at the winking red light on the answering machine. Reluctantly, he strode over and pushed the button. *Better to deal with the inevitable family conflicts than try to escape.* The tape rewound, and two messages played.

"Hi, it's your mother. I'm calling to see when you're returning to New York to visit. You don't want to leave your future wife alone too long. She's a looker. You don't want a looker to be looking. Call me."

He hardened his lips into a straight line. *Doesn't Mom know Amy would never cheat? She's perfect. I'm the complete mess.*

Beep.

"Hey, baby, it's Amy. Your mom keeps calling me and nagging me to come over for dinner, so that's where I'll be tonight. Please, call us there. We all love and miss you. Bye."

The beeping stopped.

He heaved a sigh. The clock on the stove read five-thirty. His mother served dinner at five, and Amy always left to go home at six-thirty. He would have to return the call soon.

First, he needed a shower. He hated the sticky feel

of sweat against his neck and the strong body odor emanating from his pores. In the oversized bathroom, he turned on the water. While the water heated, he gathered a set of clothes and placed them on the rack beside the toilet. Stalling, he unfastened his prosthetic, sat on the bench inside the shower, and raised his face to the pelting hot water. He hated his life. Nothing ever changed. Amy always waited patiently while his mother always nagged. He lathered soap over his body. Thoughts untangled in his mind. Never use the word "always" one of his many psychologists warned. Scrubbing until his skin felt raw, he winced. Do not use the word "never" either, another psychologist said. Extremes don't exist. He rinsed off and toweled dry. *My world is different. Everyone wants me to become a different person, and I only want someone to accept me as I am.*

After he dressed, he strode to the refrigerator for a bottle of water. Cool liquid swirled against his tongue. While standing over the sink, he peeled and ate a banana. Still hungry, he scooped a handful of raw walnuts from the glass jar on the counter and munched them before picking up the landline phone that came with the furnished apartment and dialing his mother's house.

On the third ring, his mother answered. "Finally, you called. I thought you were dead."

He chuckled, fighting the instinct to hang up the phone instead. "Not dead. Just asleep. I take naps on the weekend."

His mother clucked. "They make you work too hard at that law firm. You should come home and work for Steve."

He didn't want to work for his cousin, especially not in a criminal law firm. "I'm not an attorney, Ma. I review contracts and note the inconsistencies. I don't negotiate like Steve does."

"Why do you work so many hours?"

Why do I have to lie? He ran his fingers through his hair. *Why can't I tell her I'm not working? I'm hooking up with strangers I meet online or running so fast I hope to break the sound barrier and disappear.* He bit his lower lip and shook his head. *I can't tell the truth. What would my mother think? She'd tell Amy. I can't hurt Amy.* A knot in his stomach tightened. *Doesn't matter whether or not Amy knows the truth, I know. Good fiancés don't cheat. I wouldn't want her cheating.* "I agreed to those terms in my contract."

"When is that contract up?"

He stared at the calendar. "September."

"Before or after Labor Day?"

"Before, Mom."

"Why don't you visit? We miss you."

Striding to the window, he gazed at the Atlanta skyline, which wasn't as big and brilliant as New York. "I miss you, too."

"Here's Amy."

A moment later, Amy's bright laughter filtered through the line. "Hey, baby. How've you been this week?"

Grimacing, he fiddled with the blinds, closing and opening them as the last rays of the sun peered between the skyscrapers. "Just peachy."

She sighed. "That good, huh?"

Releasing the cord, he sank onto the edge of his mattress and stared at the pattern on the hardwood floor planks. "I'm getting night terrors again."

"Oh, baby."

Cringing, he closed his eyes. He hated when her voice softened with compassion. The tone sounded too much like pity, and he hated sympathy. "Don't worry. I have an appointment to see a psychologist specializing in post-traumatic stress disorder."

"Do you think seeing another psychologist will help?"

He viewed therapy a lot like the lottery—if he worked with enough professionals, the right one would cure him. He opened his eyes and shrugged. "Worth a try." Glancing at a framed photograph of them during happier times, he shifted the conversation. "What about you? How are things going?"

"Fine. I'm putting together an exhibit for the gallery. I think you would like this one. It's more expressive than Emotion One and Emotion Two."

Recalling the splotches of bright red and yellow paint on ten foot canvases hanging in the gallery where she worked, he laughed. He couldn't believe they both sold for five hundred thousand dollars each. "Are these different colors?"

"Even better. They're oval-shaped eggs made of saffron and dyed blue."

He nodded. "Blue saffron eggs." Were they the size of real eggs or were they oversized like *piñatas*?

"I like the artist, Robert McKenzie. I met him last week at his studio. The eggs are just the beginning of a wonderful collection he's creating based on a clash between American consumerism and Russian art. He's really quite brilliant. I can't believe I convinced him to show with us when he's had offers from MoMa and Henry, our biggest competitor."

The bright enthusiasm in her voice comforted him. "You sound happy."

"I *am* happy. McKenzie is so interesting. I can't wait for opening night. He'll dazzle everyone."

The last artist Amy adored was a Korean immigrant who worked with metal and wood. When the artist retired a few years ago, he gifted Amy with a life-size sculpture of a man and a woman chained to the Devil, which took up most of the living room of their apartment. He tensed his shoulders, sensing something slightly different about her excitement over McKenzie. "Maybe I should get some time off and visit."

"Oh, yes, please do." She sighed. "I can't wait for you to see our apartment. I hired someone to paint the walls."

A prickle of fear skipped across his scalp. "Why?"

"I want to celebrate the holidays in our new home."

Clutching the phone tighter, he remembered briefly discussing whether to sell the apartment and move to the suburbs after they were married, but he thought nothing had been decided. "What color?"

"Beige. The real estate agent said neutral colors sell best."

After standing, he paced. "I don't want to sell."

"How else can we afford to start a family?"

He frowned. "We're too old. I don't want to be seventy by the time my child graduates from high school."

"We can adopt a teenager." She choked on a sob. "If you didn't keep getting cold feet, we would be grandparents by now."

He threw up an arm and shook a fist. "I don't have cold feet. I have panic attacks. A huge difference exists between them."

A moment of silence echoed across the distance.

Rubbing his forehead, he closed his eyes. "I'm sorry." *One thousand one*. Breathe in. *One thousand two*. Breathe out. "I didn't mean to yell."

"You don't mean a lot of things, but you keep saying them anyway."

He flinched at the angry tone of her voice. "Like what?"

"You say you'll visit, and then you don't. You're all talk, and no action."

A muscle in his jaw twitched. *She doesn't understand. She didn't work in a battlefield. She didn't lose a leg. She didn't have to change her life. She's beautiful, whole, and happy—things I will never be again.* Heat stabbed behind his sore eyes. *I should have never returned the call. Let her and my mother worry. Let them believe I'm missing in action.* He squeezed the air out of his lungs. *Focus on the present moment. Don't dwell on the past.* He breathed in and counted. *One thousand eight*. "Why do you say things to push me away?" He broadened his stance. "Do you want me at the gallery opening or not?"

"Listen," Amy said. "It's getting late. I have to go. Talk to you later this week. Okay, baby?"

Baby. At least, she wasn't that angry. She called him by his pet name. "We can't avoid these issues forever."

"We won't. I promise. Good night, baby."

Her voice sounded a little too bright and a little too hopeful, neither of which mirrored his feelings. After the call ended, he strode to his desk and started his laptop. With trembling fingers, he logged into his PerfectFit.com account to see if anyone had winked. No luck. He slammed shut the lid. Rapping his fingers against the desk, he considered uploading another picture. Maybe one taken five years ago before gray hair covered his crown. Or he could change the text. Describe himself as a hero. Anything as a last-ditch effort to reclaim a bit of dignity before becoming a married man without the courage to tell his wife he didn't want her remodeling the apartment to sell without first consulting him.

Opening the lid, he logged again into the site and created a different persona—someone just like him, only better. But the changes in his profile wouldn't save. He banged a fist against the table, and the laptop shook. *One thousand one*. Breathe in. *One thousand two*. Breathe out. Maybe the universe intervened with the computer problems to remind him he should be grateful for the woman he had, not the woman he wanted. *Don't be ridiculous. I know enough about computers. This glitch is a programming problem, not divine intervention.* After clicking on the website's tech support link, he read the hours of availability between six a.m. and midnight Monday through Friday. Why not the weekend when everyone sought a date?

He clutched his hair with his fists and contemplated placing an ad on a national website which offered tech support twenty-four hours every day. By the end of the night, he might have a handful of winks, a couple of live chats, and maybe a date. A flicker of relief died with despondency. Someone he knew might also stumble upon his profile and alert Amy or his mother. A ripple of anxiety inched across his scalp. *I'll call tech support in the morning.* He powered off the machine. After removing the prosthetic, he lay on the cool mattress with his arms crossed over his chest. A restless twitch irritated his muscles, and he stared at the ceiling, wishing he was in the sensual comfort of a strange woman's arms. A feeling of emptiness radiated from the pit of his stomach. *Who am I fooling?*

Chapter 3

On Monday morning, Maddy sat in a maze of cubicles at PerfectFit.com, scrolling through her emails. She wanted to escape into other people's romantic problems and not deal with her own. As a supervisor in the technical support department, she managed a rotating cast of customer service representatives responsible for answering calls from clients on how to secure a date through maneuvering through the website. Sometimes, if a client became increasingly disgruntled or if a problem could not be fixed, the customer service representative transferred the call for Maddy to resolve.

While reading an email about a computer system update, she sipped a bittersweet mocha topped with foamy whipped cream and nibbled on a chocolate donut, brushing away the crumbs from the keyboard. Within minutes, a green light flashed on her work phone. She picked up the internal call. "Maddy, here."

"I have someone who wants to speak with a supervisor," Tina said.

Maddy lifted her eyebrows. Tina was a seasoned customer service representative who rarely passed her phone calls to management. Why did her voice sound so heavy? "Are you all right?"

"I'm just tired of the profile problem," she said. "I'm losing patience."

Maddy groaned. Ever since a software update to the website, only supervisors could edit and save public profile changes. The glitch resulted in an increase of customer service calls and unrelenting frustration among the staff. "Don't worry. I won't allow them to affect your reviews. Research and development own the problem, and not you." She bit into the sugary donut and chewed the flaky fried dough. Swallowing, she nodded. "Put the caller through."

A moment later, Tina transferred the caller.

A click sounded in her headset. "Hello, I'm Maddy, Tina's supervisor. How may I help you?"

"I can't update my profile," the caller said.

A woman's husky voice rasped over the line. Maddy opened an advanced checklist on her monitor and scrolled to the section on profile problems.

"I want to change the wording, not the picture," the woman said. "I have a great picture. I just need the words to match."

"What is your user name?" Maddy asked. She always began the conversation with the basics of identifying the person and the problem. The routine provided a sense of comfort in an otherwise tense situation. Plus, she liked to imagine the caller's physical appearance based on their login before accessing a photograph from the database. Sometimes her guess was right. Other times her intuition was wrong.

"Gaga Girl," the woman replied.

She's short, blonde, and a singer. Maddy typed the handle into the search tab and waited for the woman's profile to fill her screen. She flinched. *How could I be so off base?* Gaga Girl was a twenty-five-year-old graduate student at Emory University studying biomedical engineering. She was pretty with dark hair, creamy brown skin, and a bright smile that could light up a small room. The words beneath her photo read, "Looking for love in all the wrong places. I'm a single girl in my mid-twenties wanting to settle down. Are you strong, debonair, and handsome? Give me a call."

Maddy grimaced. Why did women write clichés and expect unique suitors? She poised her hands over the keyboard, ready to type. "What do you want your profile to say?"

"Hmm…I need something simple yet sophisticated to reel them in and leave them wanting more."

Maddy sighed. Why couldn't callers come up with their own words? The cheat sheet on her monitor only listed the steps to change and save text. Her job skills didn't include creative writer for hapless daters. "Do you have something written down?"

"Yeah, but I can't get the curser to replace what's already on the screen."

Highlighting the text, she hit the delete button, making the words disappear. "Programmers are working on fixing a bug in the system, so in the meantime I'll have to change the text. Just dictate what you want me to write."

"Hmmm…let me see. Where did my draft go? Oh, yes, I found what I wrote." She cleared her throat. "I want my title to read, 'Sweet and sassy' and the body to read, 'Just an ordinary girl looking for an extraordinary time. From Midtown movies to Buckhead shopping, I'm the girl for you.'"

Maddy typed the words into the box, scanning for

typos. "That's it?"

"Yeah, that's it."

Saving the text, she refreshed the screen. "How does that wording look?"

A moment of silence stretched between them.

Finally, Gaga Girl sighed. "Something's missing, isn't there?"

After scooping a handful of M & M's candy from the bowl, she popped three blue ones in her mouth and sucked the sweet candy coating until the gooey chocolate center oozed against her tongue. She reread the unimaginative text. How could she help this caller? Thinking, she sipped the lukewarm mocha. "Speak about yourself as if you were talking to a girlfriend."

"Why?"

"If I know a little bit about you, then I can jazz up your profile."

"Is this feature something y'all will bill me for at the end of the month?"

Maddy winced at the pitch of Gaga Girl's skeptical voice. "No, of course not." Every now and then, the thought of earning a bonus for every single hit flitted through her mind—kind of like the bonuses Darren made whenever someone clicked on his ads for male enhancement drugs. "I'm helping you get exactly what you want."

"Oh, all right." She sighed. "Now you're talking. After I graduate next June, I'll be researching full time at the university. I want a steady boyfriend I can take to my parents' house for dinner and my girlfriends' houses for lunch. The last boyfriend was good in bed, but he was not good with much else. He possessed class and style, but he couldn't hold a conversation. I'm not asking for someone as educated as I am, but his vocabulary needs to include something besides football. I'm an atheist, so I don't want any religious freaks. I dated a Southern Baptist once, and the relationship ended poorly when he took me to church and asked me to sing. He was white. I'm black. He just assumed I could sing and dance like Queen Latifah, but I can't carry a tune and I have two left feet." She chuckled.

"I hear you." Maddy smiled. "The world is full of people who make assumptions."

"Exactly," Gaga Girl said. "I'm full of contradictions. I can put together an outfit but not a meal. I can clean a house better than anyone, but I haven't a clue about home decorating. I can laugh at a joke, but I can't tell one. I'm book smart but street stupid. I'll be able to buy my own house someday, so I don't need a sugar daddy. I'm looking for a long term monogamous relationship that doesn't have to end in marriage. I'm not afraid of handling the tough stuff in life, but I don't want to be bogged down by troubles either."

As Maddy listened, she nodded. "Okay, I think I can come up with something." She erased the text and started typing. "Styling on the runway, hopeless on the dance floor—that's me. Talkative and reliable—that's you. Not looking for marriage, only monogamy. Sugar daddies don't apply. I'm educated and financially independent but hopelessly weak in the arms of a riveting conversation."

"Not bad," Gaga Girl said. "I think I'll give the new profile a try."

"Great." A swell of pride filled her. *Not bad for a rookie writer.* "I hope you get a lot of winks."

She laughed. "If I get a date, I'll call you. What's your direct line?"

Maddy grimaced. Company policy forbade employees to disclose their last names or their direct phone numbers. "Just email me." She rattled off her email address.

"You got it, girl."

After she hung up, Maddy removed her headset and strode around the department to check on her staff. Stephanie, a student with fluffy hair and baggy clothes who worked only Mondays and Wednesdays, stuttered over a rush of words. Maddy stopped and motioned to slow down the conversation.

Nodding, Stephanie acknowledged the gesture. "Sir, let me see if I understand. You're having problems changing your password. Tell me what you see on your screen."

At another cubicle, dark-haired Roberto bobbed his head. "I hear you." He pointed to his screen. "Click the refresh button, and your screen will reload."

He's so much more relaxed after our one-on-one session last week. Maddy smiled.

Roberto gave a thumbs-up.

From a center cubicle, stocky Chad crouched over his keyboard typing. "See what more you can do with a premium subscription? Now those videos of you describing your needs and wants in a romantic partner will attract attention, and more attention means more winks, and more winks mean more emails, and more emails mean more phone calls, and more phone calls mean more first dates. I went on almost one thousand first dates until I met my wife, and I met her at PerfectFit.com. It'll happen for you. We're running a special today if you sign up for our premium service. You'll get everything I've shown you for the low monthly fee of nineteen dollars and ninety-five cents. That cost is less than a dinner for two. You can cancel at any time by emailing us, okay?"

Maddy loved listening to Chad's calls. He racked up more sales than any other person in tech support, but he could also solve any problem in five minutes or less. In the three years he worked at PerfectFit.com, none of his calls were escalated to her or any other supervisor. His exceptional blend of technical expertise and people skills was why Maddy chose to have new hires shadow Chad, although she knew Chad struggled to remain focused on the new hires since he longed to be the one on the phone, helping customers and closing sales.

Through the glass doors of the office space, broad-shouldered Darren waved his beefy arms overhead. Ever since a psychiatric office moved into an office space upstairs, the doors were locked for security purposes.

She tensed her jaw in a closed-lipped smile. Was he here to apologize for not making love to her last night? Or would he only taunt her with more criticism and bad news? For a long moment, she paused before swiping her badge over the lock to open the door.

Darren swept her into his arms and smacked her lips with a swift kiss. "Ready for lunch?"

She glanced around the room, bristling with irritation. Where was her co-manager, Rick? Was he smoking on the roof again? At least, her addiction to food kept her at the desk. "I can't go until someone replaces me on the floor."

"I'll wait." He stepped into an empty cubicle. "My boss expanded my territory to include the Rockies. I'm leaving tonight for three weeks in Denver to break into a new market. This lunch will be our last meal together until I return."

She stiffened her stance. "You just got back from Washington D.C. How can they fly you out to Denver? Don't labor laws require twenty-four hours between shifts?"

He shoved his hands into his pockets and rocked back on his heels. "The labor law is eight hours between shifts but only for hourly employees. I'm exempt."

"Exempt from a normal life." Frustration mounted against her ribs.

He hardened his gaze. "I'm tired of you grumbling about my job. Must we have the same fight every time before I leave?" He balled his hands into fists. "You knew when we got together I was a traveling salesman." He pointed across the room. "Go stay with your sister so you won't be alone."

She held her breath, and her stomach growled.

"You sound hungry."

Anger heated her face, and her jaw twitched. She nibbled all morning, from the frosted cornflakes for breakfast to the donut and mocha for a snack and the M & M's between phone calls. The knot of frustration, disappointment, and fear balled up inside her, and the acids in her stomach churned. "All I do *is* eat, especially when I want something else."

He placed a finger over his lips. "No one needs to know I've been a little negligent in that area."

"A little?" She raised her eyebrows. "If sex was food, I'd be anorexic by now."

Wrapping an arm around her shoulders, he guided her through the maze of cubicles. "Why don't we go back to your desk and wait?"

She wriggled away. How dare he try to comfort her? Didn't he know she needed him at home, and not selling in Denver? Why couldn't he get a real job like hers?

Noticing the green light blinking on her phone, she groaned. Another escalated call just when she needed a break. After finding a seat for Darren, she grabbed her headset, pressed the green button, and smiled. "Maddy here."

"I have a caller who wants to talk to a supervisor," Andrea said.

"Put the caller through." Whenever Andrea became flustered, she transferred a client to a supervisor rather than troubleshoot. *I hope this problem is easier to fix than my love life.* Anxiety filled her body with heaviness.

Darren scooted closer and placed a hand on her knee.

A shocking bolt of resistance extinguished the tingle of pleasure in her lower back. What could she do—drag him into the storage closet for a quickie? Brushing aside his fingers, she answered the ringing phone, which activated the automatic timer. "I'm Maddy, Andrea's supervisor. How may I help you?"

"I'm having problems changing the text on my profile," a man said.

If only upper management would grant the staff permission to edit profiles, then she wouldn't have to field these phone calls. "What's your user name?"

"The General," he said.

Maddy typed. "We have over a hundred members with The General in their user name. Are any other words, numbers, or symbols included?"

"404Runner."

As she typed, she repeated his user name aloud. A photograph of an attractive man in his early fifties appeared on the screen. Wavy salt-and-pepper hair fell over a high forehead above soft brown eyes and a genuine smile. A zip of energy zigzagged through her. She liked him. He looked friendly and approachable. Why would an attractive man need a dating site? Glancing at the clock on her phone, she focused. "I'm sorry, sir, but our programmers are working to fix a bug in the system preventing users from changing their profile text. Luckily, I can alter the wording. What would you like your profile to say?"

Darren leaned over and nuzzled Maddy's neck with his nose.

A cold shiver raced down her spine, and she scooted away. *Why couldn't he have been this affectionate last night and not now while I'm working?*

"I'm tired of the whole online dating thing," TheGeneral404Runner said. "Nothing but crazies out there. Like the woman who took an urn to a first date because she said she wanted her mother to meet me. Seriously? What type of sane woman does that?"

Maddy hunched her shoulders. *Oh, no, this guy is cute, but he's a talker. I don't have time to talk.*

Rule One: Never engage a caller in a long conversation.

She glanced at the timer on her phone. The department's goal was to complete all calls within five minutes. "Maybe you'll attract a different type of woman once we change your profile text."

"Maybe I should just close my account."

Rule Two: Never let a customer close an account. Always solve a caller's problem.

Wearing a wireless headset, she scooted back her chair and rose. "Let's start over."

Darren seized her hand.

Frowning, she shook her head, tugged her fingers out of his grasp, and walked away. "Tell me, what type of woman are you looking for?" Striding up and down the aisles with her hands clasped behind her back, she could almost pretend she was alone with the caller on a walk.

"I'm not looking right now," he said. "That's why I want to change my profile. I don't want any hits while I take a break. I just want to focus on myself. Cook some good vegan meals and go for long runs. Enjoy life. None of this first-date nonsense where she says she's one hundred pounds and what she means is she's one hundred pounds overweight when you meet her at the coffee shop. I don't mind dating a fatty. I've dated plenty. I just mind when they lie. The lying is a real turn-off."

She clenched her stomach and bowed her head. A curtain of hair hid the humiliation heating her face.

"Why do you call them fatties?"

"Sorry for not being politically correct. Overweight. Plus size. Curvy. Whatever. Fat is fat, right? Why can't we speak the truth anymore?"

Across the room, Darren stood and walked toward her.

Maddy strode in the opposite direction, slowly weaving her way back to her cubicle. Sitting behind her desk, she smiled at the caller's profile picture before she read the tagline: Lonely runner seeks someone to jog through life with. Prefer friends first.

She sighed. He was a sweet romantic. How could any woman resist that tagline? Just look at him. Who could reject that full head of hair and those puppy-dog eyes?

Darren resumed his place beside her.

She narrowed her gaze.

He lifted his hands and smiled.

Warmth filled her chest. In spite of the travel and the misplaced affection, she still loved him.

Returning her attention to the caller, she scratched her chin. "Let me hide your profile. You can call us back when you're ready to restart."

"What if I don't want to start up again?"

As a supervisor, she could make more judgment calls than the rest of the staff in determining when to bend company policy. Often, she stuck to fine print on the refund page of the website, but every now and then she softened to the needs of the client. "We can cancel your subscription and refund you from the day your profile became hidden, okay? Just email me at Maddy@PerfectFit.com."

"Sounds reasonable."

The timer on the phone read four minutes. "I have another caller on the line waiting to be helped, so I'll hide your profile until you email me, okay?"

"Perfect."

"Great." She tugged her lips into a smile. "Thank you for calling PerfectFit.com where romantic dreams come true." Maddy ended the call, removed her headset, and forwarded her phone to Rick who just stepped into the room. Leaning over, she grabbed Darren's hand. "Let's go to lunch."

He curled his fingers through hers and stood. "Listening to you with that last caller resurrected memories of what first attracted me." A bright light sparkled in his black eyes. "I'd come here for a sales meeting and be stuck in the lobby waiting. One day, I was so bored I snuck out of the reception area and followed an employee into the call center. That's when I stumbled into your department. I was mesmerized by your voice—so calm, so self-assured, so eager to please, and so endearing."

Satisfaction tingled throughout her body. She squeezed his hand and smiled. Between resolving two good calls in a row and Darren's compliment, she let out a breath, her spirits lifting. Slinging her purse over her shoulder, she glanced at her almost-empty bowl of M & M's sugar-coated chocolate candies. A fleeting thought of TheGeneral404Runner meeting a woman who brought an urn to a first date triggered a twinge of sadness. *I didn't fix anyone else's romantic problems.* She straightened her shoulders and wove her fingers through Darren's hand. *Maybe I'm on my way to improving my own.*

****

Five blocks away in a Peachtree legal office suite, Greg leaned back in his leather executive chair. He wore the same tired blue suit he dragged across country to every other temporary work assignment he could find, but the tie was new and a gift from Amy. He stroked the silk brocade imprinted with the swirling, bold primary colors of the artist Zan-Zen, who Amy discovered last year. The artist's commercial success translated into a men's clothing line that art critics hailed as profane, but Greg appreciated the constant reminder of his beloved while he worked. *I'll learn how to be faithful.* A pang of relief hit his solar plexus. He spoke with Maddy, a tech support manager at PerfectFit.com, who agreed to hide his online dating profile. A twinge of doubt clouded his hopefulness. *Oh, why didn't I have the courage to just cancel my membership? I don't need other women. I just need Amy, right?*

Since he created his account three months ago, he received thirty-three winks resulting in twenty-two online chats and a dozen face-to-face dates. Most of the dates started with Saturday morning jogs in the park and ended with cocktails for the women and water for him at the Sundial. A few dates progressed to dinner at Ray's and art exhibits in Midtown. The relationship progressed to sex with only one date.

Even though the sex had been as flat and tasteless as stale soda, Greg longed for the physical intimacy again and again. He overlooked the woman's half-hearted interest, choosing to focus on how she obeyed his requests.

Everything progressed harmlessly until the third week of dating. Lying side by side after an evening of love making, Greg fell asleep. Deep into a night terror, he woke with his hands around her neck. When he heard her scream, he tightened his grip.

Gasping, she flailed her arms and legs. She punched and kicked until he released her. After rolling out of bed, she dressed and disappeared into the night.

The next day he called to explain his night terrors, but she would not listen.

"You almost killed me!" she had shouted on the phone. "I should report you to the police."

Since the night terror strangulation attempt, he could not find a date. Although he frequently used the online dating site's winking emoji to signal his attraction to a woman, no one winked at him. The desolate rejection coupled with the nagging guilt over the upcoming wedding forced him to temporarily suspend his account. He only hoped his three-thirty appointment with the psychologist at the United States Department of Veterans Affairs would ease his night terrors and deliver him into a pattern of sound sleep.

A knock on the office door jolted him from his thoughts.

Leaning forward, he straightened the papers on his desk. "Come in." Attorney Larry Jackson, known by all the other attorneys as LJ, strode into the room. Greg's boss was a tall, lanky man much like Greg but with creamy brown skin and fathomless black eyes. He always smelled of jasmine and cedar, and his suits were always ironed. Fanning a stack of papers in his slender hands, he smiled, showing off glossy white teeth.

"I have three sets of contracts for your review."

Greg extended a hand and grasped the pages. He welcomed a heavy workload, which helped focus his thoughts on subjects other than his problems. Reviewing contracts between corporations and government agencies for compliance segued well with his military background and legal studies. If he finished his degree and passed the bar exam, he could setup his own office in New York and settle down with Amy.

"I like the quality of your work." LJ drew back a chair and sat, crossing his right ankle over his left knee. "Would you consider a permanent position?"

Widening his gaze, he swallowed. *What about Amy?* "I might, depending on the offer."

"Full time, full benefits, and four weeks of vacation." He broadened his smile.

What about New York? What about the wedding?

LJ uncrossed his legs and rose. "Think about it. I don't need to know today, but next week would be good."

After he left, Greg closed his eyes and felt the slight thud of his heartbeat against his ribs. *If I tell Amy about the job offer, how will she react? Will she accuse me of running away again and not facing my problems?* He stroked the tie, wishing he caressed her silky blonde hair. *If I don't say anything, will I regret keeping another secret like I've been keeping with the website and the other women?* A knot of pain seized his chest. *Oh, how can I learn to live my life fully with one woman without the need to run away from the shadows of the past?*

****

Maddy and Darren sat in their favorite booth at Ted's Montana Grill. Before they arrived, Maddy suggested they dine at The Skinny Minnie, which a co-worker swore served only tasty, low-calorie American food, but Darren didn't want to try a new restaurant. As she slumped against the red leather seats next to the dark-wood paneled walls, the smells of sizzling steaks and greasy fries triggered a craving for all the fatty, high-calorie foods that kept her overweight.

A server stopped by to take their orders.

Darren pointed to the menu. "I'll have the chili cheeseburger with onion rings."

"I'll have the same." Maddy set her menu on the table and studied the listing of beverages. *Oh, how I wish I wasn't going back to work. I'd order my favorite IPA*. She sighed. "And a regular soda."

"Whoa." Darren seized his menu and scanned the offerings. "Why don't you have the kale salad and water?"

She clenched her jaw and squeezed the napkin in her lap. How dare he order the richest, juiciest, highest-calorie burger and ask her to eat a salad? "I'd rather have a burger."

"But you have to lose weight before the wedding."

"How can I when you take me here?" She waved an arm around the room. "If you're treating me to lunch, please take me some place without temptation." She narrowed her gaze and lowered her voice. "I also need you to change careers, stay home, cook meals, and cater to my *other* needs."

Folding his arms on the table, he leaned forward.

"Eating a hamburger and onion rings amounts to your entire calorie count for the day. How many times do I have to tell you to make better food choices?"

"You shouldn't have to tell me anything." She forced a tight grin. "You should make us all happy and order the same healthy meal you want me to eat." She glanced up at the server and pointed to Darren. "Bring me whatever he's having."

Darren shook his head. "I'm not changing my order to make you happy. Your happiness is your responsibility."

"How can I be happy?" She widened her gaze. "You come home, and you leave again." She pouted. "And we didn't even have sex."

"If you didn't leave the house a pigsty, then I wouldn't have to clean." He narrowed his eyes and deepened his frown. "Are you stuffing your face to spite me?"

Glancing up at the ceiling, she heaved a sigh. "I ordered a chili cheeseburger and onion rings. You make it sound like I'm having an all-you-can-eat buffet."

He placed a finger over his lips. "I meant to keep this a surprise for your birthday, which is only six weeks away, but I don't think the gift can wait."

The server returned with a glass of water and a large regular soda.

She sipped the cold liquid sugar in the glass and waited for Darren to continue talking. Part of her didn't want to hear what he might say, if what he said reflected anything he already voiced. She removed the straw from the glass and gulped a mouthful of the sweet, bubbly soda. As she set down the glass, icy coldness slid down her throat and transformed into a pool of warmth in her belly, an inadequate substitute for the loving tenderness she craved.

Stretching an arm across the table, he grasped her hand. "I spoke with your brother—"

She stiffened. "Oh, no, this conversation better not be about boot camp." Whenever she gained a pound on the scale, Darren threatened to send her to exercise boot camp.

"Only six weeks." He squeezed her fingers. "You'll get in shape and look fabulous in the wedding dress you bought online."

She tugged away her hand and crossed both arms over her chest. "I'm not going."

"Oh, yes, you are." From his breast pocket, he removed a brochure and slid the glossy paper across the table. "The opportunity to get your body fit is my birthday gift."

Studying the brochure, she sighed. "I'd rather have a sack of coals. At least, if I squeeze hard enough, I'll get a diamond."

"*You* are a diamond in the rough."

Darren, the smooth-talking salesman who ranked number one east of the Rockies, fought hard to stay number one in her heart.

He grabbed her hand and kissed each finger. "Let boot camp find the diamond for us."

Staring at their intertwined fingers, she wished for unity in their lives. How could they become one of those couples who worked out together, traveled together, and planned their lives together? They only ate together. The tiny diamond on the third finger of her left hand winked with a challenge. Go to boot camp. Lose weight. Have sex again.

The server delivered their chili cheeseburgers and onion rings.

Releasing her hand, Darren lifted the chili cheeseburger.

As he ate, she studied his sumptuous mouth and his dexterous hands. *I wish my metabolism was as fast as his.* Swallowing the last mouthful of soda, she plucked an onion ring off the plate and shoved it into her mouth. The crispy greasy batter crunched against her teeth. *If I become fit, thin, and sexy in time for the wedding, will I live happily-ever-after?*

Chapter 4

While waiting for the psychologist, Greg sat in the reception area of the Atlanta VA Medical Center, flipping through a two-year-old magazine. He hoped he would learn techniques for overcoming the night terrors.

A half hour later, a woman in a white lab coat stalked out of a room.

The staccato clip of her heels against the linoleum sounded like artillery. Rat-a-tat-tat-tat. He lurched out of his chair, his heartbeat racing.

The woman extended a hand. "Hello, I'm Dr. Diana Carter. I'll be seeing you today."

Exhaling, he shook her hand. "Gregory Power."

"Shall I call you Gregory or Greg?"

Thrusting back his shoulders, he lifted his chin. "Captain Gregory Power."

Dr. Carter consulted the chart before she arched an eyebrow. "You're retired, aren't you?"

Exhaling, he nodded. *Why pretend to be someone I'm not when I'm here?* He pulled his shoulders low. *If I remained in the war, I would have retired as a general.*

She led the way into her office and shut the door. "Have a seat wherever you feel comfortable." She waved a hand toward the patchwork couch near the window and the leather recliner near a tiny wooden desk cluttered with papers.

The room smelled stale like day-old coffee. Gray watery light leaked into the room, casting shadows on the thin industrial carpet. He slumped against the squashy springs of the couch then changed his mind and settled into the hard recliner. He crossed his right leg over his left prosthetic and studied Dr. Carter. She was tall and thin with dark hair pinned back in a low bun. When she sat at her desk, she slid a pair of black-framed reading glasses up the bridge of her narrow nose. She tugged her thin lips into a straight line and curled delicate, long fingers around a medical file. She wore no jewelry. He couldn't tell if she was single or a lesbian.

Frowning, she flipped through his chart. "After you lost your left foot in Iraq, you were diagnosed with post-traumatic stress disorder." Glancing over the rim of her glasses, she lifted her eyebrows. "You were honorably discharged but don't receive full disability because of your ability to work, correct?"

"I'm employed as a paralegal for a law firm in town. I specialize in document preparation and review." He bit his lower lip and sighed, still caught in the dilemma of whether or not to tell Amy about the offer of permanent employment. "I'm a contract employee, although my boss just extended a long-term position complete with benefits."

Frowning, she nodded. "You would have to sell your place in New York, correct?"

"Only if I accept the position." He shrugged. "I haven't decided yet. My mother and my fiancée live in

New York."

"Tell me about them." She leaned back in her swivel chair and repeatedly clicked the end of her pen.

Rat-a-tat-tat.

"Please, stop doing that." He shifted in the recliner, a slow-burning anxiety forming at the base of his skull. "It's triggering."

"What's triggering?" Leaning forward, she positioned her pen above the medical chart.

I don't believe these elementary questions. He widened his eyes. "Are you new? Or did you just not read my chart?"

"I have twenty years of experience." She straightened her spine and pursed her lips. "I don't always believe what other psychologists write, especially when I am unfamiliar with whom they are and what they know." She tapped the pen against the chart. "You've moved around so much and seen quite a few doctors. I need to determine how much of what I read is true and how much is not."

He uncrossed his legs and pointed. "That clicking sound you make with the pen and your heels annoy me. They sound like gunfire."

She raised her eyebrows. "How does gunfire make you feel?"

"Angry." He balled his hands into fists. "I want to kill someone."

"Is that reaction because of your PTSD or bitterness over your lost foot?"

"Both."

"I see." She scribbled a few notes in the medical chart. "You've been off all medications for several years. Why?"

"I attended rehab for drug and alcohol dependency." Leaning forward, he placed his hands on his thighs. *I'm wasting time. I could be running.* He glanced out the window at the slate gray sky and guessed the temperature hovered around fifty degrees. *The weather is perfect for a run near the mills.*

She closed the file and removed the glasses. "How may I help you today?"

"I'm having night terrors." He clasped his hands between his knees and shuddered. "A few weeks ago, I almost strangled a woman in my sleep. I don't want to wake up with someone dead in my bed."

Placing a hand against her chest, she drew in a sharp intake of breath. "You almost strangled your fiancée?"

"Not Amy." He slumped against the chair and buried his face with a hand. Did he really need to talk about his online dating? Didn't all guys chase women? A dark cloud of anxiety roiled closer. No, not all men pursued women with the same purpose. Most men sought a partner who cared and understood them. Amy didn't understand, but she cared. When he searched online, he longed for something else in someone else— a momentary escape from the shadows of despair. *I beat drugs and alcohol. Why not this problem with sex?*

Swallowing, he squeezed his hands tighter. "A woman I met online. She was just a fling to keep my mind off things, you understand. I love Amy with all my heart. I just can't live in New York without thinking of all the things I lost—we lost—because the hurt won't go away." As tears welled in his eyes, he silently cursed. *Why can't I keep myself together?* He swallowed the tension in his throat. "I thought once my father died I'd be ready to settle down, but since I've been offered a permanent position here, I'm torn."

"Talk about your father." She leaned close. "What type of man was he?"

Dark laughter escaped from his throat. "He was a draft dodger during Vietnam. His excuse was he was old, almost twenty-five, and engaged to my mother. I swear sometimes I think he married her and I was born just so he could avoid the war. I didn't respect him. Thought he was a coward. He hated me. I was always wrong." Glancing away, he blinked his eyes until the moisture dried.

"How is he related to your night terrors?"

Unclasping his hands, he slapped his thighs. "They started again right after he died."

"What are they about?" She frowned. "Do you remember any details or images?"

He nodded. "Mostly about the war. None about him."

She pinched together her eyebrows. "Why do you think they resurfaced once your father died?"

Leaning back, he chuckled. "Isn't that your job to tell me?"

She consulted his chart. "You have a long history with PTSD."

He raised his arms. "I've tried everything: herbal supplements, dietary changes, meditation, and relaxation. I run six miles a day. Nothing helps. I still can't sleep more than three hours at a time, and every time I wake up feeling like I'm back in the sandbox."

Bowing his head, he clutched his hair in his hands. "I just want the nightmares to stop."

Silence filled the room.

Dr. Carter tapped the blunt end of her pen against her lower lip. "How about you build some muscle? You're pretty tiny for a foot soldier."

"I wasn't infantry." He straightened his spine. "I was a captain specializing in computer-generated warfare strategy. I led the ground troops because no one could find the other captain. My commanding officer sent me. I obeyed orders. No questions asked." As his thoughts returned to that early morning in the desert, he flinched. He wore night vision goggles, a heavy bulletproof vest, and boots with a hole in one sole. Sand gritted between his toes. The wind whipped and howled. With his crew, he crawled on his hands and knees over the dunes. A blast lit the sky. Pain seared through his body. Rubber burned into his flesh. For a moment, he couldn't feel his calf and thigh. With his elbows, he dragged his broken body through the sand.

A lieutenant radioed the tankers, demanding help.

He would never forget the look of horror on the faces of his fellow soldiers when they found him weak from shock, trembling all over, before he blacked out.

When he woke in the makeshift Army hospital, he asked for Amy. When the Army sent him home, he couldn't look into his mother's face because her eyes were swollen shut from grief. Fearing disappointment, he could not make love to Amy. At the lowest point, after a transfemoral amputation, he didn't want to live anymore, because he agreed with his father. He should have died in the war. No one needed a man who was broken, damaged, and disabled.

Dr. Carter shuffled through a stack of papers on her desk. "I know you run six miles a day, but I'm suggesting something different." She handed him a brochure for Strong Gym located a few blocks away. "Boot camp might heal you."

He lifted his eyebrows. *Boot camp?* He crumpled the glossy paper in his tightened fist. "You're crazy."

"No, I'm not." She straightened her spine and smiled. "The technique is a form of reverse psychology. You place yourself in a familiar situation with an unfamiliar result. You enter boot camp expecting to train for a war. You emerge from the experience having conquered the war within. New memories replace old memories, which force the night terrors to end."

Her reasoning made sense. Unfolding the crumpled brochure, he studied the pictures of men and women exercising with rubber bands. He hoped the doctor was right, and he could reprogram his mind. He longed to be free of his old life so he could create a new life with the ones he loved. "Okay." He nodded. "I'll give boot camp a try."

She pointed toward the brochure. "You must go every day for six weeks."

He pinched together his lips. Wasn't the gallery opening on a Thursday night? He promised Amy he would attend. He could fly out after boot camp and return on the first flight after the show. "Can't I miss one day?"

"I'm sorry." She shook her head. "You reprogram your mind to eliminate the night terrors only through uninterrupted consistency, persistency, discipline, and focus."

Sighing, he rubbed his forehead with a hand. *Oh, great. I hope Amy understands. I don't want another fight about my selfishness. If I miss opening night, she will be disappointed. If I miss boot camp, I'll have night terrors.* A dark cloud of despair settled against his shoulders. *Oh, why can't I find a way to meet both of our needs at once?*

****

That night, Maddy careened her four-door sedan across her sister's circular driveway and squealed to a stop beneath a drooping magnolia tree. She sneered at the line of luxury vehicles parked outside Jane's sprawling Georgian estate in Druid Hills. She thought when Jane invited her over for dinner she would be eating with the family and not babysitting Jane's children while Jane entertained high-profile guests. She gripped her hands on the steering wheel to stop her body from trembling. *Maybe I should turn around and go home and face the night alone.* When she thought of her niece and nephew waiting for her, a pang of guilt squeezed her chest. *I better stay. I don't want to disappoint them.*

Maybe she would leave after the children were tucked into bed. *Who cares if I promised Darren I'd spend the next two weeks with Jane? Why suffer her unbearable superiority when I can stay home and eat chocolate chip ice cream in front of the TV and drink cheap wine until I fall asleep?* A pit of fear plunged deep into her stomach. *How will I lose the weight and save my relationship if I just keep doing what I've always done?* Remembering her overnight bag in the trunk, she sighed. *I guess I'll stay.* She grabbed an arsenal of food from Pig-N-Chik BBQ, ambled up the steps to the porch, and rang the doorbell. The last rays of pink and orange sunlight shone through the dense foliage surrounding the mansion. Cool evening air prickled the skin on her bare arms.

Kiki, the twenty-year-old Swedish *au pair*, opened the door and smiled. "I'm so glad you're here. I have a date with a medical student, and I need to get ready." She ushered Maddy into the spacious marble foyer with the double spiral staircases leading to the house's east and west wings. She pointed down the hall toward the formal dining room. "Miss Caroline and Mr. Collin await your presence."

Maddy envied Kiki's porcelain doll skin and body of an Amazon. No wonder she dated medical students, and not young men at the Pig-N-Chik like Maddy dated when she was her age. Maddy shuffled across the marble foyer, the rubber soles of her shoes squeaking. When she stepped into the formal dining room, the Persian rug muffled her footsteps.

With hands folded in their laps, four-year-old Caroline and three-year-old Collin sat on the Queen Anne chairs before the mahogany dining table built for twelve people. Three place settings graced one end of the table.

Tension knotted at the base of her spine. *I'm glad I bought fast food.*

As soon as the children spied Maddy, they burst into smiles.

"What did you bring us?" Collin clambered to his knees, his neck craning to see the bags in her hands.

"How long are you staying?" Caroline lifted her eyebrows. "I want to have a tea party with Mr. Bear."

"I want to show you my airplane."

"I need a name for my new doll."

"I want you to read me a bedtime story."

"Let's eat first." Maddy dumped the bags of fast food on the mahogany table and removed the plastic plates and forks, stacking aside the fine china. *Oh, I forgot to buy drinks.* She strode into the adjoining kitchen and searched the cupboards, only to find even more expensive china and real silver in the drawers. Sighing, she grabbed two crystal glasses and filled them with milk from the stainless steel refrigerator.

Returning to the dining room, she placed the glasses on the table and kissed each child on the top of the head. "Something for you." Strolling back into the kitchen, she grabbed an open bottle of merlot that smelled like expensive fruitcake and one of the dozen wine glasses from the white granite countertop. "And something for me." She carried the bottle into the dining room and poured the velvet-red wine into the glass. She sipped the smooth, full-bodied raspberry taste. *Mmm. Delicious.* Jane always possessed the best taste and the best budget.

"What are we having?" Caroline asked.

"Guess." Maddy lifted the cartons out of the paper bags.

Collin clapped his hands. "French fries."

Caroline widened her gaze. "Fried chicken."

"Both wrong." She scooped dollops of macaroni and cheese, corn off the cob, fried okra, and pulled pork onto each plate.

Collin and Caroline tugged their plates to the edge of the table and sighed.

"I'll bring fried chicken and french fries next time." Maddy slumped into the Queen Anne chair at the head of the table and licked the sweet and spicy barbecue sauce off her sticky fingers. *Mmm-mmm.* Nothing tasted better than the Pig-N-Chik.

Caroline sat on her heels. "Who's saying grace?"

Placing her hands together, Maddy closed her eyes. "God's neat. Let's eat."

The children giggled before picking up their spoons and shoving corn into their mouths.

"I'm bombing the macaroni." Collin waved a spoonful of corn over a mountain of macaroni and cheese. Turning over the spoon, he pelted the macaroni with corn that spilled over the plate.

Oh, no. Jane will kill me for letting her kids ruin her rug. Frowning, Maddy disciplined Collin by swatting his hand. "Please don't play with your food."

"Ouch." Collin tugged his hand to his chest. He thrust his lower lip into a pout before spearing his fork into the pulled pork.

Halfway through dinner, Maddy swallowed the last mouthful of merlot. She rose on wobbly legs and tottered into the kitchen in search of another bottle.

Jane stood at the counter next to Remy, the tall, dark-skinned Cajun chef with big eyes and glossy white teeth, who arranged tiny sandwiches on a silver platter. From her perfectly coiffed platinum hair to her designer heels, everything about Jane shouted privileged housewife. Even her perfume smelled of fresh gardenias this late in the evening. Jane turned and widened her gaze. "Why, Maddy, you know you can ring the servants' bell if you need anything."

Maddy grabbed another bottle of merlot off the counter. "I prefer to help myself."

Jane tugged the bottle out of Maddy's hand. "*This* wine is for my guests. Why don't you have a glass of milk with the children?"

How dare she treat me no better than her children? Crossing her arms over her chest, Maddy broadened her stance. "Because I'm an adult, and I prefer wine with dinner."

Jane forced a tight smile. "Remy can get you a nice bottle from the cellar after he serves the guests."

"Yes, ma'am." Nodding, he lifted the silver platter full of tiny sandwiches and sauntered toward the parlor.

Crossing her arms over her chest, Jane leaned against the granite counter. "You look exceptionally flushed. Are you coming down with something?"

"I'm fine." Maddy touched her cheeks, pretending to inspect her health. Why did the blood always rush to her face when she drank an entire bottle of wine?

Stepping closer, Jane narrowed her gaze. "Have you been drinking?"

Maddy stumbled back on teetering legs. A swoosh of lightheadedness swept through her, and she grabbed the counter for balance. *If she wanted me to watch the children, she shouldn't have invited me as a guest.* Tinkling laughter floated from the parlor, and a flare of indignation rose up from her chest. *I should be in that room celebrating with those adults, not substituting for the* au pair *who has a hot date with a future doctor.* She stood tall and refused to answer.

Jane leaned over and sniffed, raising her eyebrows. "You *have* been drinking."

Guilt washed over Maddy. She spun and tottered toward the swinging door.

Lurching, Jane seized her arm. "You're *already* drunk. How can you behave this way in front of my children?"

Panic thumped through Maddy's veins. Twisting her arm free, she staggered into the dining room. *I've got to get out of here. I don't care if I have to stay home alone. I don't need my sister's judgment.*

Collin launched an aerial attack of corn across the Persian rug.

Gasping, Jane clutched her pearls at the base of her neck. "What's happening?"

At the sound of his mother's voice, Collin dropped his spoon armed with corn, plopped into his chair, and folded his hands into his lap.

"Where's Kiki?" Glancing around the room, Jane frowned. "What happened to the food Remy cooked for the children?"

Caroline lifted her chin. "Kiki told him Auntie Maddy planned the meal."

"*This* food is not dinner." Jane swept an arm above the dining room table littered with the remnants of fast food. "*This* meal is junk, and it's all over my Persian rug." She rang the service bell against the wall.

Remy appeared in the doorway. "Yes, ma'am."

Jane narrowed her gaze. "Please tell Kiki to take the children upstairs to get ready for bed. Have Johanna clean this room as soon as possible. But call Peter first. Ask him to pick up Maddy."

Remy bowed his head, turned, and left the room.

A bolt of fear crashed through Maddy. *Not my brother's house.* Big, burly, and full of no bullshit, Peter lived a strict and healthy lifestyle. He also owned a gym. The one time Maddy stayed overnight, he forced her to attend his early morning fitness class. *I'd rather be home alone than in a room full of sweaty strangers in tight workout gear bouncing around to obnoxiously loud dance music.* She shook her head. "I refuse to go to Peter's house. If you don't want me as a guest, then I'm going home." Stooping, she kissed each child on the forehead. "I'll see you both later. Please remember to be on your best behavior for Kiki and your mommy."

Caroline quivered her lips. "What about the tea party?"

Sorrow ached in Maddy's chest. "Tell Mr. Bear I'm sorry I left early."

Collin tugged on her shirtsleeve. "You didn't see my airplane."

She frowned and patted his head. "I promise I'll see your plane next time."

With her hair swept into a towel turban and a robe cinched around her waist, Kiki strode into the formal dining room. As she glanced around at the chaos, she lifted her eyebrows. "What happened?"

Jane waved toward the table. "The children are finished eating. Please, get them ready for bed."

Kiki pointed to her turban and robe. "I'm getting ready for a date."

Jane swept an arm across the dining room table full of barbecue sauce and the carpet sprinkled with corn. "Johanna will relieve you as soon as she finishes cleaning this room."

Sighing, Kiki tugged the children by their hands. "Let's go."

Alone, Jane swiveled toward Maddy. "I can't believe you acted so irresponsibly."

Maddy flared her nostrils. Blood pulsed in her temples and knocked against her ribs. "I can't believe you deceived me into coming as a guest when you really wanted a babysitter." She gestured toward the mess. "Are you mad about your rug? I can pay for the dry cleaning."

"I'm not angry about the rug." Jane lifted the empty bottle of merlot. "I'm upset about the drinking and the fast food. You're a *horrible* example for my children."

Anger churned in Maddy's stomach. "At least I eat with your children."

Jane widened her gaze and touched her chest. "How dare you judge me? I'm not just hosting a dinner party. I'm planning the fiftieth anniversary Tour of Homes and Gardens this year."

"That's right, Mrs. Important." Maddy narrowed her gaze. "That's why Kiki is in charge of raising your children."

Jane gasped.

Maddy seized the keys from her pocket and staggered into the foyer. Every muscle in her body tensed.

"You're not drinking and driving." Jane tackled her sister.

"Don't tell me what to do." Wrestling, Maddy pinned Jane against the front doors.

Jane tilted back her head and screamed. "Remy, help me!"

Keys jangled in the front door lock. "Is everything all right?" Chris asked from outside.

Leaning her cheek against the door, Jane closed her eyes. "Honey, Maddy has me pinned to the door. She's threatening to drink and drive. I need Pete to take care of her. I don't want the children seeing her like this mess."

Remy darted into the room. "Miss Maddy, please let your sister go."

Maddy tightened her grip on Jane's upper arms. *Doesn't she know I'll never be perfect like her?* She wanted her sister to wake up with purple thumbprint bruises blooming against her alabaster skin. "She needs to apologize first, and let me go home."

"You're not drinking and driving."

She's always criticizing me. Maddy squeezed her hands tighter against her sister's arms. *Nothing I do is ever good enough.* The same battle begun as children— Jane thin and pretty and Maddy fat and clumsy— escalated into adulthood with no peace in sight. She shook her arms. "Then you're not going anywhere either."

Remy tugged Maddy's arms until her grip loosened.

Panting, Jane lurched away.

Chris unlocked the front door and stepped inside. "I should have been a psychologist, not a neurologist." He wrapped both Maddy and Jane into his arms for a group hug. "I could have cured you both of fighting."

Maddy narrowed her gaze. *Jane's a hypocrite. Why*

doesn't she condemn her husband? After all, Chris was a short, bald man in his late forties. Squirming out of the embrace, Maddy tumbled out of the house. Cold night air bit into her skin. She staggered across the porch. Bracing a hand on the railing, she skipped down the steps.

In the distance, a pair of headlights cut through the darkness.

Chris and Jane bolted out of the house and jogged down the steps.

The headlights to a pickup truck swerved to a stop a foot before Maddy. She swiveled, widening her eyes. *He almost hit me.* The driver's door swung open, and a compact, muscular man hopped out. With his sleeves rolled up, he flexed his burly arms chiseled with blue veins. With each step, the muscles in his legs strained against the seams of his jeans.

"What's going on?" He stepped between Maddy and her four-door sedan.

"Uncle Peter!" From the porch, Caroline and Collin yelled. They ran across the circular driveway and flung their arms around his legs.

"We thought you weren't coming." Caroline tilted back her head.

"Did you bring us anything?" Collin lifted his hands.

Maddy darted toward her car and fumbled with the keys to the door.

Peter shook off the children. He seized Maddy around the waist and hoisted her over his shoulder.

Fast food and wine swooshed in her stomach. She kicked and punched him. "Let me go."

"Don't go." The children chased after them.

"We'll be back some other time." Peter flung Maddy into the passenger side of the truck and slammed the door.

Jane ran over to Peter and hugged him. "Thank you so much. We owe you one."

Peter lurched out of Jane's embrace and hopped into the truck. "We're family." He gunned the engine and shifted into reverse. "You owe me nothing." As soon as Peter drove onto the main road, he glanced over at Maddy. "Will you talk?"

She bowed her head. Her stringy hair covered her face. The familiar pattern of anger, guilt, and shame from another night of binge eating and drinking powered through her. "Nothing to talk about." She folded her hands into her lap and gazed out the window.

"Drinking and driving is something to talk about."

"I wasn't driving." In spite of denial, heat flamed her cheeks.

A huff of breath escaped his lips. "Why don't you and Jane stop talking to each other? You've never gotten along, and I'm getting tired of breaking up your fights." He turned on the radio. A sad country song about love gone wrong warbled. "I know you're the middle child, but I always thought you'd be the first of us to grow up."

A flash of warmth eased the discomfort of her shame. *Someone from my family paid me a compliment. Maybe I'm not as bad as Darren and Jane make me out to be.* She glanced at his dark silhouette and lifted her eyebrows. "Why?"

"You feel too much." He clenched his hands on the

steering wheel. "Doesn't that give you more emotional intelligence to deal with things?"

She shrugged and turned away, resting her forehead against the cool window. "I won't go to boot camp."

He turned down the road to the warehouse he converted into a home and a gym. "I don't think you have a choice."

Maddy stared at the headlights from oncoming traffic. The heaviness of the fast food and wine fatigued her. *I hate my family. I hate Darren. I hate myself.* Closing her eyes, she groaned. *What if Peter's wrong and I'm not emotionally intelligent? What if Darren and Jane are right and I am a loser?* She opened her eyes and blinked at the lights surrounding Strong Gym.

Fear clutched her chest, and her stomach churned. She swiveled her gaze from the gym to her brother. Sweat dampened her palms. *I'm trapped.* Blood thundered in her ears. *Oh, how will I get out of boot camp? I'll just fail.* Tears pricked her eyes, and she squeezed them shut, struggling to contain the mounting pressure in her chest. *Oh, why do I have to change? Why can't I be loved for just being me?*

Chapter 5

Beep-beep.

Greg rolled over and slammed a fist against the alarm clock. He swung his legs over the side of the bed and sat.

Five-thirty.

Faint gray light leaked into the room through the blinds.

The sheets stank of sweat. Sighing, he ran fingers through his tousled hair. Last night he woke three times from the same dream in which he shouted at the driver of the Humvee to speed up as a shower of bullets rained down. For a moment, he considered crawling underneath the covers and drifting back to sleep.

Beep-beep.

Again, he punched the alarm clock into silence.

Boot camp.

At eighteen, he had enlisted in the Army. At the time, he lived with his parents in a brick house in a quiet suburban neighborhood in Long Island. The day he left for basic training, he faced his father at the bottom of the stairs in the foyer.

"You don't have to go, son. I have money to send you to college. No draft is active. Heck, I bet the conflict will end before you arrive." Frowning, he crossed his arms over his chest. "Tell them you've changed your mind. No one will care."

Glowering, Greg shifted the backpack against his shoulders. "I care." He pointed to his chest. "I want to go."

"Why?"

The sadness in his father's brown eyes troubled him more than the conviction stirring in his heart. All of his life he played at war from the board game Risk to the computer game Eastern Front. More than anything, he enjoyed the strategy behind an attack, examining all the possibilities and choosing the one that made the most sense. His goal wasn't to earn money for college but to establish a career. He didn't want to wait for the next war or the next draft. He wanted to protect and defend the country now. "This job is my version of the American Dream."

"To be a hero?" A sneer twisted his mouth. "Why not become a firefighter or a police officer? At least, you can stay around and raise a family."

The tension between pleasing his father and following his heart knotted his stomach. Nudging past, he opened the front door. "I have to go."

"If you leave, you aren't welcomed back."

For a second, Greg considered staying, enrolling at the junior college, and studying for a safe profession. But the siren sound of training for war blared. He stepped around his father and jogged down the path toward Amy's car. He slipped into the passenger's seat and slammed the door. Glancing back at the house, he saw his father standing in the doorway.

His father shook a fist and glowered. "I don't know you anymore."

Amy placed a soft hand on Greg's rough knee. "Don't listen."

Staring at the house as Amy drove away, he leaned his forehead against the warm window. The summer sun was already blazing in the clear sky, and a trickle of salty sweat grazed his cheek. He swallowed, feeling the loss of his father's love and the emptiness left in his chest. "Hard not to take in what he says."

"All children want to make their parents proud."

Turning toward her, he squeezed her fingers. "Do you understand why I have to go?"

A smile played at the corners of her lips. "Since you were a kid, you've dreamed of joining the military."

Oh, God, how I'm going to miss that sweet smile.

"I'm here for you, baby. I support you in making your dream come true."

At the time, neither of them had known the dream would turn into a nightmare.

Reaching for his everyday prosthetic, he wondered if he should wear his running blade. A rash of goose bumps rose on his arms. *Nah, I'll just adjust my gait and body weight, and hopefully, no one will notice I'm different.* He hobbled into the bathroom to empty his bladder and brush his teeth. At the last moment, he skipped the shower. Who at the exercise class cared if he stank? He slipped into a pair of sweats, not wanting to draw attention to his left leg by wearing shorts, and laced up his running shoe.

In the kitchen, he grabbed a bottle of water from the refrigerator and a protein bar from the cupboard. He shoved his wallet into a side pocket and jangled the keys in his fist. Glancing around the studio, he felt a wave of sadness. No father barricaded the door, begging him to stay. No girlfriend slipped her fingers into his hand, encouraging him to go. He was alone. The room was a witness. The unmade bed stank of sweat. The motor in the refrigerator clacked and hummed. Turning, he stepped into the hallway and locked the door behind him.

Would boot camp heal his broken spirit, or would he die outrunning his past?

****

Maddy dreamed of having sex with a stranger at the Pig-N-Chik BBQ. She slathered pulled pork over her bare breasts, and the stranger lapped the sauce off her nipples. Moaning and groaning with pleasure, she woke with both hands shoved between her bare legs.

Faint sunlight streamed through the high windows of Peter's living room. A drumbeat rattled against the wall and echoed like a second heartbeat in her chest. Voices rose above the music.

Boot camp.

She widened her gaze and squirmed from under the covers of the sofa bed. The room spun. A wave of nausea pitched her stomach. She pressed a hand to her mouth and closed her eyes. A headache bloomed between her temples.

I need to get out of here.

Tugging a shirt over her head and shoving her legs into jeans, she pawed through the tangled sheets, searching for her purse.

Peter bounced down the staircase and tossed a set of workout clothes onto the adjacent coffee table.

"Time to work out."

Shaking her head, she scrolled through the contacts of her phone for the number of a ride-sharing service. "I'm going home."

Peter ripped the phone out of her hands and held the gleaming talisman above his head. "You're exercising first. Your fiancé enrolled you for six weeks of torture, and that regime begins today."

"Don't I have until my birthday to start?" *What kind of gift is enforced exercise?* She stood on her toes, stretching for the phone.

Frowning, he pivoted away. "Another recruit joined yesterday, so he needs a partner." He flashed a crooked smile. "That person would be you."

"I'm tired, and I'm hungry." She dropped into the nearest chair and groaned. "I need coffee and an egg sandwich."

"After class, I'll make you breakfast and drive you to Jane's house to pick up your car." With a clipboard, he swatted her bottom. "Hurry up! I need you outside in five minutes."

Grumbling, she slipped into the bathroom to change. *Why am I doing this nonsense?* The extra large T-shirt hung from her shoulders. She squeezed the rolls of fat on her sides and sighed. *I'll never lose the weight.* The pair of baggy sweatpants hid her thick legs. *I'll never be pretty like Jane or strong like Peter.* With a rubber band, she tied her long hair in a pony tail. *I'll always be Fatty Maddy.* Bending, she laced her running shoes.

Before she stepped outside, she snuck into the kitchen and poured a cup of coffee. She searched for cream in the refrigerator but found only a carton of almond milk. Wincing after three sips, she dumped the flat, watery coffee into the sink. Peering through the window of the kitchen door, she spied the members of the boot camp class. Which poor soul was her partner?

****

On the pavement outside Strong Gym, Greg shifted his weight from hip to hip, waiting for instructions. Warm air left his lungs and hit the colder air that made tiny clouds. He rubbed together his hands, wishing he remembered his gloves.

A couple of minutes later, a burly man with a buzz cut jogged to the front of the group. "Good morning, class. For those whom I haven't met, I'm Peter Strong, owner of Strong Gym. Today, we have two new recruits who will be partners. The first is Gregory Power from downtown Atlanta." With a buff arm, he lifted the clipboard and pointed. "Please welcome him to boot camp."

A round of applause sounded.

Warmed by the welcome, Greg waved and nodded.

Peter motioned to his left. "Class, please welcome the second late recruit, my sister, Madeline Strong, from Emory Point."

The woman waved. "Please call me Maddy."

Another round of applause erupted.

One glance at the overweight woman in her mid-thirties, and Greg shuddered. *Why do I get paired up with the walking body pillow and not the leggy blonde or the buxom brunette?*

Stepping closer, Maddy squinted. "Don't I know you?"

Frowning, Greg thought a moment. "Your voice sounds familiar." He rolled his shoulders at the possibility they'd met and had sex but he forgot. Was she one of those women he met online and chatted with before turning down an offer to meet in person?

She widened her gaze and pointed. "You're TheGeneral404Runner."

Oh, shit. She recognized him. Scanning the length of her shapeless body, he sighed. Was she the woman with several odd jobs who only dated on Wednesdays or the woman who couldn't leave the apartment until she potty trained her new puppy? He didn't recognize her face. Did she post an altered photograph online along with a misleading tagline of curvy woman seeking slender man?

He strained his memory for a few seconds, thinking over the many women he spoke to over the last couple of weeks before he finally placed her. "You're Maddy from PerfectFit.com." No wonder she ridiculed him for calling overweight women fatties.

She tilted back her head and laughed. "What a coincidence."

He cringed. Not only was he waking up early to drive across town to work out with a bunch of strangers, but he was paired up with Fatty Maddy, the gym owner's sister. Everywhere he turned, the walls collapsed around him. Why did he listen to that damn psychologist?

Setting aside the clipboard, Peter clapped his hands. "Okay, class. We're warming up with three laps around the building. Remember to stick with your partner." He lifted a whistle toward his mouth. "Get ready. One, two, three. Go." He blew the whistle.

The sound recoiled like enemy gunfire. Greg bolted into a sprint. He bounced off one foot when he ran, his left leg stiff and light.

"Wait up." Maddy's voice trailed after him.

Glancing over his shoulder, he slowed his gait. Breathe in. *This class isn't a war.* Breathe out. *This warehouse is a gym.* Breathe in. *These people are not enemies.* Breathe out. *These participants are classmates.*

"Finally." Maddy exhaled. Huffing and puffing, she moved with slow steps.

Seeing her foot land hard and flat against the concrete, he winced. *She doesn't know how to run.* Watching her swing her arms against the rhythm of her stride, he shook his head. Pity squeezed his chest. *Teach her.* "You look winded." He slowed to a walk so she could stop and catch her breath. "Inhale through your nose and exhale through your mouth."

Air sputtered from her lungs. She clutched her sides. "Why does everything hurt?"

Placing a hand on her back, he recalled how he trained new recruits. "Place your hands on your hips. Practice breathing. Most importantly, keep moving."

She obeyed.

Together, they finished the first lap around the warehouse.

"Go ahead." She waved toward the other participants. "I'm giving up." Turning, she limped toward the warehouse.

"No, you're not." He gripped her arm. "No one surrenders in my troop. We're finishing these laps

73

together."

She narrowed her gaze and stiffened her body. "Keep running without me. I'm not part of your troop." She yanked away her arm and clutched her waist. Bending over, she gasped and choked.

Frowning, he remembered a new recruit throwing up in basic training from running too hard. "You're making things worse." He tapped her shoulder. "Stand at attention. The air can't move through you if you're all balled up." Even if he didn't like her, he would never abandon her. "Listen, Strong. For six weeks, I am your general. You listen and obey. Understand?" He waited until she rose in acknowledgment. "I've been where you are, and I know from experience the pain won't stop unless you keep moving." He placed a hand on her upper back. "Just two more laps to go."

"Leave me alone." She shook off his hand. "You're not my general." She pointed toward the other runners. "Go ahead without me. I can't finish."

"Yes, you can." He offered his hand. *Never let a soldier give up.* He steeled his voice into a command. "Let's do this run together."

She stared at his long, slender fingers then toward his feet. With wide eyes, she turned and stuttered. "You're an—an—amputee."

A feeling of weakness overcame him. For a moment, he wanted to confess, tell her everything from start to finish about the war he fought, and the war he continued to fight deep within, always losing. "Let's finish together, Strong."

She wrapped her fingers around his hand and nodded. "Okay, General."

Gazing at her flushed face, he squeezed her hand. *Sturdy bones*.

She flashed a smile.

Good teeth. He softened his gaze. *She might be fat, but the foundation's good.* Over his military career, he trained men with worse bodies and transformed them into lean, mean fighting machines.

Slowly, they walked.

The other participants jogged around them. Most of the group finished their second laps and started on their third.

"We'll never make it." Maddy shook her head. "We're so far behind."

"Don't worry." Holding her hand, he quickened his pace. "We'll make it, Strong."

She limped beside him with heavy footsteps.

Don't give up. He steeled his gaze and tightened his grip. *Maybe Dr. Carter was right. I need Maddy as much as she needs me.* Her weakness triggered an involuntary reaction to take charge and lead, something he hadn't felt since the war.

Chapter 6

Two hours later, Maddy called Darren while driving to work through the Clifton Crunch.

Pick up, pick up. She gripped the steering wheel with one hand, the phone wedged against her ear with the other hand, hoping no highway patrol officer witnessed the illegal action. The vents blew warm air into the car. From glancing at the clock on the dash, she calculated the time in Denver—six o'clock in the morning. If Darren followed his typical schedule, he should be returning from the hotel gym.

"Hullo?"

His voice sounded groggy.

"It's Maddy. I just finished my first day of boot camp." A cramp in her leg twitched from three rounds of squats, and her lungs still burned from running.

"How was it?" He stifled a yawn.

"Terrible." She didn't want him to know about the frisson of excitement prickling her skin once discovered she was paired with Greg, the handsome caller who wanted someone to jog through life with, friends first. "I woke up too late for breakfast so I was crabby and hungry. My partner and I were the last ones to finish the warm-up laps." As she remembered the tasks inside the gym, heat burned her face. "Our strength was tested. I didn't know Pete wanted us to carry a sandbag with our partner, so when he blew the whistle, I hugged that sandbag to my chest and ran across the gym by myself. Everyone stared. I was so embarrassed."

He chuckled. "Sounds like you're just a little over-eager and a little stronger than you thought you were."

Shaking her head, she turned down the road toward her office building. "The guy I'm paired up with is a little out there. He thinks he's my general. Looks like he lost his left leg, but he can still run. He ran faster than me."

"Did Pete give you a diet to follow?"

Remembering the packet of information, she winced. "He gave the class a booklet with extra exercises and running assignments plus comparisons of different diets for whatever fits your needs."

"Follow it."

Tension rippled across her shoulders. He sounded just as bossy as Greg. Resentment burned in her stomach. *Damn.* She forgot to buy another bag of M & M's for her candy dish at work. "How are your sales?"

"Too early to tell."

The confidence in his voice flagged. Was he actually struggling to woo away doctors from their existing sales representatives? "I'm sure you'll convert them. You always do." She smiled.

"We'll see." He yawned again. "What happened with your sister last night?"

Anger knotted her stomach. Biting her lower lip, she steered into the parking lot. "What did she tell you?"

"You experienced a meltdown at dinner and drank

a whole bottle of wine."

She gripped the steering wheel so tightly her fingers hurt. "Are you judging me?"

"No, I'm concerned."

The tone of his voice mirrored his words. Heat tingled in her cheeks. *I behaved poorly and broke my promise about staying with Jane.* "Please, don't worry. I'm okay."

The silence widened the loneliness. For a fleeting second, she remembered the General's warm, strong hand around her palm as they jogged around the warehouse.

"Are you staying with Peter?"

The harsh tone of Darren's voice sliced through the memory of tenderness. She searched for a parking spot. "Actually, I'm staying home."

"Alone? Are you sure you can handle it?"

She sighed. "I'm not a toddler. I'm an adult. Of course, I can handle it."

"What about your binge eating and drinking?"

Humiliation flamed her cheeks. "I have to go." Slipping into a parking space, she turned off the engine.

"Okay, Porky. I love you."

She grimaced over the nickname. "Love you, too." After the call ended, she sat inside her car a moment longer. Her co-workers left their vehicles with their hands laden with coffee mugs and paper bags full of muffins or sandwiches. Shame filled her. Why did she always feel empty and alone? Her family lived within a ten-mile radius and her fiancé was only a phone call away. A rumble erupted from her stomach. Placing a hand against her waist, she worried if the remaining M

& M's would last until lunch, or if she would have to buy a single-serving package from the vending machine during her morning break.

****

That same day, Greg sat at his desk at work preparing a legal document when his cell phone pinged with a text message.

"Can you video conference?" Amy asked.

While typing a response, he spotted a picture of Amy with her platinum blonde hair, sparkling blue eyes, and ivory skin on his computer screen. Clicking on her picture, he accepted the call. "I have to warn you I have a meeting in one hour." He stood and shut the office door. Sitting, he leaned forward and crossed his arms on the desk. "What's going on? I thought we were chatting tonight."

Amy stood in the gallery's warehouse dressed in a white shift dress looking like a Christmas tree angel. She clutched the strand of pearls around her neck. "I have to work late to setup for Thursday's opening." She sighed. "Are you coming tomorrow night or Thursday morning?"

He pinched the skin between his eyebrows. "Ah, sweetheart, I wish I could, but I can't leave while I'm in therapy."

Her eyes wide, she stepped forward. "Can't you miss one day?"

Shaking his head, he sighed. "I can't. I'm expected to complete all six weeks."

Blinking, she turned her cheek. "That's so typical of you. Promising something you can't deliver."

"I never promised anything." A vein throbbed in

his neck. "We didn't decide if I would attend the opening just like we didn't decide on whether to sell the apartment." He pointed toward the screen. "You assumed what you wanted."

She flared her nostrils, a deep pink flushing her cheeks. "I did not assume anything."

"Yes, you did." *If we're selling the apartment, I should take the permanent position here. We could buy a house in Druid Hills.* Biting the inside of his mouth, he kept his lips shut. If he mentioned the job offer, the fight would escalate. "Why did you call?"

"Doesn't matter anymore." Bowing her head, she mumbled.

"Don't put words into my mouth." Exhaling loudly, he ran his fingers through his hair. "What you say matters."

Stepping aside, she pointed to a row of framed photographs.

He clenched his hands into fists, and his jaw twitched. Years ago, when he learned to walk again, he and Amy traveled around the world. At every stop, he took pictures. The joy of capturing a wondrous moment buoyed his spirits, and he returned from their travels eager to embark on a career as a professional photographer. But after hearing his father dismissed the idea as foolish, Greg stored the framed photographs in the attic of his parents' house and enrolled at the university to become a lawyer. Two years later, he dropped out of school and took a job as a paralegal. Leaning closer, he studied the photographs of glaciers, mountain ranges, and fjords. As bittersweet nostalgia flood through him, he relaxed his hands, and his lips curled into a faint smile.

Amy stepped in front of the photographs. "What do you think of having your own exhibit next year?"

He swallowed, and a spike of anxiety zipped through him. "Who gave you those?"

"Your mother did. Last Sunday, when we were at dinner, she said the agent for the estate sale found them when they were packaging your father's belongings. I asked if I could have them." She stepped aside and swept an arm across the photographs. "This collection would be great for next spring. Who knows? You might be inspired to take pictures again."

He rubbed his forehead and grumbled. "I don't know. My father said—"

She leaned forward until her face occupied the entire screen. "When will you stop listening to your father? He's dead. You're living."

Tears pooled in his eyes. "I just don't think I can."

Shaking back her long platinum hair, she looked like a white unicorn, mythical and magical. A pang of guilt squeezed his chest. *What did I do to deserve this good woman?*

A slow smile spread across her face, and her blue eyes sparkled like sapphires. "I don't care how much you protest. I'm recommending these photographs for our spring show next year. If the photographs are well received, then we can showcase the photographs you will take on our honeymoon in the Mediterranean." She stepped back.

"Okay, you win." He slackened his shoulders. "I'm warning you I'm out of practice. I haven't picked up my camera since I started college. I'm not even sure where I packed it."

Waving a camera, she laughed. "You'll just have to come up on the weekend to get it."

Heaviness descended on his shoulders, and he bent his head. "I can't." *I should tell her about the job offer and invite her to visit to see if she could imagine living here.* "I have too much work."

The smile faded from her face. "I guess I'll service and ship the camera."

Sitting back, he widened his gaze. "You can't afford that expense."

"Consider the camera tune-up an early wedding present from your mother."

He pressed his lips into a straight line. *I should have known they conspired together.* "Anything else you want to discuss?" Wondering if enough time remained, he glanced at the clock against the wall. "My meeting starts in five minutes."

Tilting her head to the side, she puckered her lips. "Oh, yes. How is that new therapy going?"

A low groan escaped his throat. "I hope this therapist isn't a quack like all the others." Leaning back, he crossed his arms over his chest. "She prescribed boot camp as a form of reverse psychology. She swears old memories will be replaced with new ones, and my night terrors will go away."

Remembering the events of the morning, he laughed. "So I get paired up with the gym owner's sister, some fatty who should be a contestant on a weight loss competition. Girl can't run a mile, but boy, can she lift. After our warm-up, they took our measurements and tested our muscle strength. We were supposed to assist our partner with carrying an eighty-pound sandbag across an obstacle course like we were saving a child from a burning building. When we're called, the girl doesn't wait. She tosses the sandbag over her shoulder and runs like she's robbed a bank." He shook his head. "Unbelievable part is she finished the course before anyone else." A cloud of thought distracted him. "Who knows? Maybe the therapist is right. If I can whip her into shape, then maybe the night terrors will go away. I'll start dreaming of being rescued by a girl instead of being run over by a tank." Glancing at the clock, he leaned forward. "I've got to go, sweetie. Good luck with the gallery opening. I'm sorry I won't be there."

"Wait a minute." She waved a hand. "Are you really helping this woman lose weight?"

Smiling, he shrugged. "Sure, why not? Replace old memories with new ones."

"Good luck with that mission, soldier." She smiled wider. "Talk to you over the weekend. Love you." She blew a kiss.

The display of affection momentarily soothed him. *I'll tell her about the job offer another time.*

****

Maddy sat in her cubicle at work, eating a cheeseburger and fries. Between the choice of being home alone or staying overnight with her brother, she elected to take an additional shift until midnight. The green light on her phone blinked. She wiped her hands on a napkin and depressed the button. "Thank you for calling PerfectFit.com where romantic dreams come true. This is Maddy. How may I help you?"

"I hate your company for ruining my life." The caller sobbed.

Maddy stiffened her back. More disgruntled callers surfaced late at night. Between a tough day at work and no luck in the dating game, the callers unleashed their frustrations on the nearest person. Every year, a team of licensed psychologists trained the entire technical support staff on how to calm, reassure, and solve a problem within seconds. Breathing in deeply, Maddy reached for the candy dish and scooped out a healthy serving of M & M's. *Looks like a long night. Thank goodness I stopped at the corner store between shifts.* "What's your user name? I'll need to pull up your profile."

"I'm 911LostGirl," the woman said.

Who gives herself a loser name? No wonder she's a basket case.

The account showed a terminated status with a full refund issued yesterday. Maddy sucked the hard coating off the M & M before chewing the soft chocolate center. "Do you have another user name?" She reached for another handful from the candy dish. "This account has been canceled."

The caller gasped. "That loser boyfriend canceled my account without telling me."

"I can try another user name."

"That *is* my only user name."

She polished off the second handful of candy and grabbed the rest of her hamburger. "We can set up another account and create a new profile."

"Why bother? He'll just cancel my subscription like he canceled this one." She exhaled. "I told him I'm not cheating. I just need to keep open my options, you understand. After all, I don't see a ring on this finger. You want me faithful then pay for a wedding. I'm not some girl who's happy being a baby mama. I want the fairy tale."

Amen, sister. She placed the caller on mute while she chewed the last bite of the juicy hamburger. Closing her eyes, she savored the beef, melted cheddar cheese, pickles, and tomatoes slathered with ketchup, mustard, and mayonnaise on a soft bun. After she swallowed, she wiped her mouth with a napkin and released the mute button. "I understand your frustration." Nodding, she scrolled through the details. "We issued a refund check yesterday to a street address on Peachtree Court."

"Damn it!" the caller screamed. "He's home when the mail comes. Now that son of a bitch will cash my refund check, too."

She clicked on the additional details screen. "We can put a stop payment on the check and issue you a new one at another address. I'll just have to confirm your social security number and mother's maiden name."

Sighing, the caller rattled off the information.

Maddy ended the call and disconnected her phone from the queue after forwarding the caller's information to the accounting department. A quick glimpse at the clock against the wall alerted her to the time—ten o'clock. She stood and stretched her back before grabbing her purse from underneath her desk to take a ten-minute break.

After a quick trip to the restroom, she strode into the empty lunch room. The smell of microwave popcorn lingered in the air. The starkness of the plain, whitewashed cabinets and stainless steel sink always reminded her of a hospital cafeteria. Setting her purse on the sticky table, she removed her cell phone and checked for messages. She listened to Darren's sturdy voice asking her to call him during her break in response to her text message letting him know she worked until midnight.

She typed a brief text.

—*Is it too late to call?*—

A moment later, her phone rang.

"Hey, Porky," Darren said. "I can't believe you're working overtime. We don't need the extra money. You should be getting your beauty sleep. You have boot camp tomorrow."

She groaned. An ache pinched her ribs each time she breathed. "I want to quit."

"Don't."

His voice sounded harsh and commanding. She flinched. Why did he care so much about her weight? What about her feelings?

"If you keep attending boot camp, you'll look fabulous, and I won't have the strength to keep my hands off you."

To stop the impulse of crying, she bit her lower lip. *How dare he bribe me?* She shifted her stance. "How's Denver? Any luck with sales?"

"Denver is beautiful. I'll have to bring you here sometime." He sighed. "I just got back to the hotel not too long ago. I dined with an urologist who's working on an internal solution to the external one I'm selling him. He swears the technology will put my company out of business in ten years. He suggested I go back to school." He laughed. "I told him I've already taken that route. That's when he said I might have to revisit that path again."

A flicker of hope lighted in her chest. "Maybe he's right. You should start looking for something close to home, so you don't have to travel. Especially once we have kids."

"No hurry. The technology won't be available to the public for another ten years."

Ten years. The tiny hairs on the nape of her neck bristled. She gripped the phone tighter and adopted her customer service voice. "I'm thirty-five. My age is considered high-risk for a pregnancy right now. If we don't have kids within the next five years, we'll have to hire a surrogate or adopt. Are those options what you envision for our future?"

"I wish you'd stop worrying. This line of work is very lucrative. I'm sure you'll get pregnant once we're ready."

She lifted her eyebrows. "How can I get pregnant when we never sleep together?"

"Why do you keep pressuring me for sex? Can't you wait until after the wedding?"

September was five months away. What did he expect her to do? Practice celibacy? Maybe she should focus on something else like the children they often talked about having someday. "You're gone every two weeks. How can you raise a family if you're never home?"

"You're not angry about starting a family. You're upset because we didn't have sex before I left."

Heat flamed her cheeks. Why did he always see through her arguments? Tears pooled in her eyes. "Don't you find me pretty?"

"I will after you lose the weight."

She gulped a breath of air, and her chest tightened with pain. "Losing weight is hard when you're not home to help me."

"That's why you started boot camp. By the time I get home, you'll be slim."

Memories from this morning's boot camp returned, and tears streamed down her cheeks. "I can't run."

"Well, if you go every day, you'll get better."

Pain tensed her jaw. *Why doesn't he understand?* "I don't want to run." With the back of a hand, she wiped her face. "Running hurts my body."

"If you don't run, then stop eating the crap you eat."

She gasped. "What about the crap you eat?"

"I make time to work out on the road. Every hotel has a gym, and I use it. I order no dressings on salads, only grilled chicken or fish, and save the bad food for a once-a-week cheat meal."

"Like when you're home." She placed a hand on her hip and broadened her stance. "I don't want to fight tonight."

He sighed. "When I'm not home, I want you to take care of yourself."

Frustration mounted. She tightened the phone against her ear. "Quit your job. Then I won't need to take care of myself when you're not home."

"Don't be ridiculous."

"No, I'm not." Anxiety fluttered in her stomach.

She peered out the doorway to ensure her privacy. Months of battling back and forth over the same issues snowballed. Dryness parched her throat. "I'm tired of this lifestyle. If you don't get a job that does not require frequent travel, then we should cancel the wedding. I don't want to be a miserable bride waiting at home for her prince charming who's gone two weeks out of every month conquering another kingdom. I want a stay-around-town husband who values each moment he has with his wife."

"Get your head out of the clouds and stop watching those romantic movies. We can't live off your income."

"I'm serious, Darren." She glanced at the clock, and her chest tightened. *Only two minutes left before I have to return to the phones.* Realizing she could regulate her overwhelming emotions using the same techniques she learned in boot camp to control her muscles, she breathed in deeply and exhaled slowly. "I need you here."

The balance of their relationship suspended in the ensuing silence.

"I'll think about it."

She sighed. Would he really think about finding a new job close to home? Or was he only placating her so he could enjoy a peaceful night's sleep? She glanced at the clock. Less than one minute before she needed to solve someone else's romantic problem. Tension knotted her shoulders. "I have to go back to work...I love you." Another stretch of silence stitched between them.

"I love you, too," he said.

Does he even know what those words mean? She

ended the call and rinsed her face with cold water from the kitchen sink. Dabbing her cheeks with a paper towel, she wondered how she could fix everyone else's love life except her own.

Chapter 7

The next Friday night, after work, Greg joined his boss and a few co-workers for cocktails at a private midtown club. The dimly-lit dining room echoed with the murmur of dozens of concurrent conversations. An aroma of sizzling steaks from the early-bird special filled the thick air. Sitting in a booth with his back toward the wall, Greg nursed a club soda on ice.

LJ clapped his shoulder. "This guy might be joining us permanently." Turning to Greg, he winked. "Right?"

"I haven't decided." Guilt swept over him. When Amy called this morning to tell him about the success of the gallery opening last night, he neglected to mention the job offer. *Maybe we'll discuss the permanent position over the weekend.*

"I'll give you another week." Standing, LJ waved the group toward a closed door at the back of the room. "Let's party."

Greg grabbed his club soda and meandered along with a handful of other male co-workers dressed in suits. Striding into a smoke-filled room, he coughed and squinted. Four poker tables crowded against each other. Several men hunched around one of the tables deep into a game. Three women in tight evening dresses lounged on the black leather sofa. Their sharp manicured nails dangled like red talons. They didn't look like anyone's wife or girlfriend.

He swallowed and glanced around, wondering if he should linger or lunge for the door. The scene propelled him back to the service after basic training and before deployment. On the weekends, recruits would mingle at the local bar, drinking shots and smoking pot in the bathroom. Sometimes, they pooled their money together to hire a prostitute for an hour or two. "I have to go." With a flushed face and trembling hands, he set his drink on the nearest table and turned.

"Not your type of party?" LJ narrowed his black eyes.

Greg forced a smile. "My idea of fun is running."

"Marathons?" He arched his eyebrows.

"No, just running."

"You live like a monk." Shaking his head, he chuckled. "Okay, Power, see you on Monday. Hope this outing doesn't sway your decision about the permanent position."

"Not at all, sir." *Boys will be boys*. Most men, he knew, were boys. *But I'm different. I can't stay faithful because of PTSD*. Tossing his jacket over his shoulder, he strode through the private club and stepped into the cool, clear night. Breathing in the fresh air, he thought of Amy.

While driving back to his studio apartment, he called. The phone didn't ring but switched over to voicemail. Worry clutched his chest. Amy always picked up whenever he called, no matter what time of the day or night. Frowning, he left a message. "Hey, sweetheart, I'm thinking of you. Wondering what you're doing tonight. Call me, okay? Love you."

When she didn't respond to his voicemail that night, he thought she might be sleeping, exhausted from working long hours. But when he called again over the weekend, she didn't answer.

On Sunday night, he called his mother.

"I haven't seen her, sonny." His mother sighed. "I keep telling you to visit. Mighty lonely here without you."

"Have you tried calling her?"

"I left a message on Friday to ask about the gallery opening. She called back when I was at the grocery store and left a message saying the event was spectacular. Everyone really liked the artist. He was friendly and accommodating like you."

Like me? A cold shudder vibrated through him. *Was Amy seeing another man?* He shook his head, dismissing the thought as quickly as it surfaced. *Not Amy.* She was his perfect woman.

Alone with his anxiety, Greg woke at three-thirty in the morning, punching his pillow. He could not remember the night terror. Sitting, he gasped, his heartbeat thudding against his ribs. Sweat dripped from his forehead. Through the chinks in the closed blinds, the silver glow of the full moon illuminated the otherwise dark apartment. *Where's Amy? Why won't she return my calls?* He buried his head in his hands and sobbed. *I'm still getting these night terrors. Why isn't boot camp working?*

Swinging his legs over the mattress, he fastened the prosthetic and hobbled over to the desk. Turning on the computer, he waited. On the login page of

PerfectFit.com, he typed his user name and password.

Access denied.

Remembering Maddy temporarily suspended his account, he rubbed the wrinkles in his forehead.

In a new email, he typed.

Dear Maddy,

I'd like to resume my subscription to PerfectFit.com. I've considered the alternatives: eating alone, running alone, and sleeping alone.

After consideration, he deleted "sleeping alone" and replaced the phrase with "conversing with a therapist." Shaking his head, he deleted "conversing with a therapist" and typed "talking to strangers."

As he gazed at the blinking curser, dark clouds of depression overshadowed him.

Three-forty-five in the morning.

Too early to run.

Too late to return to bed.

He picked up the phone and called Amy. The phone didn't ring, just clicked over to voicemail. The mailbox was full and could no longer accept any messages.

A prickle of fear inched across his scalp.

Where was she? Was she kidnapped? Raped? Murdered?

He called the gallery and left a message on voicemail asking someone to call him about Amy. Staring at the unsent email, he reread the message. With trembling fingers, he typed, "I need a friend, Maddy. I'm tired of being alone." As soon as he hit the Send button, he held his breath and waited for the thunder to stop raging through his chest. *Will I ever stop feeling so helpless?*

****

The following morning, Maddy stripped naked and stepped on the bathroom scale.

A thrill of victory pulsed through her. Since starting boot camp, she lost three pounds.

Not bad.

Since the waistband of her jeans still dug into her skin, she guessed the weight loss was mostly water, and not fat.

Three pounds was three pounds.

At work, she replaced the M & M's with chocolate-flavored almonds. Ten almonds constituted a serving size. Worried about overindulging, she counted ten almonds and placed them into the candy dish in the morning and replenished the dish with ten more almonds after lunch.

Following the Strong Gym's booklet to healthy weight loss religiously, she drank only water after the first cup of coffee. No soda. No mochas. No beer. No wine. From the grocery store, she bought a one gallon jug and filled it with water at the start of the day. She didn't go to sleep at night without drinking the last drop. At first, she woke up several times a night to go to the bathroom, but by the end of the week, she mastered the gallon of water a day habit, often finishing the last cup before dinner.

Instead of stopping for fast food, she walked to the organic grocery store in Emory Point and bought romaine lettuce, cucumbers, tomatoes, celery, and a can of tuna for lunch and chicken breasts, broccoli, and green beans for dinner. Dessert alternated between low-fat pudding or a cheesecake-flavored rice cake.

After a week of exercising, she could move her arms and legs without feeling like they were made of rubber. When she breathed, air filled her lungs without her ribs aching. She smiled at her reflection in the bathroom mirror. *Maybe I can lose the weight, after all.*

A current of anxiety pricked her skin, and she frowned. *Would the weight loss, however minor, be enough for Darren?*

****

Two minutes after six o'clock, Greg stood with his hands on his waist, pacing back and forth across the pavement outside of Strong Gym while the rest of the class started the three warm-up laps. Cars lumbered into the parking lot. Panic from last night carried over to this morning. Every muscle in his body tensed. *Where is Maddy?* Frustration knotted his shoulders. *Did she quit?*

"I'm here." Waving her arms in the air, she darted across the parking lot with her purse flapping against her back. She shoved her belongings into a cubby and started jogging. "Sorry I'm late. Traffic was bad."

Fear melted the muscles in his neck, and he nodded. "Leave fifteen minutes earlier tomorrow."

She bit her lower lip and returned the nod. "How far behind are we?"

"One lap."

A groan escaped her lips.

"Don't worry." He grabbed her hand and matched her pace. "We always finish."

Widening her eyes, she picked up the pace. "Your hands are shockingly cold like a jolt of caffeine." As soon as he released her hand, she cupped her mouth to stifle a yawn. "I don't know why I'm still tired."

Flashing a sideways glance, he wondered. *Did she suffer from insomnia or nightmares or some other condition?* "I'm tired, too. I've been up since three-thirty this morning."

Golden sunlight crested over the building, illuminating the sharp features of his face. She squinted. "Why were you up so early?"

"Night terrors." Compulsion forced him to explain. "By-product of serving in the war, thank you very much." He hoped the bite of sarcasm would deter her.

She cocked her head to the side. "In which war did you fight?"

"Gulf War." He pumped his arms back and forth. "I served in Operation Desert Sabre, replacing another officer in field operations when he went missing. After I lost my leg, I was sent home." With each exhale, tiny clouds of warm moisture dissipated in the cool breeze.

She stared ahead and said nothing.

"Can't sleep without strangling my pillow." *Why am I confessing?* She wasn't a therapist; she was a boot camp partner. He pumped his arms faster and lengthened his stride. *Maybe I can keep talking and still lose her.* "Almost killed a woman last month when she fell asleep beside me. I'm afraid if I go back to New York and marry Amy, I'll strangle her while she sleeps."

She jogged faster. "Why are you sleeping with women you meet online when you already have a fiancée?" She swatted his arm. "You're a scoundrel."

He flinched from the brusque slap. *How dare she*

touch me? She doesn't know me. We just met last week. Why the judgment? Scowling, he balled his hands into fists. "You don't know what you're talking about, Fatty. Cheating is for married people. I'm not married." Dipping his chin to his chest, he bounced one step closer to the building. "I should probably call off the wedding."

She glared. "What's stopping you?" She smacked his arm again. "My name's Maddy."

He chuckled.

With both hands, she shoved him against the wall of the building.

Hot breath spat in his face.

After pressing his body against the concrete, she thrust her chin at his face. "Don't ever call me Fatty. Or I'll beat you to a pulp." She tightened her grip on his balled-up T-shirt. "Understand?"

For a moment, all of the air squeezed out of his lungs. Narrowing his gaze, he gave her a shove. "Leave me alone."

Stepping back, she shook a stiffened finger. "You started this conversation, General."

Why did women always assign blame? He ground his teeth. "I'm ending this talk right now."

A long moment stretched between them.

Turning, she resumed jogging.

He joined her.

Their shoes slapped against the pavement, and their breathing matched their strides.

Rounding the warehouse a second time, Greg thought about how he was supposed to be replacing old memories with new ones and not reliving the past again through his confessions to a stranger. Something inside of him softened. "Maybe we can help out each other."

She narrowed her gaze. "How?"

"I teach you how to run, and you teach me how to build some muscle."

As she jogged, she peered closer and panted. "Why?"

He waved a hand back and forth between them. "Because for five more weeks, all we've got is each other."

Shaking her head, she sighed. "I doubt running will help me."

"I run almost every day." He thought about his long runs along the creek alone. "Running helps clear my mind." He steadied his gait.

She matched his movements. "Why do you need to build muscle?"

He widened his eyes. "Because I'm embarrassed when my female partner races through an obstacle course with an eighty-pound sandbag and wins."

She laughed. "When we were little, I used to beat up my sister. Peter broke us apart every time. If we didn't have Peter, I would have ended up an only child."

He sensed the deeper feeling in her voice. "Why are you angry?" He rounded the building. *Only one more lap to go.*

Huffing and puffing, she shrugged. "I guess I never thought of my behavior as a reaction to anger. I always thought of my actions as defending myself against the unfairness of life." She tipped her lips into a crooked smile. "My fiancé says I'm fat. I prefer to think of the extra weight as body armor to protect me."

He shook his head. "Fat is fat. It won't protect you."

"What will?"

You can defend a country against an enemy, but you cannot offer protection when the enemy is yourself. "I don't know." Pumping his arms, he exhaled. "I wish I did."

She shortened the length of her stride. "What about you? Why are you here?"

He slowed to almost a walk. "My therapist sent me. She thinks I can replace old memories with new ones and learn to sleep through the night."

"Is her theory working?"

Her eyes loomed large and blue, innocent with the inquiry. The truth dampened his spirits, and he squirmed. He hated the directness of her question. Failure haunted him at every word. Staring at her, he changed the topic. "How much weight do you have to lose?"

She jogged with heavy steps. "According to my fiancé, every pound I've gained since the engagement." Grumbling, she shook her head. "He's stopped having sex, because I'm fat. I asked him to quit his job last night, because I hate being alone. I'm afraid he won't, because he probably travels to avoid me." She inhaled deeply and exhaled slowly. "I'm doing my part, though." Smiling, she tapped her belly. "So far, I've lost three pounds."

He rounded the corner, finishing the final lap. Stopping by the warehouse, he placed his hands on his waist and paced back and forth. "Don't stop moving just yet. Let your body cool off."

She paced beside him with her arms crossed over her head to allow more air into her lungs.

For a long moment, he studied her. Sweat beaded against her flushed forehead. In the baggy sweat suit, she looked as shapeless as a ball of dough. No wonder her fiancé stopped having sex. Guilt squeezed his chest. *Why do I sleep with other women when the most beautiful woman in the world loves me? Is Maddy right? Am I a scoundrel?*

Loud music drifted from the warehouse.

"Ready?" She nodded toward the free weights. "I'll show you how to build muscle."

Wiping the sweat off his forehead with the back of his hand, he followed her into the suffocating warehouse. *We are two broken people who need help.*

Maddy stacked twenty-pound weights on both sides of a barbell.

Lingering beside the bench, he tipped his head to the side. *Can we rescue each other without making things worse?*

Chapter 8

As Maddy drove through the Clifton Crunch on her way to work, early morning sunlight glinted off the metal trim of the sedan inches away from her bumper. Heat powered through the vents, and the radio played a sickeningly sweet love song. She snapped off the music and gritted her teeth. She hated gridlock. Eager to diffuse her frustration, she called Darren on a hands-free device. She wanted to tell him about losing three pounds and ask if he decided to find a new job that didn't require travel. The phone rang several times before switching to voicemail. Sighing, she punched a button to disconnect the call without leaving a message.

He's probably at the gym. Another thought entered her mind, and she tensed her jaw. *He's at breakfast with another woman.* She envisioned him sitting across the table from a thinner woman at an all-you-can-eat breakfast buffet, and churning burned her stomach. *I bet he lets her eat anything she wants without criticism.*

At the next light, she punched speed dial to call Darren again. The phone rang and rang until the reassuring lilt of his voice greeted her on voicemail. She waited to leave a message, her heartbeat thudding in her ears before the annoying beep. "Hey, Dare, I want to tell you some good news—I've lost three pounds." She didn't mention the remaining pounds she needed to lose. "Hope you've processed last week's conversation." Then she recalled the ultimatum. A mixture of dread and anticipation squeezed her chest. "Call me, okay? I'm not working double shifts this week." *Why don't I have a strategy to occupy the hours between work and sleep when boredom and restlessness claw at my stomach, begging me to eat and drink?* "Let's see how many more pounds I can lose before you get home, okay?" She blew a kiss, wishing for the soft warmth of lips against lips. "Love you. Bye." As soon as she ended the call, she wondered how she could stop the thoughts flitting around her mind without a handful of M & M's.

****

As he waited for his ten o'clock appointment with Dr. Carter, Greg gripped the phone tight against his ear and leaned forward in the vinyl chair in the waiting area of the Atlanta VA Medical Center.

Amy's voice floated through the phone. "Hello, baby, I'm returning your call from this weekend."

Knots loosened across his shoulders. "Hey, sweetie, I was worried about you. Is everything all right?"

"Everything's fabulous. I've never been so busy. I forgot to charge my phone." She sighed. "McKenzie's opening was successful. All of the pieces sold by Sunday night."

"Incredible." He exhaled. *See? Nothing to worry about.* His perfect woman worked. She didn't date another man. He smiled. "No more saffron blue eggs."

She laughed. "We'll have to showcase his next collection early. I'm stopping by his studio to see how far along he's come."

"Mr. Power."

Glancing up, he acknowledged Dr. Carter with a nod. "I have to go, sweetie. My ten o'clock is here. Talk to you soon, okay?"

"Love you."

"Love you, too." He ended the call and rose. He arched his back, and a bolt of pain shot down his leg from the dead lifts Maddy demonstrated this morning. He winced. *Do I have a bottle of ibuprofen in my office desk?* For now, he would endure the pinched nerve from overworked and underused muscles. Hobbling, he followed Dr. Carter to the office at the end of the hall. The room still smelled of day-old coffee. Taking a seat on the scratchy couch, he folded his hands. "I have to tell you boot camp isn't working. I'm still getting night terrors."

She crossed her legs at her ankles and withdrew a sheet of paper from her clipboard. "Don't give up. I have a visual to describe the process."

Clutching the paper, he examined the bell jar curve. The vertical axis was marked "anxiety," and the horizontal axis was labeled "exposure."

With a pen, she pointed. "When you make a major change, experiencing anxiety is normal. Often the feeling of anxiety is overwhelming at first. Sometimes, you see an onset of panic attacks, or in your case, night terrors." She ran the pen across the horizontal line. "With more exposure over time, the anxiety lessens and becomes more manageable. The panic attacks cease, and the night terrors go away." She tapped the pen against the vertical axis. "With boot camp, the goal is to expose you to a new set of experiences over a set period of time, once a day for one hour. Each time you show up for class and complete your assignments, the repetition and duration neutralize the brain's chemical reactions. Eventually, the anxiety disappears." Smiling, she leaned against the back of her chair.

He stared at the bell jar curve. "So, you're saying I have to endure five more weeks to get from here"—he pointed to the height of the curve—"To there." He traced the flat line at the bottom of the page.

After setting aside the pen, she nodded. "The process is called habituation." She pressed together her lips and folded her fingers into a steeple. "If you give in to the anxiety, the panic attacks and the night terrors increase. Soon, you have a history of failures." She frowned. "My worst-case scenario was a man whose anxiety prevented him from obtaining employment, because he always canceled the in-person interview. Over a period of six weeks, I exposed him to a series of in-person interviews he was not allowed to cancel. The interviews began as short three-minute meet-and-greets and evolved into a standard fifteen-minute job interview. Over time, the panic attacks subsided. Eventually, he landed a job." She smiled. "From what I've heard, after several years he is still free of panic attacks."

No wonder I can't marry Amy. Recognition dawned. *Each time I say no, I am reinforcing the anxiety.*

Clasping her hands, she leaned forward. "Does any of this information make sense?"

"Absolutely." Nodding, he studied the bell jar

curve. "I'll attend boot camp for the remaining five weeks." A shiver of anxiety rippled up his spine. *I hope I can end this nightmare, for Amy's sake and mine.*

****

"Thank you for calling PerfectFit.com where romantic dreams come true. This is Maddy. How may I help you?" She glanced at the cell phone on the desk. Two hours lapsed since she left a message. Why wasn't Darren returning her call?

"I can't change my profile," the caller said.

How long will the programmers take to fix the problem? "I'm sorry for the inconvenience, but a bug in our system won't allow text to be saved from the user's end. Fortunately, I can change the words." She positioned her hands above the keyboard. "What's your user name?"

"RoseAndGarden101," the caller said.

Maddy located the profile. A thirty-something woman with luscious, midnight black hair and smooth mahogany skin flashed a moonlit smile. Her tight body looked as perfect as a gymnast. Why would a woman as beautiful as RoseAndGarden101 need to frequent an online dating site? She grabbed a chocolate-flavored almond. "What do you want your profile to say?"

"Hmm…I want to attract the right guys, so I want something thoughtful and funny."

Most guys won't read the text anyway. They'll find her picture attractive and send her a wink. "Why don't we write something short and snappy above your picture?"

The caller sighed. "I don't know what to say."

"Tell me a little bit about yourself."

106

"I have two careers as a horticulturist and a journalist," RoseAndGarden101 said. "I'm writing an article about the Tour of Homes and Gardens this year."

Oh, goodie. Maybe I can persuade this caller to feature Jane's gardens in her article. Maybe then she will forgive me for being a bad influence on her children and extend the offer of dinner with the adults. Wine included, of course. "My younger sister showcases her home and garden every year. She lives next door to the house featured in the movie *Driving Miss Daisy*."

"Oh, I know that home. Italian cypresses line the circular driveway and the bougainvillea wind up the pillars on the porch, right?"

"That's the one." Maddy glanced at the time. Three minutes passed. She needed to redirect the call. "So, how about we write, *Stop the Presses to Smell the Flowers*, as your headline and in the body write, *Never too busy to garden and write. Looking for...* What type of partner are you looking for?"

"A tall, dark, and handsome man," RoseAndGarden101 said.

"You're a writer. You can come up with something better than a cliché."

"I'm journalist, not a romance novelist."

What makes you think I'm a romance novelist? If I was, then why would I be working here? Maddy tapped the keyboard. "Okay, how about this line: *Looking for the right person to appreciate the finer things in life. Taller, darker, and better looking than me*?"

"Sounds good," RoseAndGarden101 said.

"I'm sure you'll get plenty of winks, but if they

don't result in great dates, please send an email to Maddy@PerfectFit.com. We'll work together to select the right words to find you the right person." She smiled. "Thank you for calling PerfectFit.com where romantic dreams come true." Pressing a button to disconnect the call, she checked the time. Five minutes.

As soon as Rick stepped back into the room from his break, Maddy waved to let him know she wanted to disconnect her phone from the queue. Once he acknowledged her, she logged into her work email account. She scrolled through the inbox and stopped at a message from TheGeneral404Runner. *Why was he contacting her?* She trembled. Clicking on the link, she read:

Dear Maddy,

I'd like to resume my subscription to PerfectFit.com. I've considered the alternatives: eating alone, running alone, and talking to strangers. I need a friend, Maddy. I'm tired of being alone.

TheGeneral404Runner

Exhaling, she shook her head. *What a jerk. How dare he ask to resume his subscription when I know he's engaged? What type of person does he think I am? Obviously, he doesn't know me. I believe in fidelity, married or not.* She clicked "Reply" and selected a standard response from the company templates, personalizing the necessary fields.

Dear TheGeneral404Runner,

Thank you for contacting PerfectFit.com where romantic dreams come true.

Based on your email, your request can be met through our online companion site, Find-A-Friend.com.

Your contact information will be forwarded, and a customer service representative will assist you shortly. Your account will be terminated, and your subscription will be pro-rated. Please wait six to eight weeks for the reimbursement to show on your credit card statement.

Good luck in your search for the perfect person.

Sincerely,

Maddy

On the desk, her cell phone vibrated with a message. Unlocking the screen, she scanned the text from Jane.

—See you at church on Easter Sunday. Brunch afterward at my house—

A bristle of frustration inched across her shoulders. Quickly, Maddy typed.

—Will think about it. Working right now. TTYL—

Setting the phone on the desk, she cupped her eyes with the palms of her hands. When she glanced up, she nodded to Rick who waved to signal she needed to take a break. She stood and stretched, feeling the tightness in her ribs and hamstrings from this morning's run. Grabbing her purse and phone, she waddled into the lunchroom. She didn't want another cup of coffee or another donut. Instead, she wanted something more substantial to carry her beyond the next minute and the next hour, something enough to propel her through the next year and maybe even the next decade. Staring at the dirty linoleum floor, she wondered what that something might be.

"Hey, boss, what's happening?" Chad strolled into the kitchen and bought a soda from the vending machine. After cracking open the lid, he leaned against the counter and took a sip. "Have you heard the latest news?"

She suppressed a groan. Chad was the best customer service representative on staff, but he was also the biggest gossip. Crossing her arms over her chest, she crammed her lips into a tight line. "What now?"

Chad lifted the soda above his head in a mock toast. "The company's selling to Global Dating Conglomerate."

"No way." She gaped. Why would a large corporation buy out their small boutique business?

Nodding, Chad gulped the rest of the soda and crushed the empty can in his fist. "GDC is looking to deepen their portfolio with successful local businesses. They already bought two other online dating sites. Now they're buying us."

To steady her trembling legs, she clutched the back of the nearest chair. A grumble erupted from her stomach. *Stay calm. Have a glass of water. Be focused.* "Will we lose our jobs?"

"I don't know." He shrugged. "The offer hasn't been accepted yet. Curtis in accounting is running the numbers right now."

A momentary relief overshadowed worry. Sinking into a chair, she folded her arms on the table. "Well, I don't think Global Dating Conglomerate will buy a broken website."

He tossed the crushed soda can into the recycling bin. "The programmers are fixing that glitch with the profile text."

Laughing, she shook her head. "They're taking too

long. I've been fielding profile calls for the past three weeks."

He jerked his head toward the clock on the wall. "I have to get back to work."

After he left, Maddy grabbed her purse and withdrew her cell phone. She typed and sent a text to Darren.

—*Need to talk about work*—

She cupped the phone in the palm of her hand, waiting for the buzz of a responding text or the lilting ring of a return call.

Nothing.

After filling an empty cup with water, she returned to her desk. She slumped into her chair and stared at the blinking light on the queue. Anxiety bubbled up from her stomach and seized her throat. Plunging her hand into the candy dish, she scooped the remaining chocolate-flavored almonds and shoved them into her mouth. As she chewed and swallowed, she opened the bottom desk drawer and rummaged around for the bag to satisfy her craving for chocolate. She ate two more handfuls before guilt clenched her stomach into a knot, and she dropped the remaining almonds into the bag.

I cannot gain back the weight I've just lost.

She crumpled the bag into the bottom desk drawer. Tension knotted in the pit of her stomach, and she closed her eyes.

What can I do if I don't eat my feelings?

Maybe she could talk to someone to quell the panic thumping in her chest. But whom could she talk to if Darren wasn't available?

She glanced at her phone. Not Jane. She didn't

work. She wouldn't understand the dilemma of job insecurity. Flipping through the contacts in her phone, she frowned. Not Peter. He owned his own business. No one could eliminate his position.

Sighing, she set aside her phone and stared at the monitor on her desk. Maybe she should take her own advice and subscribe to Find-A-Friend.com.

Fear rippled over her skin. How could she register for the affiliated website without her account being monitored by the IT department? She would have to submit her credit card number to start a subscription, and she didn't have a prepaid credit card. Maybe she should pick one up at the grocery store on the way home.

Another thought crowded into her mind. She could send her phone number in a message to her boot camp partner but not from her work email on her work computer, but through her personal email on her cell phone. Her heart knocked against her chest, and her palms dampened with sweat. Company policy prohibited employees from contacting a customer outside of the company's phone or email system.

Righteous indignation invaded her body. She pinched her lips tightly. *Calling him for personal reasons is not against company policy.* A cloud of guilt cast shadows on her argument. Another grumble of anxiety erupted from the bottom of her stomach. *I met him first through the technical support line. His account may be canceled, but if he registers for Find-A-Friend.com then he's still a customer. I could be fired. I won't have to worry about the company buyout. I'll only have to worry about finding a new job.*

Tired of arguing with herself, she grabbed her phone and stepped outside the office building into a valley of balmy afternoon sunlight. In the parking lot, in the safety of the front seat of her stuffy car, she logged into her personal email account on her phone and, with trembling fingers, typed a message.

Dear General,

Please disregard the previous message I sent you from work.

Don't worry about being alone. You have a friend in me.

Maddy

A co-worker leaving for lunch strolled past her car and waved.

She clutched the phone to her heaving chest and returned the gesture with her other hand. Alone again, she lowered the phone and typed her cell phone number. She reread the message three times before pressing the Send button. An illicit thrill zipped through her, and the anxiety disappeared. Anticipation buzzed from her fingers to her toes.

Chapter 9

What a day. Greg slipped out of his jacket and hung it in the closet. He sank on the edge of the bed and untied his shoes. Even after taking two ibuprofen, he ached from his lower back to his upper thighs. *Maybe I will have to skip my run tonight.* He sighed. The long hours stretched ahead like a vast desert.

I need a woman.

Logging into his email account, he scrolled through the messages in his inbox for a response from Maddy@PerfectFit.com. The generic business letter filled him with rage. How dare Maddy cancel his account and refer him to Find-A-Friend.com. He didn't want a friend. He wanted a woman to indulge his sexual fantasies. No long conversations. No lingering eye contact over cocktails. No chaste kiss goodnight. Just honest-to-goodness anonymous sex to beat away the hours until pink daylight.

One thousand one. Breathe in. *One thousand two.* Breathe out.

Grabbing his cell phone, he called the technical support number but received voicemail. "Thank you for calling PerfectFit.com where romantic dreams come true. Our technical support line is available Monday through Friday from six a.m. to midnight. If you have reached this message during normal business hours, all of our technicians are on the phones assisting other customers. Please stay on the line, and your call will be answered by the next technician."

I don't want to wait. I need help now.

Ending the call, he clutched his hair with his fists.

I could go to a bar. I could pick up a stranger.

The effort to make small talk filled him with dread. Picking up the phone, he called Amy. The phone rang several times.

"Hi, it's Amy."

"Amy?" He leaned forward.

"You know what to do."

The sweet sound of her voicemail greeting filled him with hopelessness.

Beep.

He did not leave a message. *Who else can I call?* Scrolling through his contacts, he dialed his mother. The phone rang again and again. "You've called the Power family." Finally, his father's voice filled the space. "We're unavailable at the moment, but if you leave your name and number, we'll return your call."

Beep.

Again, he did not leave a message. Setting aside his phone, he returned to his email account. Reading only the sender's information and the subject line, he scanned the unread messages.

Sam from Tire & Smog: Monthly Smog Special and Tire Rotation.

Delete.

Hildegard from Fast & Healthy: Subscribe to Thirty Minute Meals.

Delete.

Tony from Active Runners: Decrease Your Race Time.

Delete.

Madeline Strong: No Subject.

He pointed the cursor next to the message, ready to click the Delete button. Why did the name sound familiar? Madeline. Strong. Strong Gym. Madeline. Maddy? Was she emailing about boot camp? Or harassing him about being a bad human being for wanting to resume his account with PerfectFit.com? Swallowing, he clicked to read the message.

Dear General,

Please disregard the previous message I sent you from work.

Don't worry about being alone. You have a friend in me.

Maddy

For a long moment, he stared at her phone number. *I have a friend in the body pillow girl who can carry an eighty-pound sandbag across an obstacle course in record time*. He clenched a fist. Having sex with her wouldn't be his first choice. A wave of nausea roiled his stomach. The option was actually terrible. Maddy was the gym owner's sister. The gym reported to Dr. Carter who reported to the VA. If he violated any code of conduct and decorum, he might lose his benefits.

But I won't be alone tonight.

He unclenched his fist.

If I call her, what will I say?

Several random thoughts flitted through his mind. *I'm angry you closed my account with PerfectFit.com. I wanted to hook up to take the edge off the loneliness.*

No, blunt honesty never worked.

Why do you want to be my friend? I'm a cheating bastard who can't keep his hands to himself. I registered for a local online dating site, and not one of the national ones, because I didn't want any of my single family or friends to recognize my picture and tell Amy about my habits. I don't want to lose her, but I don't want to give up anything to keep her. My boss told me I have another week to decide if I want a permanent position. If I choose to continue my temporary employment, my contract will terminate at the beginning of September or sooner if my boss finds someone to replace me. My boss wants a commitment. Amy wants a commitment. Why does everyone want a commitment? No, the long version sounded too whiny.

Aren't you supposed to be a good fiancée and not befriend men you meet at boot camp? No, he didn't want to come across as a big brother.

He fiddled with his phone, turning the slender case over and over in his hand.

Hey, my back still hurts from those dead lifts. Now I can't run. And I can't hook up with anyone online without starting an account on another website. Why the hell are you ruining my life? Yes, that explanation sounded right. He needed to blame her for everything. She contacted him. He didn't reach out. Therefore, whatever transpired was her responsibility.

Taking a deep breath, he punched the digits into his cell phone and waited as the phone rang.

****

Maddy furrowed her forehead at the tinny sound of her cell phone buried at the bottom of her purse on the coffee table. The living room, dark from closed blinds, created the sensation of being inside a womb. She wiped her sticky hands full of pulled pork juice on her jeans and lurched for the remote, turning down the volume of the romantic movie on TV. As she rummaged for her phone, she gritted her teeth, anticipation trembling her hands. She answered without glancing at the caller ID. "Hey, Darren."

"Maddy Strong? Is that you?"

She frowned. The man's voice didn't belong to Darren. Anger prickled her skin. Why didn't Darren call? Was he enjoying happy hour with a ton of single women at a bar or having an early dinner with a potential client?

"Do I have the wrong number?"

The man's voice sounded familiar. She lifted her eyebrows. "Is this the General?"

"Yeah, it's me." He sighed. "What are you doing?"

After tucking her feet beneath her hips, she surveyed the damage in the living room. *I'm eating junk food for dinner, drinking way too much beer, watching a sappy movie with a happily-ever-after ending, and wondering why Darren is too busy to return any of my texts or phone calls.* Shame splashed her face. "Nothing." The lie left her mouth easily. She crumpled a fast food wrapper and threw it on the coffee table. "What about you?"

He paused. "Nothing."

The listless tone of his voice intrigued her. *He's lying just like me.* She shifted against the sofa cushions and tipped back her head to stare at the shadows on the ceiling. "Sounds like we're both doing a whole lot of nothing." A laugh escaped her lips.

"Yeah." He snickered. "Why don't we do a whole lot of nothing together?"

Every hair on her body rose on end. Her smile disappeared. She turned off the TV and switched on the light beside the sofa. Maybe she shouldn't have given him her phone number. "Are you coming on to me?"

He exhaled. "I don't know, Maddy. I'm pretty messed up. I can't commit to anyone or anything. I'm stuck." He grunted. "Plus my back hurts from those dead lifts."

"Your back shouldn't hurt from dead lifts." In the pool of lamplight, she examined the messy room. If Darren was home, he would ask her to throw out the trash, vacuum the carpet, and dust the furniture. "You should feel the burn in your hamstrings." She recalled Greg bending over from the waist and lifting the weight with one swooping motion. "I bet you locked your knees. You've got to keep your knees loose. Otherwise, you'll lift from your lower back. Your leg muscles are stronger." She relaxed her shoulders, comfortable discussing a benign topic.

He grumbled. "Easy for you to say. You have two functional knees."

How stupid could I be? He's disabled. A twinge of pity rippled through her. She placed her fingertips against her forehead. "I'm sorry. I guess dead lifts weren't the best move to show you."

"My back hurts so much I can't run tonight." He paused. "If my back doesn't get better overnight, I'll be limping through my workout tomorrow morning."

Who will run with me? She stood and gazed at her

bare knees. *How would I feel walking with only one leg?* She bent from the waist and ran sticky fingers over her knee cap. *What else am I taking for granted?* A moment of tenderness flooded through her, and she softened her stance. *I need to help him get better.* "Have you iced your back?" She gathered the empty wrappers and beer bottles off the coffee table, then shoved them into a garbage can.

"I don't have an ice pack."

"Try a bag of frozen vegetables. Peas are best. They conform to just the right spots."

"Are you hungry? I haven't eaten dinner yet. We could go out and meet somewhere."

Embarrassment flushed her face. "I've already eaten. But I can meet you somewhere for drinks."

"I'm a recovering alcoholic. I hate sitting in a bar sipping on sparkling water unless I'm meeting a girl."

"*I'm* a girl." Indignation stiffened her jaw. She crumpled the last wrapper in her fist.

"You know what I mean."

Tears crested in her eyes. *Of course, he meant an attractive girl. He wasn't talking about me.*

"Well, maybe tomorrow we can go out to dinner."

The sound of his voice stretched across the distance and tapped her out of her misery. She glanced at the calendar on the refrigerator. The square was blank, as blank as her heart. "I'm free." Every fiber in her body tingled with the possibility of making a new friend. "Where and when do you want to meet?"

"How about Ray's?"

She frowned. The seafood restaurant was always too busy, too overpriced, and too loud. "How about Pig-

N-Chik?"

He whistled soft and low. "That's a whole lot of meat."

Annoyance bristled against her skin. *I hope he's not some health nut.* "What do you like to eat?"

"Vegetables, chicken, and fish. No dairy. I break out."

"You sound high maintenance." What restaurant would cater to his needs?

"I'm healthy." He paused. "I'm fifty-two, but my doctor says I have the body of a twenty-eight-year-old."

Oh, great, an egotist. She yawned. After all of her efforts to eat clean, she succumbed to binging on too much fast food and alcohol. She only hoped she avoided regaining the three pounds she lost. "Why don't we wait and give our suggestions tomorrow morning?"

He chuckled. "If you're worried about the money, I'll pay."

"I'm not worried about money." She grimaced. "I'm worried you think this dinner is a date."

"Don't worry. We are not on a date. We're friends."

A slight heaviness settled in her stomach. "That's what your profile said, 'Friends first.' " Shaking her head, she sniggered. "What your profile should have said was, *Engaged man seeks fling.*"

"I was honest. I never said I was available for anything other than friendship."

She shook her head. "I doubt that woman you almost strangled stayed overnight because she's your friend."

"True." He cleared his throat. "But you're no better. Don't most companies forbid you to contact clients from your personal account?"

She blushed. Shame buckled her knees, and she sank into the sofa. Bowing her head, she rubbed her brow. "I needed someone to talk to."

"Don't you have any family or friends? What about your fiancé? Shouldn't you be talking to him?"

Tears welled in her eyes. She dabbed her cheeks with a soiled napkin. "Darren wasn't available." Sadness quivered in her voice. "I have no friends. I can't talk to family. They just don't understand."

"And I do?"

Sarcasm dripped from his hard voice. Every muscle in her body tensed into knots. When she sent the email, she hoped he would understand her situation without the need to tell him anything. But he was a boot camp partner, and almost a stranger. Humiliation powered through her. *When did I become desperate?*

****

Miles away, in his studio apartment, Greg sat on the edge of his mattress and ran his fingers through his hair. *Why am I being hard on her? She's just lonely.* He softened his jaw. "Listen. I'm sorry for being a jerk."

"You're right. Calling you from my personal number *is* against company policy. I could get fired." She sniffled. "But I was willing to take the risk since the company's being bought out, and I could lose my job anyway."

Hearing her sobs, he shuddered. *She's more alone than me. At least, Amy and my mother listen.*

She inhaled. "I just needed someone to talk to so I

would not eat and drink my way back to the weight I lost."

He straightened his spine, and a muscle in his lower back twitched. *She lost weight?* He failed to notice because she wore baggy sweats. If she sported a tight tank and clingy shorts, he would have said something to encourage her progress. Exhaling, he smoothed a palm against the cotton comforter, pretending he caressed his hand over her hair. "I'm sorry, Maddy. I'm an insensitive bastard. Explains why I'm not married. No one deserves someone like me."

She hiccupped. "What about Amy? She's been waiting to marry you for as long as I've been alive. Isn't that true love?"

Trembling, he brushed aside the silent tears streaming against his cheeks. Why was he crying? "I don't know." He swallowed. "I don't want to upset you more, so why don't we just say goodnight?"

"Don't go."

The desperation in her voice touched him.

"I don't want to be alone," she said.

Deep inside his soul, dark clouds of despair billowed close. *I can't let this poor girl see how broken I am. She has her own problems.* Turning his head, he gazed out the window at the bruised sky. Loneliness overshadowed him. *Will I regret being truthful?* He swallowed the resistance in his throat. "Me, neither."

The silence ached between them. For a moment, the weight of responsibility crushed his chest. If he pretended to be her general and she played along as his troop, then he needed to defend and protect, and not pillage and destroy. He must respect her as a human being and not treat her as an object used to satisfy a fleeting desire like he treated all the other women he dated. Hot shame invaded his face. *I don't think I'm capable.* He scratched the back of his neck. "Listen. Being friends is not a good idea. Everyone will get hurt in the long run. We should stay boot camp partners and nothing else, okay?"

She sobbed. "I need help. I can't lose weight if I keep doing what I'm doing."

Tightness squeezed his chest. He needed help, too. "I can't marry Amy. Every single time I try, I have a panic attack." He trembled. *Oh, shit, I'm opening up.* He breathed in deeply. *What if she hangs up?* He squeezed his eyes shut and pressed forward. "My situation is hopeless. Sometimes, I think my father's right, and I would be better off dead."

She gasped. "Why would your father say something so heartless?"

He opened his eyes. *She's here. She's listening.* Confidence swelled in his chest. "He didn't want me to go into the military. Having a crippled son was worse than having no son at all."

"Wow." She exhaled. "I can't imagine my parents ever saying something that harsh. And I wasn't an easy kid either."

Lightheaded with hunger, he stood and strolled over to the kitchen. "I hope you don't mind, but I need to eat. I promise not to talk with my mouth full."

"No problem."

Rummaging through the freezer, he found a box of veggie burgers. He placed one on a paper towel and stuck the frozen disc in the microwave for ninety seconds. Staring out the window at the night skyline, he clutched a fist over his chest to quell a pang of loneliness. He recognized the same separateness he experienced growing up in a world full of adults. "I was an only child."

"Lucky you."

He frowned. "Why is being an only child lucky?" He envisioned the thrill of bonding with siblings.

She snickered. "You avoid fights. I grew up in the middle. I should have been the peacemaker, but Peter, the oldest, took that role. Jane, the baby, was an instigator. I was a bully. My parents didn't intervene enough."

Pressing the speaker button, he set the cell phone on the kitchen counter as he made a sandwich. He spread mustard on two slices of whole wheat bread. Stacking pieces of lettuce, tomato, and pickles on one slice, he slid the hot veggie burger on the other. Thrusting the pieces together, he took a bite and chewed. He imagined a different life with brothers and sisters to cushion the emotional blows from his father. "I wanted siblings."

She chuckled. "No, you don't. My sister Jane thinks she's perfect. We got into a fight, because I fed her kids junk food and drank a bottle of her good wine. You've met my brother. He's no piece of cake."

Shrugging, he took another bite, chewed, and swallowed. "I don't know him, but he comes across as a decent person who is truly interested in helping people with their health."

"I guess." She sighed. "Thanks for taking the time to talk. I feel better somehow."

Hearing the gratitude in her voice, he smiled. The warmth of intimacy comforted him. "Thanks for letting me eat while talking."

"Are we still going out tomorrow night for dinner?"

The possibility of greater connection thrilled and terrified him. "Sure." He shrugged. "But not Ray's, correct?"

"Right," she said. "I want to go someplace casual."

Finishing the veggie burger, he scooped a cup of homemade apple crisp into a bowl. *Where can I take her?* He needed a restaurant that served healthy food in a relaxing atmosphere, not a date place or a pick-up bar. "How about we decide tomorrow during boot camp? When I wake up at three in the morning, I'll think about some place to eat."

"I'll probably be up, too." She sighed. "When I eat and drink too much, I always have problems sleeping."

He took the phone off speaker and tucked it against his ear while carrying the bowl of apple crisp. Perched on the edge of the mattress, he wished Maddy sat beside him. "If you're up, call me."

"Only if you don't expect me to talk dirty."

A half smile lifted his lips. *Actually, that scenario wouldn't be too bad.* Hot shame scalded him, and he winced. *Be respectful and stop thinking like a cheating bastard.* With the bowl cradled in his lap, he separated the apples against one side of the bowl and the crumbled sugar topping against the other. "Don't worry, Maddy. We're just friends."

"Okay. I won't worry."

Hearing the trepidation in her voice, he set aside

the bowl on the nightstand and shifted the phone to his other ear. "You're lying." *How can I get her to trust me?* He softened his shoulders. "You're more worried than I am."

She gasped. "You're worried?"

"Of course, I am." He barked nervous laughter. "I have problems talking to attractive women. I keep thinking of ways to seduce them instead of focusing on the conversation."

"You should have no problems talking."

She's right. I shouldn't. But I do. When he listened to her voice, he felt like he stood on the end of a diving board. A thrill of anticipation zipped through him every time he opened his mouth. "What worries you?"

"Hmm…" She paused. "You're my first friend. I'm not exactly sure what I'm supposed to do."

Was she serious? He felt a pang of loneliness clutch his chest. *She's more like me than I thought.* Internal darkness brightened with swatches of hope. He cleared his throat. "Maddy?"

"Yes."

The strength in her voice built up his confidence. "Just be yourself." Hesitancy vibrated in the silence. *Am I asking for too much?* A jolt of panic raced through his veins, and he clutched the phone tighter. "Maddy, are you there?"

"I'm here."

"Can you be yourself?" He wanted to know her as much as he wanted her to know him.

"I'll try."

Hearing the doubt in her voice, he frowned. "No trying. Just be."

She exhaled. "Okay, I'll be myself as long as you'll be yourself."

"Sure." As soon as he spoke, he realized the reciprocal agreement sparked a new set of worries. *I lied about being a general.* Pain squeezed his chest. *Do I tell her the truth?*

Chapter 10

At midnight, Maddy heard the phone ring. She scrambled to sit in the king-sized bed, grabbing the phone off the nightstand and glancing at the caller ID. *Darren. Thank God, he finally called.* With her heart beating against her throat, she pressed the phone against her ear. "Hey, Good Looking, I was almost asleep. What took you so long to return my call?"

"Sorry, Porky, but I've been busy."

Sighing, she worried if Darren spent the night eating dinner and having sex with another woman. She drew her knees to her chest. "You usually have time to text or call."

"These accounts are different." He exhaled. "I'm up against a sales rep from the largest drug manufacturer in the United States who has cornered the market for years. Prying these urologists from a known drug and a known sales rep is harder when you're new to the territory and the drug you're selling has only recently been FDA approved."

"I'm sorry to hear you're struggling." She stroked the cotton comforter, wishing she stroked Darren's bare arm. "I miss you."

He sighed. "Are you home alone?"

Of course, she was. Where else would she be? "Yes."

"Why aren't you at your sister's?"

Tension tightened her jaw. "I told you about our disagreement."

"She already forgave you. You've been invited to church and Easter brunch this Sunday."

Jane must have sent him the same text. Did he respond and receive an apology? Or was he assuming the invitation meant all was forgiven? Anger flared deep inside, and she pointed to her chest. "Why should I go? She needs to say she's sorry first. If I'm supposed to be living healthy, then I can no longer ignore things that need to be resolved. Our fight can't be glossed over with invisible forgiveness."

"You were a guest in her house. You drank her good wine. You pinned her against the door." He gulped a breath of air. "You should be apologizing, and not her."

How dare he obtain information from her siblings and throw it in her face? Fury stirred in her stomach. Shaking her head, she sighed. "She cares more about tending her garden than raising her children."

"You have no right to judge. You aren't a parent."

The sharp tone of his voice sent a sudden coldness throughout her body. *Oh, no. Not the childbearing talk.* She closed her eyes. "When we have children, I'm not pawning off their care to a twenty-year-old au pair. I'm raising them. I'm not inviting Jane to have dinner with my children while I entertain work colleagues in the parlor. I'm having an old-fashioned family dinner with good wine for everyone."

"That bottle of wine you drank cost three hundred dollars."

Three hundred dollars. A sharp intake of breath caught in her chest. She narrowed her gaze. "Jane served several bottles to neighbors. Why are neighbors worth more than family?"

"Your sister is in charge of the fiftieth anniversary Tour of Homes and Gardens, a historic, monumental event featured by every major news outlet." He sighed. "Maybe I should have sent you to rehab instead of boot camp for your birthday."

She widened her gaze. "I'm not the only one who drinks in this relationship."

"What relationship? You gave me an ultimatum last week to either quit my job or call off the wedding."

"At least I gave you a choice." A frisson of fear crinkled her scalp. *I bet he's calling off the wedding.*

"What do I have to look forward to if I resign and stay home every night?"

The question rattled her. After three years together, she thought he would not need ideas on how to spend time as a couple. "We could work out, eat healthy meals, and enjoy each other's company." A moment of silence confirmed he processed the information.

"Okay. But what about the message you sent about work?"

She bit her lower lip. Should she tell him? Probably not right now. "Just a stressful day."

"Every day answering calls from romantic psychos is a stressful day. You seem to enjoy it, so I don't know why you would send me a text about needing to talk without having something specific in mind." Silence ensued for a beat. "C'mon, Porky, tell me the reason why you left that message."

Closing her eyes, she exhaled loudly. "The company's selling to Global Dating Conglomerate, if the price is right."

Tension tugged between them.

"So, if I quit my job and you lose yours, then who will pay our rent?" Darren broke the silence.

She scrunched a handful of the cotton sheet in her fist. "I didn't know anything about the company selling when I asked you to find a job that does not require travel. I heard about the buy-out afterward, and the news is just a rumor right now, okay?" Exhaling, she uncurled her fingers and raised a hand. "Besides, we can both get new jobs. The market hasn't been better. The economy is booming, and inflation is low."

"You're sounding like an economist and not a soon-to-be-unemployed tech support manager."

For a moment, she imagined how unemployment might feel—free and lighthearted in the moment but burdened by financial woes every time she needed to purchase groceries or pay the utility bills. Why couldn't she feel freedom without worry? Because she wasn't filthy rich. The amount in her savings barely covered three months of expenses in an emergency. "I'll start looking for a replacement job tomorrow."

"We could move to Kauai," he said. "We could live with one of my cousins until we figure out things."

The reality of island fever sparked resistance. She shuddered. "I'd rather not live with relatives."

"Well, the option is better than being homeless."

Unshed tears clotted her throat. Wishing Darren was here to hold her, she hugged her knees to her chest. "As long as we're together."

He yawned. "It's getting late. I should let you sleep. How's boot camp coming along? Peter said you're kicking butt in the gym."

"I'm doing okay." Why did Darren find time to contact her brother and her sister but not enough time to contact her during the day? A prickle of irritation lodged beneath her skin. "I have a great work out partner who has become a friend."

"Hmmm… As long as I've known you, you've never had friends."

She bit her lower lip. Why had she mentioned Greg? "Well, I guess it's never too late to start."

"Just be careful. Not everyone is who they appear to be."

She grimaced. "Okay." Was Greg not who she thought he was? "I'll be cautious."

"Night, Porky."

She tensed her shoulders. Why didn't he call her Maddy anymore? She swallowed her question, consciously choosing to avoid the topic until he returned home. "Night, Darren."

****

Buzz-buzz-buzz.

Greg fumbled for the cell phone on the table by his bed. He swiped the alarm and squinted at the time in the watery light.

Five o'clock.

Wondering if he slept through the night, he closed his eyes for a long moment. He couldn't recall any dreams or night terrors. Yesterday, after talking to Maddy, he iced his back with frozen peas. At ten-thirty, he brushed his teeth, washed his face, and crawled into bed.

He rolled over and stretched against the soft sheets. The muscles in his back lengthened, and his body tingled with freshness. Thoughts of Maddy drifted through his mind, scrambling his feelings. A flush of warmth traveled over his skin. *I can't be attracted. I hate fatties.* Seconds later, the feeling faded, and a blanket of calm settled. *Home.* Not the bright lights and the cacophony of the city-type of home, but the deep in the soul knowing one belongs type of home. *Maddy.* She made him feel safe.

He snuggled against the pillow and listened to the hush of traffic several stories below the studio apartment. Every day for the last few months, he woke with anxiety. Why the sudden sense of peacefulness? He was over fifty years old. Shouldn't he have experienced every possible emotion by now?

Buzz-buzz-buzz.

He picked up the cell phone and deleted the alarm. Holding the phone to his chest, he stared at the blank ceiling and listened to his heartbeat.

Time for boot camp.

He smiled.

Time to see Maddy.

He wondered if she looked forward to seeing him.

****

Maddy careened into the parking lot at a quarter-to-six. Dark clouds roiled in the sky, and a thick mist blanketed the pavement. She jogged to the warehouse and stood in the doorway, rubbing her arms with her hands while she waited for boot camp to start.

"Enjoying the second week?" Peter tapped the

clipboard against her shoulder and winked. "Heard you've lost a few pounds. Good job, sis."

"Thanks." She winced. After stepping on the scale this morning, she gained back the three pounds she lost and added two more to the amount she needed to lose. She pointed to the sky. "Do we skip the warm-up if it rains?"

Laughing, he shook his head. "We run a fourth lap."

She glowered.

In the distance, the General strode toward the gym. He wore a navy blue jogging suit and carried a water bottle.

Maddy waved.

He saluted.

The gesture sent a thrill of excitement through her. *We're having dinner tonight. I won't be left alone to binge eat and drink, packing another five pounds onto my tiny frame.* She turned toward her brother. "Excuse me, but I'm joining my partner." Jogging, she met Greg at the edge of the parking lot. "Where are we eating tonight?"

"Good morning to you, too." He chuckled. "Do you always think about food?"

She narrowed her gaze and playfully slapped his arm. "Not always."

He tugged her pony tail. "What else could you possibly think about?"

"The same things you think about." She sidled over to the bars inside the warehouse and stretched her hamstrings before the morning run.

He joined her, grabbing the bars with his hands and

leaning into a calf stretch. "I doubt you think about reciprocal clauses in legal agreements or how to keep a residual limb from chaffing."

"True." She nodded toward his lower body. "How's your back feeling?"

"Better." He stood and stretched from side to side. "Must be the frozen peas. Ibuprofen didn't help."

Peter waved toward the class. "Everyone ready?"

The group clapped and cheered.

Don't rain. Maddy bounced back and forth on the balls of her feet in the cold drizzle. *I'm not sure if I can run an extra lap.*

"I want four laps around the warehouse. Four." He lifted his whistle. "Ready, set, go!"

Standing still, she quivered.

Greg grabbed Maddy's hand then quickly let go.

As she jogged beside him, she felt a cloud of sadness pass over her once his fingers left her skin. Why didn't he want to hold her hand longer? He usually held her fingers until a quarter of the way through the first lap. Should she voice her displeasure? He told her to just be herself. She cast a sidelong glance. "Why did you let go of my hand?"

He shrugged. "You're running well without my help."

Lengthening her stride to match his, she widened her gaze. "I like when you hold my hand when we start our run. The gesture gives me confidence."

"Really?" Offering a crooked smile, he grasped her hand.

"Too late to hold my hand now." She smiled, savoring the intimacy of skin against skin. Reluctantly, she tugged her fingers out of his grip. Completing the first lap, she pumped her arms back and forth, keeping pace. Thinking of restaurants, she frowned. "I don't know any places serving vegan foods."

"Most places serve salads." He winked. "Except the Pig-N-Chik."

She lifted her chin. "Potato salad is salad."

"I can't eat it."

"You're allergic to mayonnaise?"

He shrugged. "I don't eat eggs."

"I give up." She groaned. "You'll have to decide on the restaurant."

****

Greg slowed his pace, allowing Maddy to finish the second lap around the warehouse beside him.

The damp morning air tingled against his freshly shaved cheeks. He missed stepping out of the shower and Amy cupping his face with her hands and dabbing kisses on the tender skin beside his lips. "Your skin is so smooth," she'd whisper.

Maddy glanced over. "What are you thinking?"

Distracted by her voice, he frowned. "Why do women always ask that question?"

"Because women are only silent when they're thinking, and women always want to know what you're thinking in the event you are thinking of them."

He chuckled. "Men are silent most of the time, not just when they're thinking."

"You were thinking." Narrowing her gaze, she pointed toward his face. "I could see your eyes darting back and forth."

Deep within the accusation flashed like lightning—

tell the truth. "I didn't think of you." He exhaled. "I thought of Amy."

"Why don't you go back to New York, get married, and live happily-ever-after?"

Why don't you just mind your own business? He shook his head. "Not so easy."

"You're making the situation complicated." Panting, she punched the air with her fists. "Just like Darren is making my life complicated."

He raised his eyebrows. "What is he doing?"

"He called at midnight, which was ten o'clock his time, with some excuse about working late because the market's tough." She huffed. "I don't understand. He found enough time during the day to call my brother to tell him about my weight loss." She pumped her arms. "He even called my sister to talk about plans for Easter."

She sounds angry. He inhaled. "Did you tell him you're angry?"

Jogging, she shook her head.

No wonder she's fat. She eats to stuff her emotions. At this rate, she'll be as big as a blimp. "You need to tell him how you feel." He shortened his stride to match hers. "Use 'I' statements like my therapist always says."

"I can't." She huffed and puffed, slowing to a brisk walk. "I don't want to get in a fight over the phone. I'm waiting until he gets home."

He walked beside her, swinging his arms by his sides. "How long until he returns?"

"A week and a half."

He whistled. "Too long." He glanced at her hand,

wondering if he should squeeze her fingers for reassurance. "You need to tell him now."

She placed her hands on her hips and breathed in deeply. "Do you talk to Amy using 'I' statements?"

"Sure." *Does a white lie count against me?* He winced. He could not remember the last time he said, "I feel," about anything to anyone.

She lifted her eyebrows. "I feel scared to take relationship advice from you."

Knotting his hands into fists, he flushed. "I want to change."

"Working out with me will not foster intimacy with her." She shook her head and sighed. "Amy must be a saint. No other woman would remain engaged for that long."

"You're right. Amy is a saint." Guilt tugged his chest. "I don't deserve her."

She frowned, walking with an even gait. "Why do you put yourself down?"

"Habit, I guess. My dad was the expert. God rest his soul." He bounced with each step.

She widened her gaze. "Your dad is dead?"

He nodded. "He died two days before last Thanksgiving."

"I thought he was still alive from the way you spoke about him last night."

"He is alive." Grimacing, he pointed to his temple. "Right here in my mind. I hear his voice."

Maddy nudged him in the ribs. "Get another voice to replace his. He's not very objective."

He felt the left corner of his mouth lift. "Maybe I should adopt your voice and think about food all day."

Narrowing her gaze, she shook a fist. "I do *not* think about food all day."

A ripple of laughter escaped from deep in his belly.

He turned the corner of the warehouse. *Third lap. One more to go.*

She swatted his arm.

The brief touch bloomed with pleasure against his skin. For a moment, he thought of tickling her side, but a quick glance at her serious expression stopped him. "Yes, Amy is perfect. I'm the one with the problem. I have a panic attack at the altar. Not once, but twice. We're scheduled to get married this fall, and I'm afraid I'll mess up again." The muscles in his thighs twitched. He longed to sprint to the finish, but he didn't want to stop talking. "Last week I was offered a permanent position with the company I'm with. I'm considering accepting, which means Atlanta would become home."

Glancing over, she raised her eyebrows. "Have you talked to Amy about it? She might want to relocate."

Gesturing toward the other runners, he lengthened his stride. "We need to pick up the pace, or we'll be last again."

Groaning, she pumped her arms and lifted her feet. "You haven't talked about it, have you?"

He shook his head. *She's capable of so much. Look how she's keeping pace.* "You're a good runner."

"Don't change the subject." She panted. "You need to talk today. See what she says." She winced, placing a hand on her side and breathing.

Why talk to Amy when she would say what she always said? "I'll wait for you." Some part of him suspected she would die waiting. "Okay," he grunted.

"I'll talk."

"No, you won't." She frowned. "I can tell from your voice you're placating me."

He flashed a guilty smile. "I hate nagging." He sprinted ahead, finishing the last lap around the warehouse.

When she finally caught up, she frowned. "Show off." Placing her hands over her head, she panted. "We haven't decided on the restaurant tonight."

From a locker inside the warehouse, he grabbed a water bottle and took a sip. "I refuse to eat junk food."

"And I refuse to spend fifty dollars."

Frowning, he waved the water bottle. "I told you I'd pay."

She crossed both arms over her chest and shook her head. "This dinner is *not* a date."

Thinking, he closed his eyes and rubbed the water bottle across his forehead. "Okay. I've got it." He opened his eyes. "How about we dine at Marlow's Tavern? They serve great salads."

She clapped her hands. "I love their hamburgers. One is by my house in Emory Point. Shall we meet there at eight?"

"How about we meet at six-thirty? Our bodies metabolize food best between the hours of eight in the morning and eight at night."

"Good to know. We'll meet at six-thirty." A line creased her forehead. "I might be a few minutes late if I don't get off work on time. My schedule depends on whether the night manager arrives promptly."

He smiled. "I'll save you a seat."

She dropped her shoulders. "C'mon. We have a

minute before Peter runs us through whatever he has planned today." She waved toward the bench press. "Let me show you something different this time."

He strode beside her, and a new set of worries sprouted. *How will I spend the evening dining with her without turning it into a date?*

Chapter 11

When Maddy stepped into the tech support room at PerfectFit.com, she sensed a change. Everyone sat in their cubicles, hunched over their computers, and chatting amicably with callers, but a heavy, cold air swooped through the room, dropping the morale by a few degrees.

After hanging her jacket on a peg against the wall, Maddy sank into her chair. As always, she logged into her computer and checked her email before joining the queue. The third message from the top said, *Urgent Work Update* with a red exclamation point. She clicked on the message and read:

In an effort to offer better customer satisfaction and service, we have decided to sell our company to Global Dating Conglomerate (GDC), the parent company of many popular online dating sites. The acquisition will take place at the end of the first quarter. Starting next week, representatives from GDC will interview existing employees to determine their best place in the new corporate structure. We anticipate this location will remain fully functioning but with more job opportunities opening in New York. We will provide more information at our company meeting next Monday.

As soon as she finished reading the email, she

blinked because the room spun. She closed her eyes and steadied her breathing. *Don't panic.* Exhaling slowly, she counted the chocolate-flavored almonds in her candy dish.

Zero.

After thrusting a hand into her purse for the company keys, she unlocked the bottom desk drawer and rummaged around for the bag. She dumped the candy into the dish. Grabbing a handful, she crunched the salty sweetness between her teeth. After the second handful, she stopped.

Ten almonds equal one serving. I probably ate three servings. Not a great start to my diet today.

She shoved the bag into the drawer, placed her elbows on the desk, and clutched her head.

What to do?

Through the anxiety fluttering in her mind, she heard the General's voice crisp and clear. "Use 'I' statements." Seizing her phone, she headed into the lunch room and sent a text message to Darren. With trembling fingers, she typed.

—The announcement is official. Company selling. Will know more Monday. I'm scared I might lose my job or be asked to move to New York. Call me, please—

She added a sad face emoji. *Oh, how long will I have to wait for his response?*

****

Morning sunlight glinted off the glass windows of the skyscrapers in downtown Atlanta. Greg jostled through the crowds on the sidewalk on his way to work. He gripped the phone against his ear, listening to Amy talk about how the sloppy, slushy snow she woke to dampened her spirits.

"I want to see cherry blossoms on trees and smell freshly cut grass," she said.

"We've been lucky with the weather down here." Greg glanced up at the cloudless sky between the buildings. "The morning mist has already burned off." He remembered the cold moisture from the drizzling clouds mingling with the hot sweat that dripped down his back during boot camp. The warm, mild air cupped his face. "But the weather will change. Starting next week, rain is forecasted for ten days straight."

"Do you have any running raingear?"

"Yeah, but I should probably pick up a new pair of trail shoes in Buckhead this weekend. During the rain, the jogging paths get muddy fast." He waited at a street corner for the light to change. "How did the studio visit with McKenzie go?"

"Actually, the visit was amazing. He already completed ten of the twelve pieces we requested. I've been so busy installing the new exhibit. I forgot to send your camera. I'll mail it today. You should get the package at work on Friday."

"Just in time for the rainy weekend." As he stepped off the curb and into the street, he snickered.

"This Sunday is Easter. You aren't running on Easter, are you?"

He flinched, his gaze darting for an escape. "Why not?"

"You should come up and visit. Have a ham dinner with your mom and me. Celebrate spring and new beginnings."

He thought about the job offer. *I should tell her*

now. Not wait. Just like Maddy said.

A moment of silence blanketed the airwaves.

"I've been waiting for months for you to visit." Amy huffed.

Recognizing her frustration, he tensed his jaw.

"If we're at your mom's house, I know you'll be thinking of your father, so maybe we celebrate at our apartment. If the pressure is still too much, come next weekend. We'll stay inside and make love all day. How does that idea sound?"

He scratched the back of his neck, his heartbeat thudding in his ears. *I should tell her about the job offer now. I should just say it.* "Umm…actually…I think you should come visit me."

"Why?"

Stopping, he leaned against the brick pillar of a building. "Because, I've, um, been offered a permanent job…and if you're here, you can have a look around and see if you want to spend our lives here instead of New York."

"Our lives *are* in New York." She gasped. "I've been at the same job for over twenty years. I'm not relocating, so you don't have to face things here."

He lurched away from the building and lunged into the stream of walkers. The challenge of dodging stray arms and legs of strangers eased the tension building at the base of his spine. *Of course, she doesn't want to move. She's never taken a chance anywhere. She's as stuck as I am.* A wave of compassion swept over him, and he slowed his pace. "I didn't say I'm taking the job. I said I'm considering."

"Consider the offer alone. I'm not moving to

Georgia."

He rubbed his forehead. Why did he listen to the advice of a woman young enough to be his daughter? "Okay, I'll tell my boss I'm declining the offer."

"No, you won't."

He shuddered from the harsh tone of her voice.

"I know you," she said. "You'll take the job. I'm just surprised you mentioned the offer at all. You usually wait until a week before I expect you to return to spring the news." She gulped a mouthful of air and choked on a sob. "When will you start including me in your plans for the future?"

"I always include you." A pang of guilt squeezed his chest. He averted his gaze, waiting for the light to change.

"Liar. You're a selfish coward who can't commit." She sniffled. "I don't know why I stay sometimes."

Maddy would agree. Searching for privacy, he glanced around the people milling on the sidewalk. A splash of sunlight glinted off the glass doors of a nearby office building. He strode across the street and yanked on the brass handle. Silence echoed in his shambling footsteps on the marble floors. The still, dry air cradled his anxious face. Finding a quiet spot by the window, he sank on a cushioned seat and steadied his voice. "I told you because I wanted to discuss the opportunity." He bit his lower lip to stop the trembling. "I wanted you to come and see the city where I'm living and working to see if you could fall in love with the magnolia trees and the lush green lawns and the wonderful schools." Bowing his head, he stared at his perfectly polished leather shoes.

"I know I've been a jerk in the past, but I'm not making any decisions without consulting you first." He tensed his jaw. *Unlike how you painted our apartment beige.* "If I take the job, then you'll move south. We'll find a great Georgian home in Druid Hills with expansive lawns and privacy. You can wake up to sunshine and the scent of freshly mown grass, not snow and the stench of garbage." He lifted his chin and blinked at the fluorescent lights. "If I decline the offer, I'll move back to New York as soon as my boss finds a replacement." He closed his eyes, wishing he could see her face and touch her arm. "Either way, I would like you to visit. I want us to decide together what works best."

The sobbing stuttered into sighs. "Okay," she whispered. "I'll think about visiting you."

As his chest expanded with hope, he loosened his grip on the phone. "Thank you, Amy. When we do things together, I feel better."

She sniffed. "You must be late for work."

A quick glance at the clock showed the time as ten minutes after eight. If he was lucky, he could dash over to his office in time for his eight-thirty meeting, but he leaned against the cushions and draped an arm across the back of the chair, lingering a moment longer. "Don't worry about whether I'm late. You're more important than work. You always have been, and you always will be."

"Since you lost your foot, I've never felt like I mattered. Everything revolves around you."

He sighed. If she was here, he would kiss her lips, stroke her hair, and hold her close for reassurance.

"Going forward, I promise we'll make decisions centered on us."

"We'll see." She ended the call.

Deafening silence rang in his ears. Panic gripped his chest. *She didn't say, "Baby." She didn't say, "I love you."* He called her back, but the call dropped immediately into voicemail. *Why did I listen to Maddy? Just because she's a woman doesn't mean she knows Amy.* He rubbed his forehead and stared at the blank screen on his phone. *Should I call Maddy and tell her the advice didn't work?* He gritted his teeth. *No, I'll wait until dinner tonight. That way she won't be able to hang up on me like Amy did.*

Chapter 12

Halfway through the morning, in the safety of the work cubicle, Maddy glanced at her cell phone on the desk. *Why isn't Darren returning my text?* Tears brushed against her lashes. The high walls shielded her face from curious co-workers. She rubbed her eyes and sniffled. *Why doesn't he respond?* During her fifteen-minute break, she called and left a message. Didn't he know she urgently needed to talk to someone about the anxiety over the company merger, so she wouldn't order a hamburger and milkshake for lunch?

Standing, she wandered into the break room, filled a glass with water, and returned to the cubicle. *Why did I let the news of the company's sale toss me into crisis mode?* A sharp pain stabbed her chest. *I love working here.* Yes, the customers could be rude and disrespectful, but when she received emails from customers who successfully found someone to love because of her help, she swelled with a deep sense of accomplishment. Romantic love motivated her more than anything else.

Forget Darren. Forget the company. Time to work. Adjusting the wireless headset, she selected the green light on the phone. "Thank you for calling PerfectFit.com where romantic dreams come true. This is Maddy. How may I help you?"

"I can't save the changes to my profile text," the man said.

She shook her head. *Why was GDC buying a broken website?* She forced a smile. "Unfortunately, the programmers haven't fixed the problem yet. I can, however, update your profile. What's your user name?"

"Fit Pig-N-Chik," the man said.

She gasped, imagining the buff stranger in her dream nibbling pulled pork off her naked body.

"Yep. I'm a body builder whose favorite cheat meal is the pulled pork plate with mashed potatoes and fried okra from the best barbecue place in all of Georgia."

"Mmm-mmm." A delicious smile curled her lips. "You sound like my type of man." She slapped a hand over her mouth. *Did I say that statement out loud?*

"Really? Are you a fitness model with a penchant for meat?"

She slumped. Should she tell him the truth? *I'm struggling to lose weight.* Or should she lie and lead him on? *I'm super sexy but too shy in front of the camera to be a fitness model.* She searched for the guy's profile and studied his photo. He looked like every other Mr. Universe with a bronze spray tan and oiled muscles. No way would he date someone like her. "What do you want your profile to say?"

A vibration emitted from her cell phone on the desk beside her monitor. Maddy swiped the screen to read the group text message from Jane.

—*Confirming Easter church and brunch. Are you coming?*—

"Serious body builder seeks serious fit woman for

serious relationship."

Through the wireless headset, Fit Pig-N-Chik's voice interrupted her thoughts. *Is he serious?* After setting aside her cell phone, she typed the words. "Go ahead and refresh your screen. Tell me if what I typed is exactly what you want to say."

She picked up her cell phone and typed.

—No—

Fit Pig-N-Chik hummed. "Do you think I say, 'serious,' too much?"

She sighed. *Of course, you do. With all the blood pumping to those muscles, nothing is left to fuel your brain.* She glanced at his photo again. Why did she care if the hulking mass found true love when he only cared about skinny women? She forced a broader smile. "You mention the word three times. Ever heard the saying three times a charm?" She tucked her cell phone next to the monitor and checked the call time. Three and a half minutes.

"Yeah, I guess you're right. I'll try this version and see if I get any winks."

The cell phone vibrated. She snatched it off the desk, expecting another text from Jane. When she read the message from Darren, she scrunched her shoulders toward her ears.

—No? Of course, you're going. It's Easter Sunday—

She narrowed her gaze. Blood rushed to the surface, and she clenched the phone. Was he marrying her or her family? She bit the inside of her mouth. Acids churned in the pit of her stomach. She set aside the cell phone, took a deep breath, and focused on the caller. "Can I help you with anything else today?"

"No, that's it."

She tightened her smile. "Thank you for calling PerfectFit.com where romantic dreams come true." *Four minutes. Not bad.* She stood, arched her back, and rolled her shoulders. Bristling, she grabbed the cell phone, turned it off, and shoved it into the purse beneath the desk. *Let's see how he feels by being ignored.*

****

The hostess welcomed Greg to Marlow's Tavern in Emory Point. The dark restaurant glowed with casual comfort. Tiny spotlights illuminated black-and-white photographs on the brick walls. Strolling to a booth toward the back of the restaurant, he admired the artwork. *I should receive my camera tomorrow from Amy.* He cringed, remembering their conversation from this morning. *I hope she doesn't hold the camera hostage, so I'll return to New York.*

Slipping across the banquette seat with his back against the wall, he studied the entrance, waiting for Maddy. She told him she might be a few minutes late, but he really wanted to see her. The scent of fresh bread and savory meats wafted through the dense air. The soft hum of neighboring conversations floated like bubbles around him. He browsed the menu, glancing up every now and then to see if Maddy arrived. He left work late and didn't have time to change, so he wore his suit and tie, although he removed the jacket and draped it across the seat beside him.

Five minutes later, she emerged from a halo of evening light into the darkness of the tavern. She wore a blue dress one size too small, her curves straining against the seams. She glanced around until she saw him. A slow, easy smile blossomed on her face.

A cold shiver traced his spine. *She's here.* Standing, he waited for her to be seated across from him.

"Have you been waiting long?" She met his gaze before she lifted the menu.

My whole life. The cheesy pickup line lit up his thoughts. Shrugging, he glanced at his watch. "Seven, maybe eight, minutes."

"The other manager was on time, but traffic is always bad through the Clifton Crunch."

He nodded. *Thank goodness, I can walk to work.*

She glanced at his suit. "You look…nice." She lifted a hand before he could open his mouth. "I know this dress is too tight, but I don't want to buy a new wardrobe if I'm losing weight."

She doesn't need to lose much for the dress to fit perfectly. He clasped his lips and studied the menu although he would order the same salad he always ordered. "How was work?"

Waving a hand, she grimaced. "Let's talk about something else, okay?"

"What happened at work?" He set aside the menu and crossed his arms on the table.

Swallowing, she stared at his knuckles. A bright pink blush covered her face, and she glanced at the scarred wooden table. With the tip of a finger, she traced the letters D+A inside an etched heart. "My company accepted a buyout. When I found out, I panicked." The rosy flush deepened to scarlet. "I ate three handfuls of almonds before I stopped myself from downing the whole bag." She shook her head and sighed. "I wish I knew how to handle things better." Lifting her head, she met his gaze. "I tried texting Darren one of those 'I feel' statements, but he never responded."

"Wow. I can't believe you took my advice, and he didn't get back to you. Doesn't he care about how you feel?" He widened his gaze and leaned forward, his fingertips grazing the knuckles on her fist. A tingle of pleasure rippled up his arm.

"Don't take advantage of my vulnerability." Frowning, she withdrew her hand. "This meal is not a date." She tucked her fist into her lap.

"I'm sorry." He lifted his palms. "I didn't mean to offend you. The gesture wasn't sexual." The lie rolled too easily off his tongue. A dry thirst tightened his throat. *Why can't I be honest?*

She narrowed her gaze.

"All right, I lied." He crossed his arms over his chest. "I'm having a hard time controlling myself." Sweat beaded against his shirt collar. "I don't know how to act around you."

She dropped her shoulders and sighed. "Just be yourself. That's what we promised each other." She stretched an arm across the table, opening a hand. "I overreacted."

For a long moment, he stared at her long white fingers and remembered his first date with Amy. He was seventeen. When he left the air-conditioned theater, the shock of the muggy summer night forced him to accept her cool, dry hand. "I don't have many female

friends, so I might blur the lines but not on purpose."
He placed a hand in her open palm and gently
squeezed. "Why didn't you call me when you couldn't
contact Darren?"

"Call you?" Frowning, she shook her head. "I don't
know. I didn't think of it."

"Call me next time." He squeezed her hand one
more time. "Promise?"

Withdrawing her hand, she nodded. "How was
your day?"

He groaned. "I told Amy about the job offer."

"And?" She crossed her arms on the table and
leaned forward.

"She said I was a selfish coward who could not
commit."

She nodded. "And?"

A flicker of annoyance glimmered. He narrowed
his gaze. "Are you saying you agree?" A crooked smile
played at the corners of her lips.

"I didn't say I *disagreed*."

He arched an eyebrow. "Whose friend are you
anyway, hers or mine?"

Raising her hands, she smiled. "Both?"

Letting his head fall back, he laughed. "You're
teasing."

"Of course, I am." She giggled for a couple of
seconds. "But an ounce of truth exists in her statement."

The words felt like a punch to the stomach.
Flinching, he shook his head. "I know I'm far from
perfect."

A server stopped to take their orders.

Waving, Greg deferred. "You go first."

Picking up the menu, Maddy shook her head. "I haven't decided."

He ordered the garden salad and a glass of water.

She arched an eyebrow. "What about protein? You can't build extra muscle without protein."

Bossy, isn't she? He glowered. "I don't eat most meats."

"You said you eat chicken. Add a side of grilled chicken."

Grumbling, he modified his order. "Your turn."

She pouted. "I really want a pint of beer and a double cheeseburger, but I need to lose weight. Should I order the same as you?"

Shaking his head, he pointed toward the menu. "You can have the hamburger. Order a single, no cheese, and no mayonnaise. Extra lettuce, pickle, tomato, and mustard. Salad, no fries. Water, no beer." He waited for the server to nod before returning his attention to Maddy. "Where did we leave off?"

"We were talking about Amy's comment." Maddy drummed her fingers on the table. "What did you say after she called you a selfish coward who can't commit?"

The click of fingernails against wood triggered a jolt of anxiety, spiking his heartbeat into a gallop. "Please, stop tapping the table." He gritted his teeth. "I don't want a panic attack."

Her eyes widened, and she lifted her hands. "I'm sorry."

As soon as the sound receded, he breathed deeply, listening to soft patter of his heartbeat. "Thanks for understanding." He folded his arms on the table and slumped forward. "She said she would think about visiting me in Georgia, but she hung up without calling me 'baby' or saying 'I love you,' which is something she's never done." Glancing at the scarred table, he shuddered. "I called her again but my call went directly to voicemail. I'm really worried I messed up this time." He hardened his mouth into a tight line. "Maybe she's more than a little bit right. I am completely self-absorbed and fearful, unable to settle on anything or anyone without running away." He heaved a sigh. "I always return, but I never stay."

The server delivered two glasses and a pitcher of water.

Greg poured them each a glass.

"Why don't you go visit her in New York?" She sipped from the glass of water. "Buying tickets for the holiday weekend might be tough, but you could plan something for next weekend."

Slumping, he shook his head. "Amy made the same suggestion about Easter or the weekend thereafter before I told her about the job offer." He lifted his face. "Do you girls think all alike?"

"Hardly." She laughed. "Only the best of us think alike." She winked. "Whoops. No flirting." She clutched her hands in her lap and tucked her chin toward her chest. "Honestly, you should visit her before she visits you. Make her feel like she comes first. All the romantic heroes surprise the heroine by giving her exactly what she needs and wants."

Raising his eyebrows, he studied her closer. "Romantic heroes?"

She lifted her head, smiling. "Don't you watch

romantic comedies? All the men are bumbling fools who somehow get their heads out of their butts long enough to make a grand romantic gesture to win the women they love." She clasped her hands over her heart. "Every woman lives for the grand romantic gesture."

He propped an elbow on the table and cupped his chin in a palm. "What are you talking about?"

"The grand romantic gesture is different for every woman." She touched her chest. "When I heard Darren propose at the Fern Grotto in Kauai, I knew we were destined for a happy marriage."

He sniggered. *She lives in a fantasy world.* He slapped a hand on the table. "This man is the same guy who won't return your phone calls and text messages when you have a work crisis."

Dropping her shoulders, she pouted. "No romantic hero is perfect."

"You girls are impossible." He shook his head, laughing. "You want us to give you a grand romantic gesture, but if we forget to take out the garbage, we instantly become a villain, and you start looking somewhere else for someone who will save the day."

A red blush colored her cheeks. She shook a fist. "I am not looking for anyone to save the day."

Smiling, he pointed to his chest. "Then what am I doing here, if I'm not replacing the romantic hero?"

Biting her lip, she glanced away.

"Did I hit a nerve?" He scowled.

After a couple of minutes, she met his gaze. "If your hypothesis is right, then you need to hop on the next plane to New York before Amy vanishes off into the sunset with another man."

The truth blazed between them.

The server delivered their meals. "Anything else?"

Greg swallowed, glancing from the salad and burger to the starkness of Maddy's intent face. "No, thank you. We're fine." *Fine*. The word underscored too many unspoken conversations. Nothing was fine— not Greg and Amy, and not Maddy and Darren. Feeling the tug of tension increase between them, he guessed they weren't fine either. He stabbed his dry salad, shoved a forkful into his mouth, and crunched into a bitter cucumber.

She bit into the hamburger. A dribble of juice leaked onto her chin. She mopped it up with a napkin.

For several minutes, they ate in silence.

Halfway through the meal, the server returned. "Everything still fine?"

Without glancing at Maddy or the server, he nodded.

Finished, Maddy shoved aside her plate and sipped from a second glass of water. "I thought you were different because of your leg. Doesn't trauma make you more compassionate?"

Tossing down his fork, he glowered. "Are you saying losing my foot makes me a better person?" He threw up his hands. "What a ridiculous argument. That statement is worse than the pity-fuck some women give me."

She threw her napkin on the table. "This conversation has nothing to do with pity. I don't pity you." She waved a hand between them. "We have a connection."

He squeezed his hands, blood pumping through his veins. "Through boot camp? Or PerfectFit.com?"

Shrugging, she shook her head. "I...don't...know."

Her downcast eyes melted his resistance. Yes, he felt a connection. Not necessarily through boot camp or PerfectFit.com. If he thought about their relationship long enough, he didn't know when she became the missing piece to the puzzle of his life.

Dipping her head, she sobbed.

The sight of her curled shoulders and blonde hair triggered another memory of Amy bursting into tears at the altar when he said, "I don't," instead of "I do." He glanced around to see if anyone was watching before he reached across the table and tapped her wrist. "Ah, Maddy, don't cry."

Rubbing her nose, she sniffled. "Why did you agree to see me if you knew I was only using you?"

"A general never abandons his troop." He dabbed her cheeks with a napkin. "For the next five weeks, I'm your general, and you're my troop."

She clasped her hand over his wrist. "What happens after the five weeks?"

Sighing, he gazed into the endless blue of her cloudless eyes. Desire and uncertainty tensed his jaw. "I don't know."

Nodding, she pouted. "I don't want us to end."

He extended his other arm and held both of her hands. The warmth of her skin softened into a wealth of possibilities. *I can have a non-sexual relationship with a woman.* A cloud of doubt scuttled across the sky of his thoughts. *I'm still pretending to be a general.* The lie tightened a knot in his chest. *If I tell her the truth, will she walk?* He swallowed. "I don't want us to end either."

The server returned. "Any dessert?"

He met Maddy's glance.

She shook her head.

"No." Greg released Maddy's hands and removed his wallet. "We're ready for the bill."

Maddy opened her purse. "Let's go Dutch."

"Sure." He placed a twenty-dollar bill on the table. *I want her to feel comfortable.*

The server returned with the tab.

After squinting at the total, Maddy tossed two ten-dollar bills on the table. "What a great meal." She slipped out of the booth and slung the purse over a shoulder.

Greg stood and slipped his arms into his jacket.

She smiled. "Thanks for going Dutch."

"Well, I couldn't let you wrestle me for the check, could I?" Winking, he waved her toward the exit. "I don't need you to embarrass me in a restaurant. Bad enough you embarrass me at the gym."

Giggling, she wagged a finger. "Only during burpees. You annihilate me in pull ups. How many did you do this morning?"

"One hundred five." He opened his arms, exposing his chest. "Not bad for ten minutes." As he held the door, a brisk wind tunneled through the lobby. Shivering, he followed her outside into the dark, cloudy night that smelled of jasmine. "Only one more day until the weekend."

"Two days of rest." She shuddered, crossing her arms over her chest. "What are you doing this weekend?"

"Running." He slipped out of his jacket and draped it across her shoulders. "Where did you park?"

"I walked." She pointed toward the apartment building across the street. "I live there."

Nodding, he placed a hand on the middle of her back. "I'll see you into the lobby."

"No, thanks." Tensing her shoulders, she stepped aside. "I'll walk you to your car. Where did you park?"

He pointed toward a four-door sedan. "What are you doing this weekend?"

She tugged the jacket against her breasts and bit her lower lip. "Nothing."

Turning toward her, he lifted his eyebrows. "Why don't you come and run?" *Please, say yes. I don't want to be alone.*

"I can't even jog four times around the warehouse without stopping to walk." Staring at him, she laughed. "How could I possibly jog around a creek?"

"We can *fartlek*. That word is Swedish for speed play. You run a little and walk a lot to build up tolerance for long distance running or to improve your timing for marathons." He touched her elbow and nodded. "I'll show you."

She shook her head. "I don't have any running gear."

"I'm shopping in Buckhead the day after tomorrow." He smiled. "Come along. I'll show you what to buy."

For a long moment, she stared at the pavement. "Okay." She lifted her chin. "I'll go. But you have to promise to be easy on me."

"Don't worry." He wrapped an arm around her shoulders and tugged her close. "I'll treat you like a new recruit."

She leaned into his body and groaned. "I'll be sore on Monday."

Releasing her, he shoved his hand into his pocket and removed his car keys and cell phone. He glanced at the screen and noticed a missed call from Strong Gym. *Was boot camp canceled?* As he listened to the voicemail, he motioned for Maddy to stop walking. "Hey, Greg, it's Peter Strong. I'm sorry to be calling, but I'm looking for my sister, Maddy. I don't know if you've seen or heard from her. She's missing. Anyway, if you know where she is, please call me at the gym, okay? Thanks."

Frowning, she slipped out of his jacket and folded it once. "Is everything all right?"

A cold chill ran through him, and he shook his head. "Your brother's looking for you." He met her gaze. "Apparently, he thinks you're missing."

The streetlight caught a glimmer of disbelief in her narrowed eyes. "How dare he panic? I turned off my phone, so I could get a little peace and quiet." She balled her trembling hands into fists. "Why does my family always have to check up on me like I'm some little kid who needs to be supervised instead of a grown woman who can manage herself?"

He unlocked his car and laid his jacket on the passenger's seat. "You should call him and let him know you're okay." Turning, he studied her closer beneath the pool of amber light. *She looks so small and helpless. No wonder her family worries about her. I worry about her, and she's not even mine.* He wrapped his arms around her. "*Are* you okay?" he whispered through the tangle of hair.

She leaned into the embrace, placing her head against his chest. "Yeah, I'm okay. I'll call my brother as soon as I get home." She stepped back and straightened her shoulders, her gaze zigzagging across his face. "What about you, General? Will you get any sleep?"

"Actually, I've been sleeping better since I met you." Heat flooded his face. "I mean, since boot camp started."

She tilted her head. "Heavy lifting wears you out."

You wear me out. When would being friends with a woman feel natural? For a long moment, he studied her. *She's such a nice girl. I hope I don't screw up.*

Chapter 13

When Maddy turned on the lights of her stuffy apartment, she clutched a fist against the knocking in her chest. *How much damage have I done by shutting out my family?* The beep of the answering machine chimed in the living room. She stepped inside, locked the front door, strode over to the blinking light, and pressed the Play button.

Beep. "Maddy, it's Darren. Why is your cell phone turned off? Call me."

Beep. "Maddy, Jane here. Where are you? We're all worried. Please respond before we call the police and report you as a missing person. Love you. Bye."

Beep. "Hey, Mad, it's Pete. Everyone keeps calling me to ask if I know where you are. Your phone's turned off. You're not at work. You don't have any friends." He gulped. "Anyway, you better not be with that guy from boot camp. He's psycho. The VA is paying for his classes. I know I should have never set you up as partners, but I figured you wouldn't show up for class and I'd have to work with him." He exhaled loudly. "You guys seem kind of close. I'm worried. Call me."

You're all psycho. Maddy dropped her purse on the coffee table and kicked off her flats. *My boot camp partner is the only sane person in my life.*

The urge to guzzle a beer before returning any of

the phone calls struck deep in her gut, and she flinched. *Can I blame my family for my habit of drinking and dodging the bullets of life?* She ran fingers through her lank hair and sighed. *No, I will face these assaults sober, and I'll face them now before I take a long hot bath and go to sleep.* She picked up the home phone and called Darren first.

"Hey, baby, you're home," Darren said. "What happened to your cell phone?"

"Battery died." She paced back and forth across the carpet, glancing around the room with Darren's critical gaze. The furniture needed dusting, the photographs on the walls needed to be straightened, and the carpet needed to be deep cleaned. "I'm very sorry everyone was worried. I've been so busy between work and boot camp I forgot to charge my phone last night."

"I'm just glad you're okay." He exhaled. "Jane said you might have been drinking and driving, and Peter thought you might have been kidnapped, raped, or murdered."

Why did her family always assume the worst? Tensing her shoulders, she tightened her grip on the phone. She tilted her head to the side. "What did you think?"

"You were upset about the news about work and a little angry because I didn't call you back immediately after you sent that first text this morning." He cleared his throat. "I spoke with a prestigious doctor, and the meeting lasted longer than I expected, but I got the sale. When I called, I went directly to voicemail."

She sank on the sofa and propped her legs on the coffee table. "Were you calling to tell me about your big sale, or were you calling to find out if I was all right?"

"Both."

Of course, he called about his big sale. He already sent a text about church and Easter brunch. Why couldn't he have sent a text about my job? "I feel unimportant when you respond to Jane's group text before you respond to one of my texts, especially when you know I'm trying my hardest not to eat my feelings." She crossed an arm over her chest. "I need you to be here emotionally by responding to my texts and phone messages instead of waiting until the end of the day after I've already left work to deal with things on my own."

"I'm sorry, Porky."

"My name is Maddy." She lurched to her feet and shook a fist. "Please, don't call me Porky anymore. When I'm called that name, I feel unattractive and unloved."

"Okay, Maddy." He sighed. "I wish I was there to hold you. You sound like you need a hug."

She nodded, her knees buckling with gratitude. *He understands me.* "A hug would be nice right about now."

"Well, if we were texting, I would send you the hug emoji and the kissy face emoji."

A half-smile lit her face. She softened her shoulders and uncurled her fist. After slumping into the sofa, she stretched her legs across the coffee table. "Congratulations on your first big sale during this trip."

"Thanks. I celebrated with a prime rib dinner tonight, and I'll be getting up early to work off those calories. How about you? Are you worried you might lose your job because of the company's sale?"

She shrugged, feeling the weight of anxiety blanket her shoulders. "I'll find out what's happening to the company and my job next Monday."

"Call me after you find out, okay? If I'm in a meeting, I promise I'll call you right back. Just keep in mind some of these meetings last a few hours, especially if I'm golfing. I can't return your call until after I'm off the green."

The reassurance of his words comforted her. From experience, she knew he checked his messages before and after a four-hour game.

"Tell me about the rest of your day," he said. "Where did you go after work?"

She paused, and her scalp crinkled. "I dined out."

"Alone?"

If I tell him the truth, he'll just encourage me to stop seeing Greg. I will have lost the only friend I have. "No, I ate with Tina from work."

"Tina?"

She gnawed on her lower lip, shifting uncomfortably on the sofa. "You know who she is, don't you? Short, curly hair, sits in the next cubicle, has a hard time keeping down her call times."

"Yeah, you've mentioned her once or twice, but you never go out with anyone from work."

Oh, no, he knows I'm lying. She fumbled for an excuse. "Everyone's stressed about the company takeover. You're gone, and her boyfriend's gone, so we decided to share a meal and support each other."

"Did anyone else from work meet you for dinner?"

Anxiety threatened to overwhelm her. She swung her feet off the coffee table and paced. "Why are you asking so many questions? Don't you trust me?"

"I'm worried. Pete said you might be hanging out with Greg. I don't mind you having friends, even male friends, but that guy's not all there."

"He's *not* dangerous." Stopping, she broadened her stance. A vision of Greg dipping his chin toward his chest as he talked about Amy floated across her mind. He looked so forlorn. She wanted to pet him like a lost puppy. She threw up an arm. "He's just as messed up as I am."

"You're not messed up."

A bark of derisive laughter escaped from her mouth. As she listed her faults, she curled her fingers toward her palm. "I drink too much. I eat too much. I feel too much. I can't be alone."

"Those details are all minor, and not major medical issues." He sighed. "You haven't been diagnosed with PTSD." Silence came over the line. "Do you know people with that disorder can hold innocent people as hostages before they shoot their brains out?" He huffed. "I'm serious, Maddy. I've already talked to Pete, and he says you need to stay away from this guy. He's assigning you both new boot camp partners tomorrow."

"I don't want a new partner." Sinking into the sofa cushions, she clutched her head with a hand. Blood throbbed in her temples, and a headache bloomed across her forehead. "I'll quit boot camp."

"You can't quit."

"Yes, I can." *How dare they try to control who I work out with?* She lifted her head, and the room spun.

170

"You're not here to stop me from quitting."

"I can arrange to have Pete come by every morning to haul you out of bed."

"Stop ganging up." She clenched a hand into a tight fist. "Please, let me make my own decisions."

"We would if we knew you made good decisions."

She swept an arm across the room. "I didn't choose Greg. Peter chose him." *Only because he thought I was a flake.* A tremor wobbled in her voice. He didn't need to know she pilfered Greg's information from work and contacted him through her personal email account. "I feel like you're blaming me for Peter's decision."

"Okay, I admit Peter was wrong. He lacked judgment."

"If he pairs me up with anyone else, I'll quit."

"Why are you being so stubborn?"

"Greg is helping me to stay on track." She pointed to her chest. "Don't you want me to lose weight? Don't you want me to be healthy?"

"I don't want you to be thin and *dead*."

"He won't kill me." She perched on the edge of the sofa cushions and ran her fingers through her hair. "He's a nice guy. He needs a friend as much as I do."

"When did you two become friends?"

Her silence threatened to reveal the truth. Thinking, she swallowed. She could not confess emailing her cell phone number to Greg outside of work. Darren would assume she intended on cheating, and another argument would blast away their tentative truce. "I don't know."

"Yes, you do."

She jumped from the anger in his voice. How would he know about her email to Greg?

"You befriended the guy to get back at me for not being home. You think if you continue seeing this guy, then I'll quit my job, right?"

Frustration bristled against her skin. She gripped the phone tighter. Did she contact Greg as a pawn to save her relationship with Darren? Or did she have some other motivation? A shiver ran through her. She worried both Greg and Darren might be right, and she might not know herself as well as they did. "Of course, I want you to quit your job and come home, but that reason is not why I'm friends with Greg."

"Please, stop seeing him."

"I can't." When she thought about waking up at five a.m., rolling out of bed, driving to the gym, and jogging around the building without him, she ached with loneliness. Who else would encourage her to keep the pace? Who else would slow to join her when her legs were so damn tired she could barely walk? "I need him."

"Why?"

"Because he brings out the best in me." A tear slipped out of the corner of her eye and trickled down her cheek. "When I'm with him, I don't want to drink until I pass out. I don't want to eat junk food until I'm so bloated I can't zip up my pants."

"So, you've seen him when you're drinking and eating?"

The truth seared through her body like a torch. She ran a finger beneath the collar, releasing damp heat from her skin. *Oh, how do I answer his question?* She took a deep breath to steady her quivering voice. "Working out with him during boot camp inspires me throughout the day. I look forward to getting up and challenging myself to run. I look forward to talking about his life. I look forward to becoming a better version of me."

"And you can't do any of this self-improvement without him?"

"No, I can't." She pushed back her shoulders and straightened her spine. "I need him as much as he needs me. He's not like you or Jane or Peter. He doesn't hound me or nag me or parent me. He lets me be me."

"Are you falling in love?"

She widened her eyes. *In love? With Greg?* She chuckled. "That feeling never crossed my mind. I love you, although lately, I've been questioning whether or not you truly love me or if you're just longing for an imaginary person I can't be."

"But you can give that better version of yourself to him, can't you?"

A pang of guilt stabbed her chest. She glanced around the living room. Did she sound like a lovesick woman? "How can I get you to hear what I just said? He encourages. He listens. He accepts me for who I am."

"And I don't?"

"No, you don't." She swiped a finger across the coffee table and lifted it to the light. A gray smattering of dust covered the tip. "You complain I don't clean enough. I don't eat what you want me to eat and drink what you want me to drink. I don't work out enough. I'm not thin enough. I'm not happy enough. I'm not all put together like Jane, and I'm not healthy like Peter." She sucked in a breath. "The list goes on and on."

"Okay, you win." He exhaled. "I'll quit my job and come home." A moment of silence passed. "But you better be happy."

She threw up a fist. "There you go again demanding something from me which I cannot promise you." She stood and adjusted the grip on the phone. "If you quit your job, you quit because you want to quit. Don't quit because you think I'll be happy." She tapped her chest. "My happiness is my responsibility. Before today I've just been too wrapped up in pleasing everybody else."

A long stretch of quiet filled the space.

"How long have you been unhappy?" he asked.

Sighing, she thought back over the years. Since college, she filtered the world through an alcoholic haze. Since boot camp, she experienced clarity through a change in her diet and exercise. Until now she never realized how she used food and alcohol to numb the pain of day-to-day living. "I don't know."

"Did your unhappiness start before or after we met?"

"Before."

"You can't blame me for your unhappiness."

"I'm not blaming anyone." She closed her eyes, frustration pulsing at her temples. "I love you, but I question if we're the perfect fit. I like Greg, even though you say he's crazy. I love my job, even though the company's being sold." She sniffed. "I hate my body, but I can't trade it in for a new one. I like to eat junk food and drink alcohol, but I don't like how I feel afterward." She hiccupped. "I hate my family. They're too controlling. Sometimes I think you've become as

174

controlling as they are."

"We're just worried about you."

"I know." Sighing, she opened her eyes. *If I clean up my act, then maybe I won't be controlled anymore.* "I still have to call Jane and Peter, and I want to take a long hot bath before I go to sleep. I have to get up early if I'm attending boot camp."

"Okay, I'll let you go. Please reconsider church and Easter brunch on Sunday. I know you don't get along with your sister, but I also know being with family is better than being alone."

He's trying to control me again. She shook her head. *He doesn't need to know about Greg's invitation to go running.* "Okay, I'll think about it. Good night, Darren."

"Good night, Maddy. I love you."

"Love you, too." She ended the call. Taking a deep breath, she dialed her sister.

"Hello?"

Jane's crisp voice greeted her. "It's me, Maddy." She swallowed. "I'm calling to let you know I'm fine. My phone died because I forgot to charge the battery. I dined with a co-worker and just picked up your message. You can stop worrying about me."

"Why aren't you coming to church and brunch this Sunday?"

Annoyance bristled in the tone of her sister's voice. "I have other plans." She wasn't about to elaborate.

"What other plans?"

Fear tensed her jaw. She didn't want to mention Greg. "I'm getting together with co-workers for brunch."

"On Easter?"

She glanced at the ceiling, concocting a plausible story. "We're having a picnic."

"When the newscasters expect rain?" Jane exhaled. "You're a terrible liar, Maddy. Are you just staying home and getting drunk? If you want to drink, Chris can drive you home. I don't have a problem with that arrangement. I just don't want you drinking and driving."

She folded an arm across her chest, wishing she could curl into a ball and disappear. *Now I'm the drunken relative everyone accommodates during the holidays.* She squeezed shut her eyes. "I just don't want to go. You were mean the last time I visited, and I never want to go through that type of experience again." She opened her eyes. "I'd rather be alone."

Jane sighed. "I've already forgiven you for your behavior. The children will be expecting you. You don't want to disappoint them, do you?"

"I'll think about it." She yawned. "I'm tired, and I still have to call Peter. Good night, Jane." She ended the call.

One more call then I can take my bath. She dialed Peter's home number.

"Hello?"

Peter's gruff voice drifted across the line. "It's Maddy."

"Hey, I'm glad you called. Where have you been?"

She could never lie to her brother. He broke up her fights with Jane, and he carried a sense of impartial justice based on the truth. "I was out having dinner. I already called Darren and Jane. I'm getting ready to take a bath and go to bed, but I wanted to let you know I'm safe."

"Good. I was worried." Silence barreled down the line. "Are you all right?"

The gravity of the truth weighed on her, threatening to overwhelm the delicate balance she struggled to maintain during the previous two conversations. A ringing sensation echoed in her ears. Burning gnawed her stomach. The familiar impulse to shove food into her mouth to quiet the pain jolted her attention. "No, I'm not all right. My company's being bought out, and my fiancé travels more than half the year, and I'm being hounded to attend Easter celebrations although I no longer believe in God." She clutched the phone against her jaw. A wave of panic swept over her. "Please, don't switch my boot camp partner. I like Greg. He helps me, and I help him. I don't care if he's been diagnosed with PTSD. The VA would not have enrolled him in your boot camp if they thought he was treacherous."

A moment of silence stretched between them.

"I hear what you're saying, but you need to see things from my point of view. Greg isn't Jane. I can't just separate you two from a fight. He's a vet with a mental illness. I don't know how unpredictable he might be." He took a breath. "Didn't you see what happened in Yountville, California? A vet with PTSD held three women hostage before shooting them to death. I want you to be safe."

She slumped deeper into the cushions. *He's just worried about my safety.* A trickle of anxiety leaked through her. *Should I be concerned, too?* An image of

Greg's soft brown eyes and crooked smile filled her mind. Comfort blanketed her shoulders. *He's as harmless as a puppy.* "Boot camp is a public place. You can supervise us. Outside of boot camp, I can take care of myself." As she thought, she curled her fingers with each item of risk. *He has my cell phone. He knows where I work. He knows the apartment building where I live, but he does not know which apartment number. If I only see him in public places, I should be secure.*

"What about Darren? Have you talked to him about Greg?"

"Briefly." Recalling the tense conversation, she tightened her jaw. Heat flushed her skin. "He knows he can't protect me forever. I have to make my own decisions."

He laughed. "Lately, you have a terrible track record."

"Agreed." As she nodded, she chuckled. "But I'm getting better."

Another stretch of quiet passed between them.

"Okay. I won't switch you guys." He sighed. "But I won't stop worrying either."

"I appreciate it. Night." She ended the call and placed the wireless home phone in the base.

Loneliness descended. The apartment creaked like the joints of an old woman. The clock against the wall ticked to the rhythm of her heart. *Can I learn to take care of me?*

****

Greg paced back and forth outside the gym waiting for Maddy to arrive. A buzz of anticipation electrified the morning air. Why did he feel alive when he was with her? Was her infectious laughter the reason? Or the way she tilted her head when she thought? Did her candidness give him permission to be vulnerable? Or was he relieved to know he no longer needed to impress? Whatever the reason, he craved her presence. He kept his gaze trained on the parking lot. As he paced, he exhaled tiny clouds of moisture and rubbed his hands together to stay warm.

From inside the gym, Peter loped over, carrying a clipboard. A silver whistle on a chain bounced between the chiseled muscles of his chest. With a pen, he tapped Greg's forearm. "Excuse me, sir."

Startled, Greg glanced over at the gym owner's broad shoulders and muscled thighs. Peter was short and compact like Maddy but leaned out and puffed up from eating clean and working out. An air of suspicion hovered. Leaning forward, he frowned. "Yes?"

Peter pointed toward the clipboard. "I'm switching your partner for the rest of boot camp. You'll be working out with Gunther." He nodded toward a lanky man in baggy shorts. "Maddy will work out with Lola." He lifted his chin at a pudgy woman in sweats. "Better pairings."

Frustration throbbed against Greg's temples, the first sign of a headache. He recalled the voicemail Peter left on his cell phone last night and his ensuing conversation with Maddy. He rubbed his forehead. A terrible unsettling doom, the kind he felt during the war, roared through him. Why did Peter see him as the enemy when he only wanted to help? Stepping closer, he narrowed his gaze. "Don't play games. This idea about switching partners isn't about better fits. You want to end my relationship with your sister."

Peter drew together his eyebrows and pounded his chest with a fist. "I care about her. She's fragile."

A string of tenderness wove through him. Greg nodded, remembering how small and helpless Maddy looked beneath the streetlight last night. Stepping back, he slackened his shoulders. "You have my promise to respect her."

From the parking lot, someone called Greg's name. He pivoted.

Maddy jogged over. Cool pockets of air escaped from her open mouth. She halted between Greg and her brother, glancing from one to the other. Frowning, she placed both hands on her hips. "What's going on?"

A spark of nervousness ignited within Greg. *Should I tell her? Or should I shrug off the exchange?* He didn't want to upset her, but he didn't want to withhold the truth. Finally, he lifted his chin. "Your brother suggested we change partners."

Turning toward Peter, she wagged a finger. "Did you forget our conversation last night?"

Peter grabbed Maddy's elbow, steering her aside.

She yanked away her arm. "Whatever you have to say, you can say in front of Greg."

A knot tightened in Greg's stomach. "Maybe I should go."

"Stay." Maddy placed a hand on his arm.

Warmth sizzled up his arm. He lurched backward, not wanting anyone to know he craved her touch.

Frowning, Maddy let her hand fall away. "You're not the problem." She waved her thumb toward Peter. "He is."

Peter swiveled his gaze from Greg to Maddy. "I changed my mind. I don't trust him."

She narrowed her gaze, waving her hand between Greg and herself. "If you force us apart, we'll both quit and join another boot camp, and then you'll be unable to supervise us."

Placing his hands on his hips, Peter broadened his stance. "Why are you defying me?"

"Don't baby me anymore." She glowered. "I can take care of myself." She gathered her light hair away from her face and captured the strands at the base of her neck with an elastic band. "Ready to run?" She brushed Greg's bare skin with her fingertips.

An electric jolt powered through his arm, and blood flooded into his groin. Why did his body betray his feelings? He moved aside. "I don't want any trouble with your brother."

Tight-lipped, she nodded. "If he wants us to stay, he has to listen to me for a change."

He studied her determined face a moment longer. *I'm glad I don't have siblings meddling with my life. I've enough problems with a demanding mom and an unreasonable fiancée.* Last night, after returning home from dinner, he called his mother and spoke about the job offer.

She huffed. "Are you crazy? Don't take that job. You belong in New York."

Afterward, he called Amy. The phone didn't ring but clicked over to voicemail. He wanted to leave a message but the mailbox was full. Why was Amy's phone turned off? Why was her mailbox full? He needed to ask Maddy for her insight. After all, Maddy turned off her phone because she didn't want to speak with her family. Did Amy not want to speak with him? Was he as unbearable to deal with as Maddy's family was? Or was he reading too much into her silence?

"Four laps around the building." Peter raised the clipboard and blew the whistle.

Placing a hand on Maddy's shoulder, Greg nodded toward the runners. "Let's go."

Maddy lifted her legs and pumped her arms back and forth, breathing in through her nose and out through her mouth. "I'm sorry about my brother's behavior."

"No need to apologize." Greg slowed his pace to match her stride. "We're only responsible for our behavior." A thought flitted through his mind. "We need a couple of rules to govern our friendship."

She tilted her head to one side. "What type of rules?"

The stricter the boundaries, the better the friendship, he figured. "Respect and transparency."

"I understand respect." As she continued running, she shook her head. "What do you mean by transparency?"

"No secrets." He frowned. "At all times, you can tell anyone anything about us."

"I think I already broke the second rule." After rounding the corner of the gym, she picked up her pace. "I didn't tell Darren I ate dinner with you last night. I told him I spent the evening with a co-worker."

"Why did you lie?" He deepened his frown. "We shared a meal, nothing else."

She panted. "I was afraid he would tell me to stop seeing you."

He lifted his eyebrows, shortening his stride. "Why would he care?"

"Because you're a threat." She pumped her arms back and forth. "You've been diagnosed with PTSD. A guy with that diagnosis just killed three women in Yountville, California."

Every muscle tightened. *I'm not a murderer. I'm a friend.* Still running, he gazed intently at her face. "Do you trust me?"

With tears in her eyes, she nodded. "But no one else in my family does. They think you're a menace."

Shaking his head, he pumped his arms back and forth. "No wonder." When he received treatment in New York for PTSD, a fellow veteran was dismissed from an outpatient program for physically attacking a psychologist. Most of the veterans he knew, however, processed the lingering trauma of war internally, numbing the chaos with drugs or alcohol, rather than lashing out at others with pummeling fists or loaded guns. "I'll talk to your brother after our run."

Blinking away tears, she lifted her eyebrows. "Can we still be friends?"

He exhaled, considering the ramifications of her actions. "Going forward, I need you to be completely honest with your family about everything we do and say." He flashed a warning. "If you lie, we're over. Understand?"

Nodding, she picked up her pace. "Yes, General."

Halfway through the final lap, Greg remembered what he wanted to discuss. "I tried calling Amy last night, but her phone was busy. Do you think she's avoiding me?"

"Probably." She cupped a hand against her side and slowed to a walk. "Have you booked a flight to visit?"

"No." Shame flushed his face. "I hoped to convince her to come down here."

"You need to give a little to get a lot." She inhaled, raising her hands over her head.

He placed his hands on his waist, his gaze darting back and forth across her face. "I'll think about it."

"Don't think too long." She wagged a finger. "She might run off into the sunset with someone else."

Laughing, he shook his head. "She doesn't have someone else." Whenever he thought of Amy, he envisioned her alone in their apartment or the gallery or his mother's house.

"Are you sure?" She lifted her chin. "Has she ever mentioned anyone?"

Finishing the final lap, he shook his head. "No one…" He didn't count his mom, who was family, or McKenzie, who was an artist from work. He touched Maddy's arm. "I'll be right back." He jogged over to Peter who stood at the gym's entrance. "Excuse me."

Peter raised his head and frowned.

"I understand your concern about my PTSD." He held his gaze. "I want to reassure you. I don't own a gun. I've never been admitted to an inpatient program. I've always held a job. I'm highly functional." He furrowed his forehead. "I'm here because I have night terrors. Dr. Carter thinks the exercise will help. If you'd like, I'll sign a release, and you can talk to Dr. Carter about my condition if it will make you feel better about my friendship with Maddy. Okay?"

"Listen, Power, I don't care if you're inpatient or

outpatient or even if you've been cured." Peter clutched the clipboard to his burly chest. "I don't want you hanging out with my sister after class. She's engaged to be married. She doesn't need any help messing up her life, understand?"

Clenching his hands into fists, he steadied his escalating breath. "Shouldn't Maddy decide whom she associates with?"

Peter stepped closer. "Maddy only associates with family."

Stay calm. Don't let this jerk aggravate you. He's only proving his point that you're dangerous. Greg sighed and unclenched his fists. "I'm her friend."

Peter stepped back. "Men and women can't be friends."

"Have you ever tried?" Greg leaned forward.

"Leave my sister alone."

"No." Greg spun and searched for Maddy.

She stood by the bench press inside the gym. Smiling, she waved.

Happiness flooded through him.

Who cared if Greg was a man and Maddy was a woman? They were friends who wanted to help each other step outside their comfort zones and broaden their horizons. *What could possibly go wrong?*

Chapter 14

That afternoon, an overnight package arrived at Greg's office. Smiling, he held the battered box in his hands. *She must not be as angry as I thought.* He ripped apart the box. A soft leather case tumbled into his palm. The smell of polish lingered on his fingertips. He unzipped the case and fondled the camera. The shutter used to stick whenever he wanted to take a picture with fast movement. A picture he took of Amy swinging her hair as she rode the carousel in Central Park blurred like spilled milk. Whatever happened to those practice pictures?

Turning over the camera in his hands, he adjusted the aperture to control the amount of light. The movement flowed smoothly, narrowing and widening with his touch. Next, he increased and decreased the shutter speed to test whether or not the camera would capture images in low light or with quick movement without obscuring the image. Finally, he aimed the camera at the bookcase against the wall and peered through the lens to adjust the focus.

Click.

The camera worked perfectly.

Gratitude warmed his chest, and he grabbed the office phone to call Amy. The call rolled over into voicemail. He hung up before the sound of the beep.

Fear crinkled his scalp. *Something's wrong.*

He held his breath. *Don't panic.* After picking up the receiver, he dialed the art gallery.

After three rings, someone answered.

"It's Greg, Amy's fiancé." With a sharp intake of breath, he ran his fingers through his hair. "Do you know where she is?"

"She's meeting with a collector to acquire a few pieces before an estate sale," the receptionist said. "What number shall I have her call?"

Tension eased from his jaw. "Work." He rattled off the phone number. "Please, let her know I received the camera." Smiling, he stroked the case. "Everything works perfectly, and the lenses, filters, and rolls of film are more than I expected. She and my mother shouldn't have spent so much for servicing, but I'm grateful."

"I'll let her know, Greg. Goodbye."

He ended the call and embraced the camera against his chest. The steady rhythm of his breathing matched the steady rhythm of his thoughts. *We're fine. She's just working. She doesn't want to be disturbed. She'll call me back this afternoon. Everything is fine.*

Picking up the phone, he dialed his mother. Again, the phone rang three times before clicking to voicemail. "Mom, it's me. Thanks for working with Amy to get my camera serviced. I appreciate it. Can't wait to see how the pictures turn out." He paused, wondering if his mother knew something more about Amy's whereabouts than he did. "If you see Amy, please let her know I'm thankful. I can't reach her. I know she's working a lot, but I miss her." The old familiar pain ached in his chest. He thought of Maddy's advice to visit. "Maybe I'll make a trip home soon."

The darkness rolled into his thoughts, and the familiar undertow of depression sank his spirits. Ending the call, he set aside the camera and listened to the hollow echo of silence in the impersonal office. An overwhelming desire to bolt from the building and dart into the heat of the afternoon twitched the muscles in his thighs. Remembering Dr. Carter's advice, he coached himself through the panic. *I have to visit. I have to go home and marry Amy.* A prickle of anxiety raised goose bumps on his skin. *If I don't leave soon, I might lose her.* Another thought drifted through his mind. *She's not returning my calls. She's avoiding me. Maybe Maddy is right, and I have lost her to someone or something else.*

****

After work, Maddy stopped at a grocery store and bought fresh fruits and vegetables for a homemade meal. Nothing fancy, she decided, just an apple walnut salad with a vinaigrette dressing. No beer, no wine, and no hard liquor. Instead, she would drink sparkling water with a slice of lime.

When she arrived at the apartment, she unloaded the groceries on the counter and prepared the salad before sitting at the kitchen table. She didn't want to wallow in self-pity by lounging on the couch and munching the sparse meal while watching commercials of fast food and beer.

But as she picked up her fork and speared the first piece of lettuce, she held her breath. A cold prickling sensation crawled over her skin. She was alone. Releasing her breath, she closed her eyes and said a silent prayer. *Please, help me get through this meal.*

Opening her eyes, she focused on her breathing as she chewed. One thousand one, one thousand two… By the time she finished the salad, satisfaction filled her body. *I ate alone.* Standing, she cleared the table, washed the dishes, and grabbed a light sweater for an evening walk. While descending in the elevator, she thought of calling the General. As soon as she stepped into the cool, crisp evening air, she forgot about everything. The orange sun blazed against the horizon, streaking the sky with charcoal and violet rays beneath a canopy of clouds. She gasped. Why had she never noticed the beautiful surroundings of her home?

Shoving her hands into her pockets, she strolled. *Being alone is all right.* Without the conflict of her family or the drama between her and Darren or the worry about work, she softened her shoulders. The wind played through her hair and tickled her nose. She smiled. For the first time in her life, she cherished being alone. The sensation surprised her, and she wondered if the pleasure of her own company outweighed the pain of being with others.

****

On Saturday morning, Greg met Maddy at Lenox Square in Buckhead a little after ten. Already, dark clouds threatened the sky. A cool breeze ruffled the back of his neck.

Maddy shuddered beneath her jacket. "The weather shouldn't be this cold in March."

"I wouldn't know." He shrugged. "This spring is my first in Georgia."

She strolled beside him toward the shops. "When

our family first moved here when I was ten, spring was longer and warmer, almost muggy. Summers I hated. I longed for the California coast." Maddy rubbed her arms through her jacket. "I sometimes think about moving back, if the cost of living wasn't so expensive."

"Who knows?" He nudged her elbow. "You might be out of work soon. Perfect time to leave."

She groaned. "I have to think about Darren."

"Hasn't he decided yet?" He lifted his eyebrows.

"I think he hopes I'll change my mind and marry him anyway."

"Would you?"

"If you asked me a month ago, I would have said yes. If you ask me today, I might say no." Smiling, she lifted her head. "I actually ate a meal alone and enjoyed it. I didn't freak out like I normally do. In fact, I walked around the block afterward."

"Good for you." He wrapped an arm around her shoulders and squeezed her close. "I'm proud of you."

She snuggled, burying her cheek against his chest. "You're warm."

A sense of longing penetrated the darkness within him, and he tugged her closer, bending down to smell her hair. The light floral fragrance reminded him of the first time he bought Amy flowers at the corner market near his apartment—how the sight and scent of so many different flowers overwhelmed him. He was conservative, selecting red roses, when he should have been daring, selecting lilies. When was the last time he bought Amy lilies?

"Maddy?" A high female voice pierced through the crowds.

She stopped and stiffened.

He rubbed her knotted shoulder and studied her face. "What's wrong?"

The disembodied voice drifted closer, calling out again. "Maddy. It *is* you."

A woman carrying a designer purse and a ton of shopping bags stepped out of the crowd. She was young and slender and wore lots of makeup. Her platinum hair was arranged into a chignon. When she frowned, the skin between her plucked eyebrows didn't pinch together.

"What are you doing here?"

Maddy gulped. "Shopping."

The woman lifted her eyebrows. "For a wedding dress?"

"No, for running gear." She glanced from Greg to the woman. "Greg, this is my sister, Jane." She pointed. "This is my friend, Greg."

Jane glanced up and down the length of Greg's body. Setting aside her bags, she extended her hand. A slow smile spread across her face. "I'm sorry, but Maddy's never mentioned any friends. Where did y'all meet?"

Greg shook her hand firmly. "Boot camp."

She tightened her smile. "I see." Glancing at Maddy, she frowned. "Is this the friend you're having a picnic with tomorrow instead of coming to church and brunch?"

Averting her gaze, Maddy shuffled her feet back and forth before lifting her chin and straightening her shoulders. "I'm sorry I lied. I was afraid of your judgment." She waved a hand back and forth between her and Greg. "We're running tomorrow."

Feeling the tension between the sisters, Greg intervened. "We're meeting at Lullwater Preserve at ten. Would you care to join us?"

Maddy shot him a widened glance, her mouth agape.

Jane picked up her bags. "I'm flattered you asked, but I'm celebrating the resurrection of our savior." Turning to leave, she stopped and pivoted. "How about the two of you join us for brunch? I'm serving plenty of food."

Frowning, Maddy shook her head. "Greg has a special diet—"

"We'd be happy to join you." He broadened his smile, delighted for the opportunity to spend an afternoon in the presence of a beautiful woman. "I'll prepare my favorite vegan dish for everyone to enjoy."

"Great." Jane arched an eyebrow at Maddy. "See you both tomorrow at eleven-thirty." She turned and swung her hips as she strode toward the parking lot.

Mesmerized, he stared until she disappeared. He shook his head. *When will I stop looking at women that way?*

Maddy swatted his arm. "How could you accept an invitation to a brunch I don't want to go to?"

Oh, thank goodness she wasn't reading my thoughts. He stepped aside and rubbed his arm. "We'll be hungry after our run."

"We could go to Marlow's Tavern again."

"Why go out to eat when your family's serving free food?"

She narrowed her gaze and wagged a finger. "You

don't know my family."

"Not yet." He winked, holding open the glass door of the nearest athletic store.

Grumbling, she stepped inside the warehouse.

The artificial light hurt his eyes, but the piped in music soothed his rattled nerves. He directed her toward the back of the store. "Your sister's pretty."

Shaking her head, she huffed. "She's a skinny bitch."

The spark of anger ignited a brief chuckle. "You're just jealous because she's thinner and more successful."

"She's petty and mean. She only cares about appearances."

Smiling, he wrapped an arm around her shoulders and tugged her against his side. "And you're an angel?"

Wriggling out of his embrace, she snickered. "I'm more of a porky devil."

He furrowed his brow and lifted both arms. "Don't call yourself porky."

"Darren calls me that nickname."

He grimaced. "Amy would never forgive me if I called her a derogatory nickname. Why doesn't he respect you?"

"Because I'm not like my sister." Pouting, she lifted shoes off a rack and slammed them down. "I continue to disappoint him."

He swallowed a lump of pity and placed a hand on her wrist. "You're too hard on yourself. You're doing your best, aren't you?"

She tugged away her hand and blinked. "No one in my life agrees." She shrugged and ran a hand across the mesh top of a running shoe.

Frowning, he glanced at her profile. Like her sister, she shared the same bright blue eyes, small nose, and wide mouth. Unlike her sister, she sported chubby cheeks and a double chin. If she lost weight, would she rival her sister's poised appearance? Another thought skittered through his mind. *If she was slender, might I find her irresistible?*

Holding up a shoe, she waved to a sales clerk. "May I try this shoe in a size seven?"

"Wait." Greg seized the shoe out of her hand before the sales clerk arrived. "You need something with a little more grip to run by the creek." He scanned the shoes against the wall and selected an orange and gray trail running shoe that felt as light as a roll of toilet paper. Grabbing her hand, he guided her fingers over the hills and valleys of the shoe's sole. "This shoe is the type you want to buy: water-proof, micro-engineered, and affordable. I'm getting the same brand."

"Okay." Shrugging, she handed the shoe to the sales clerk. "I trust your judgment."

While waiting, he sat beside her on a row of chairs. He clasped his hands between his thighs and pursed his lips. "Are you still upset I accepted the invitation to brunch?"

She glowered. "My family's intrusive."

The sales clerk returned with the box of shoes and laced them on Maddy's feet.

Afterward, Maddy stood and ran back and forth down an aisle.

Greg studied her gait, examining how the ball of her foot hit the linoleum and rolled to the edge of her heel. Nodding, he liked the way the shoes cradled her feet, preventing both an inward and outward wobble. She needed stability and support. "How do they feel?"

"Springy." She smiled, bouncing on her toes.

He nodded toward the sales clerk. "We'll take those shoes. May I have the same brand and style in a men's size eleven?"

While he waited for his shoes, he patted the seat beside him.

Maddy unlaced the shoes and held them in her lap. "I've never had anyone help me pick out the right shoes. I've always just bought whatever was on sale."

"Sales are good, but value is better." He flashed a smile. "Your feet will thank you."

"I thank you."

"You're welcome." He turned his thoughts toward her family. "Don't worry about tomorrow."

She shook her head. "I'll be glad when brunch is over."

What could possibly go wrong with sharing a meal? After all, he enjoyed both his mother's and Amy's company. Even when his father was alive, family meals were never contentious. A quick sideways glance caught her pinched lips and tight jaw. Maddy loved food, but she didn't love her family. She would rather eat alone. How could someone turn away from those who loved her? A bright pinpoint of light sparked in his consciousness. A prickling sensation shivered up his spine. *I'm just like Maddy. Otherwise, I'd be visiting my mom and Amy this weekend in New York.* "I'm sorry." He patted her knee. "We don't have to go."

"Of course, we do. We're committed now." Frowning, she brushed aside his hand. "Like I said, you don't know my family." She stared across the room at nothing in particular.

The sales clerk returned with a box and knelt.

Greg waved. "No need to try them on. I have a worn-out pair at home." Standing, he tucked the box under his arm and motioned for Maddy to follow him to the racks of clothing.

Silently, she strode beside him.

He stopped and flipped through a stand full of rain jackets until he found the correct size. Holding the jacket against his chest, he glanced at Maddy. "What do you think?"

"Try it on." She extended her arms to hold his shoebox and existing jacket.

Slipping his arms into the sleeves, he zipped up the jacket and modeled.

Frowning, she tilted her head to the side. "Looks fine."

He hated the apathetic expression on her face. When she was happy, her laughter brightened everything. But when she was unhappy, her darkness covered a vast terrain which mirrored his sadness. He hung the jacket on the hanger and gathered his belongings from her arms. "How long will you be upset?"

She shrugged.

Sighing, he walked over to another rack of jackets. "I apologized. What more do you want?"

"Do you trust me?" She tilted her head with a sidelong glance.

"Of course, I do." He yanked an orange rain slicker from the rack.

"Next time, please listen when I tell you about my family. I don't want any grief because of our friendship."

He examined her closely and noticed her pinched eyebrows and narrowed gaze. She looked angry and afraid, battling an enemy of which he had no knowledge. "Okay, I'll let you take the lead on your family next time." He held another jacket to his chest. "What do you think of this style?"

While holding his jacket and shoebox, she nodded. "Let's see how it looks."

The rain slicker wasn't as bulky and awkward as the first jacket.

"I like the color." She flicked her gaze toward the sleeves. "The burnt orange complements your skin and hair."

Pivoting, he glanced in a full-length mirror and agreed. "Okay. I'll buy it." Undressing, he grabbed the rest of his belongings from her arms. "Do you need anything else?"

She nodded.

He wandered over to the women's section.

Flipping through the rack of rain jackets, she flashed him a sidelong glance. "I forgive you. But don't be surprised if Jane hires someone to follow us on our run tomorrow."

He lifted his eyebrows. "Why would she hire someone?"

She held a black jacket against her chest.

He nodded his approval. "Try it on."

After handing him her shoebox and jacket, she tugged the sleeves over her arms. "She can't afford to skip church any more than she can afford to have her older sister found dead in a creek by a serial killer suffering from PTSD." She lifted her arms with her palms up in the too-tight jacket. "What would the neighbors think?"

She looked like a penguin with floppy arms and bulky legs. He chuckled.

"I think this jacket is one size too small." She waddled around flapping her arms. "I'll have to find a large."

He laughed until his sides hurt.

Catching a glimpse of her reflection in a mirror, she snickered. "I look ridiculous." She wriggled out of the jacket and hung it up. She flipped through several other selections. "How about this jacket?" She wrestled into a neon green slicker, flexed her biceps, and grunted. "I'm She-Monster."

Tears of laughter sprang from his eyes. Jane might be prettier, but Maddy was funnier. Staring at a good-looking woman might stir his emotions, but laughing until tears streamed down his cheeks felt so much better. "I won't get you angry, She-Monster."

Smiling, she removed the She-Monster jacket and found a turquoise jacket in a large. After slipping her arms into the sleeves, she modeled. "What do you think?"

The larger turquoise jacket deepened the blue in her eyes. She wasn't svelte like her sister, but she wasn't porky like her nickname. "Get it."

At the register, she handed the sales clerk her credit card. "With my job in jeopardy, I have to be careful of expenses."

"Tell Darren this purchase is an investment." He folded the jacket over his arm and set the shoe box on the counter.

"But after boot camp is over—"

"You'll be running every day." He smiled. "With me."

She lifted her eyebrows. "Every day?"

Am I being impulsive? He liked Maddy's company. Did he enjoy her presence enough to see her beyond boot camp? The idea settled like a comforting blanket across his shoulders. He shrugged. "Why not?"

Grabbing her bag off the counter, she waited while the sale clerk rang up his purchase. "I hate running."

"As much as you hate your family?" He set three one-hundred-dollar bills on the counter.

"Maybe." She shrugged.

He grabbed his bag and motioned toward the exit. "After I lost my foot, I didn't think I would walk again." Holding open the door, he winced at a gust of cool air. "For eighteen months I attended physical therapy. Then I was fitted for a running blade, and a retired high school track and field coach offered to teach me how to run." He paused, feeling a well of emotions swell in his chest. "The first few weeks, I experienced problems regulating the power of the blade against the natural ability of my foot. The blade is lighter. My foot is heavier. The blade propels me forward faster. My foot holds me back."

As he walked to the parking lot, he breathed in the fresh air. "When I finally learned how to balance between the two, for the first time since the accident, I felt free." He turned and met her gaze. "Moving on my own after believing I was nothing but a cripple liberated me." He nodded toward her bag of running gear. "I can't promise running will change your life like it changed mine, but I can guarantee you'll feel better once you start taking care of yourself."

"I already feel better." She grinned. "Thanks for the pep talk, friend."

Unlocking his trunk, he stowed his purchases. "May I walk you to your car?"

"Sure."

Silently, he strode across two rows of cars to Maddy's sedan.

She opened the passenger's door and tossed her bag on the seat. "See you tomorrow."

Pulling her into his arms, he held her until loneliness evaporated.

Stepping out of the embrace, she tilted her head to the side. "Do you ever run with Amy?"

"No."

She pursed her lips. "You should run with her in Central Park."

Run with Amy? How come the thought never crossed his mind? He always ran alone to escape. *Where was the freedom of running with his beloved?*

"If you're running with me, and I'm just a friend, you should run with her, the togetherness will mean much more." She patted his arm once before slipping into her car.

Shoving his hands into his pockets, he strode across the parking lot. Inside his car, he shoved the key into the ignition. *Was there any truth to Maddy's words?*

****

At nine o'clock on Sunday morning, Maddy steered into the parking lot near Hahn Woods. A light rain drizzled against the windshield. In the twenty-five years she lived in Atlanta, she never visited Lullwater Preserve. Glancing through the driver's side window, she glimpsed the General standing near the mouth of the trail.

He waved.

A quick smile lighted her face. She released the seatbelt, tucked her phone in a zippered pocket of her blue rain jacket, and stepped outside. A cool rain pelted her shoulders. The scent of damp earth filled her nostrils. With slick hands, she locked the car door and jogged over.

"You made it." He extended his arms and smiled, wearing the orange rain jacket and black water-repellant pants. On one foot, he wore a new trail running shoe.

"What's that thing?" She pointed to what looked like a giant fish hook where his second shoe should have been.

"This prosthetic is a carbon-fiber-reinforced polymer blade." He lifted the leg of his pants to show off the black curves. "I only wear it for running."

Squinting, she knelt to examine the blade closer. The hooked curve reminded her of a machete. "That leg looks like a weapon."

Releasing his pant leg, he chuckled. "The running blade is absolutely harmless...like me." He pointed to the trail behind him. "Ready to run?"

A quiver of nervousness snaked through her. How

would she jog three miles when she could barely jog four times around her brother's gym? She shrugged. "I guess I'm as ready as I'll ever be."

"Let's go." He grabbed her hand and guided her down the trail.

She stepped beneath a canopy of trees and plunged into another world, and a buzz of excitement zipped through her. Pockets of sunlight scattered across the moist earth, illuminating the pathway. Dense droplets of rain fell from the leaves and splattered against her shoulders. From the branches overhead, birds squawked, punctuating the steady rhythm of her breathing.

What a fine morning for a run—not too wet or too crowded—with the only other people running far ahead on the trail.

For a few minutes, after he released her hand, she pumped her arms back and forth, her legs following the same momentum. But as the sunlight disappeared behind clouds and the rain deepened into showers, the trail darkened into a tunnel of sludge. She lost her breath and her footing. Gasping, she stumbled on a rock next to the embankment and slid off the edge of the path. She felt her stomach lurch into her chest and her blood thump in her ears.

"Maddy!" He lunged for her hand before she plunged into the rushing waters below. Drawing her toward his chest, he wrapped his arms around her body. "Are you all right?"

Shuddering, she nodded beneath the hood of her blue rain jacket. Every nerve in her body felt awake and alive. "You saved me." She clutched him tighter.

"Thank you." As she panted, her breath rose in misty clouds.

"I was so scared." He brushed his mouth against her hair. "I thought I lost you."

Tilting back her head, she gazed into his eyes. The fear reflected in his dilated pupils slowly melted away. She placed a cold hand on his chest and jerked back on trembling legs until she stood on solid ground. "You're my hero."

He bent his head and covered his face with his hands.

"What's wrong?" She frowned.

"I'm having a flashback." He rubbed his eyes and sank against the embankment, drawing his legs toward his chest.

Not sure of what to do, she hesitated. The last time she witnessed a man crying she was at her parents' funeral, and Peter swiped his hand across his cheeks before steeling his shoulders. Every now and then, on the phone, she heard men sob over the frustrations of sorting through a catalogue of women online in the hopes of finding someone special. Suddenly remembering her training on how to deal with difficult callers, she knelt beside him and patted his shoulder. "Tell me."

Shivering, he shook his head. "It's too personal."

She searched his troubled face. "I thought you trusted me."

"I do." He closed his eyes and gulped back a rush of sobs. "I just told Amy, 'I don't,' at the altar at our first wedding ceremony. She pummeled my chest with the bouquet, saying, you're supposed to say 'I do.'

Then she asked why I didn't say 'I do'." With a heaving breath, he opened his eyes. "I remember white petals shaking like raindrops, scattering on the sea breeze. She hit me again with the bouquet. Her questions continued, why couldn't you have said 'I don't' to the commanding officer? And why couldn't you let the other soldiers die? The last one hurt the most, why did you have to be a hero?" Tears misted in his eyes. "She kept asking for her old Gregory back." He clutched his hair and bowed his head. "I'm afraid he died in the war."

Compassion softened her joints, and she flopped beside him. When she received the news her parents died in a car crash, she succumbed to numbing shock for a little while until a gaping hole of emptiness threatened to devour her whole. Hoping to stop the pain, she spent the last years at college stuffing her feelings with fast food and alcohol instead of grieving. Maybe Greg hadn't grieved his losses either. She rubbed his arm. "Even if the old Greg died, a new Greg is right here," she whispered.

More tears spilled from his eyes. "I'm so sad and empty." He panted. "I've nothing left to give."

"That statement is not true. You've given me confidence and hope I can lose this weight and change my life." Standing, she offered a hand. "Stop the pity party. We have a run to finish."

For a long moment, he stared at her outstretched hand. "You're right." He nodded, accepting her hand. "Let's finish our run."

In the distance, a familiar voice penetrated the woods. "Maddy."

She turned her gaze and stiffened.

A figure darted along the trail about two hundred meters away.

"That man is my brother."

Frowning, Greg crossed his arms over his chest. "Why is he here?"

She sighed. "My sister probably told him about the run. I bet he spotted my car in the parking lot and followed us to make sure I'm not harmed."

He grabbed Maddy's hand. "Let's go."

Digging her heels into the mud, she refused to move. "I can't out run him."

"You don't have to. We can lose him across the suspension bridge." He pointed toward a narrow row of slats dangling in a semi-circle above the burbling waters of South Fork Peachtree Creek.

Fear plunged to her stomach. The bridge looked flimsy, and the water looked high and wild. Surely, she would drown. "Are you crazy?"

Peter's voice roared closer. "Maddy."

Panic thickened her throat. Why couldn't her family leave her alone? Why did they always assume the worst? She glanced over her shoulder.

Her brother pounded his feet against the mulch, his arms moving like pistons at his sides. "Maddy." Raspy breathing followed the shout.

"C'mon, let's go." Greg waved toward the bridge.

Shaking her head, she stood still. After almost plunging off the side of the cliff, she could face being yelled at by her brother for an imagined wrong. "Let's wait and see what he has to say."

Peter jogged to a stop. Panting, he glanced from

Greg to Maddy. "What are you doing out here?"

She narrowed her gaze. "Didn't Jane tell you we scheduled a run before brunch?"

He placed his hands on his hips and broadened his stance. "You missed church for this?" He nodded his chin at the thin trees and the rushing water. "What about God?"

"God is everywhere." She threw up her arms and lifted her face toward the dark clouds. Rain kissed her hot cheeks. "This forest is the cathedral we have chosen to worship in." She leveled her gaze. "We'll see you at eleven-thirty for brunch at Jane's house."

Frowning, he pointed at Greg. "Is he invited?"

She lifted her chin. "Yes, Jane invited him yesterday." She arched an eyebrow. "Didn't she tell you?"

"Incredible." He shook his head. "I can't believe I missed church."

Curiosity rose within her. She tilted her head. "Why did you come out here?"

Peter spoke to Maddy but glared at Greg. "I thought you were lured here for malicious reasons."

She swatted Peter's arm. "How dare you think I was kidnapped, raped, and murdered?" She linked an arm through Greg's and tugged him toward her. "We are running."

Greg swiped the rain from his face. "Would you like to join us?"

Glancing from Greg to Maddy, he shook his head. "No, I'll see you both at brunch." Turning, he jogged back toward the parking lot.

Maddy released Greg's arm. "I'm sorry about my

brother's behavior."

"Don't be." He sighed. "You warned me about your family. Apparently, I don't listen very well."

She smiled. "You'll get better." She waved toward the suspension bridge. "Is there another path out of here?"

Nodding, he offered his hand. "We can follow the trail beneath the bridge."

She took his hand and jogged beside him into the ravine until the dirt path narrowed. Releasing his fingers, she fell behind and listened to the steady gush of the river. After a while, the dark clouds scuttled away along with the rainfall. A shaft of sunlight penetrated the foliage. She stopped running and lifted her gaze.

An American robin swooped from the branches.

The bird's cheerful song brightened her mood. *Free. I'm finally free. Now let's see if Darren will quit his job or set me free.*

Chapter 15

Greg met Maddy at Jane's Georgian mansion at eleven-twenty-five, parking next to her four-door sedan in the circular driveway. The rain started again, big wet droplets, and he sheltered them underneath a black umbrella. Carrying a vegan coleslaw salad in one hand and the umbrella in the other, he trudged up the steps to the porch and waited.

Maddy rang the doorbell.

He hoped he wasn't underdressed in a long-sleeved, button down shirt and slacks with loafers.

After tugging on her braid, Maddy straightened her floral dress.

Jane opened the door and welcomed them inside. "Kiki's on vacation in Sweden visiting her family this week, and Remy's busy in the kitchen, and Johanna is getting the children ready." Smiling, she took the bowl of salad and led them into the formal dining room. "Have a seat anywhere you'd like. I'll let Chris know you're here."

Staring at Jane's slender body clothed in a form-fitting floral dress made his face flame.

She sashayed through the swinging door and into the kitchen.

Narrowing her gaze, Maddy batted his forearm. "Stop looking at my sister like she's the main course."

"She's pretty." He gazed at Maddy's concerned face and winked. "Are you jealous?"

Flushing, she turned away.

"Where shall we sit?" He waved toward the long mahogany table.

Maddy bit her lower lip. "I always wait for the children to pick first. Seat selection is the only thing they have control over in their lives."

Moments later, two tow-headed children darted into the room.

A short, portly woman wearing a black and white uniform waddled after the children. She wagged a finger. "No running."

The children didn't listen. They flung their arms around Maddy's legs and gazed with wide eyes into her face. "Did you bring us french fries?"

Maddy chuckled and rubbed the tops of their heads. "No, I brought a friend, instead." She pointed toward Greg. "This is General Greg Power, retired Army veteran."

The boy widened his gaze and ran over to Greg. "A real war hero?"

An odd feeling of betrayal and flattery overcame him. The boy didn't need to know he was a captain discharged early because of an injury. Nervous and uncomfortable with the lie, he chuckled. "Not a hero. Just a soldier." He extended his hand. "And you are?"

"Collin." He thumped his chest then pointed to the girl. "This is Caroline."

"What a pleasure meeting both of you." He shook Collin's hand first then Caroline's hand.

"May I show you my plane?" Collin grabbed

Greg's hand and Maddy's hand. "Aunty Maddy hasn't seen my plane." He led them out of the room and into the foyer, taking one of the staircases.

Greg galloped after the boy, hobbling from one foot to the next, keeping pace with the enthusiasm.

Halfway down a long hallway, Collin released their hands and threw open his bedroom door. Darting across the room, he swooped the B-52 bomber through the air. "Rat-a-tat-tat. Rat-a-tat-tat."

Greg stiffened. Heat crawled over his skin. Rubbing his arms, he scratched the memory of sand out of his clothes.

"Rat-a-tat-tat. Rat-a-tat-tat."

"Are you all right?" Maddy touched his sleeve, frowning.

Collin crashed the plane against Greg's belly.

Stumbling back, Greg fell onto the twin mattress, kicking up his legs.

"What's that thing?" Collin frowned, pointing to the prosthetic.

Maddy knelt beside Collin. "General Power lost his left leg in the Persian Gulf War. That's his fake leg. It's called a prosthetic."

Collin widened his gaze. "May I see?"

Greg met Collin's curious gaze, and a shock of innocent wonder propelled him into a tunnel of long-buried memories of playing at war—zigzagging aerial bombings, complicated ground tactics, and the resultant glory of winning against his friends who always left a loophole in their strategies. Ignorant pleasure tingled in his fingertips, and anxiety drained from his body. Shifting into a sitting position on the bed, he lifted the leg of his pants.

"Does it hurt?" Collin touched the smooth sides of the limb.

"Not anymore." Greg released the leg of his pants and clasped his hands between his knees. "At first, I often felt prickles where my leg used to be. But my leg has been gone so long, I hardly ever think about it."

"How did you lose your leg?" Collin climbed on the mattress and sat beside him.

He winced. Should he shelter the truth from someone else's child? He pinched together his eyebrows. Would he have gone to war if he knew the facts? "A bomb blew off my foot in the desert."

Collin swung his legs. "Does your new leg have any special powers?"

Smiling, Greg laughed. "No, it's just a leg."

"If you lost your leg, how come you're not a hero?" Collin scrunched his forehead.

"I didn't save anyone."

"You saved yourself."

Shaking his head, Greg sighed. "Saving yourself makes you a survivor, and not a hero."

Collin sat straight and shook the bangs out of his eyes. He thumped his fist against his chest. "You're my hero."

Gazing into the boy's soft brown eyes, Greg felt something hard shift inside him. That old glory he fantasized about as a child returned, and the magnificence of war regained its splendor. *I love this boy*. Wrapping an arm around Collin's shoulders, he tucked the boy against his side and rubbed his knuckles against his scalp until Collin squirmed with giggles.

"Oh, there you are." Jane poked her head inside the room. "We're getting ready to eat."

Collin leaped off the mattress and ran to his mother. "The General showed me his fake leg. He lost his real leg by a bomb. I bet this fake leg can stop bullets. He just doesn't know it yet because he hasn't used it." Smiling, he ran back to Greg and grabbed his hand. "I want to sit next to the General. Okay, Mommy?"

Glancing from Collin to Greg, Jane nodded. "I'm fine with the arrangement, as long as the General says it's okay. He might want to sit next to your dad or Uncle Peter."

A frisson of tension danced across Greg's shoulders at the mention of Peter. He squeezed Collin's hand. "I'll sit with you and your aunt Maddy."

"Cool." On the stroll along the hallway and the climb down the stairs, Collin studied Greg's legs.

In the dining room, Caroline sat next to Uncle Peter, who stood as soon as Maddy, Greg, and Collin entered the room.

As he met Peter's solemn gaze, Greg tightened his jaw. The two men did not exchange words.

Sitting between Maddy and Collin, Greg waited as Jane fluttered around the table, making sure everyone was comfortably settled. He watched as she bent over and her cleavage swelled. A pang of lust filled him. *When was the last time I had sex?*

Two men carried platters into the dining room and set them on the table. "This is my husband, Chris, and my chef, Remy." Jane pointed respectively to a short, bald white man wearing a navy blue suit and red tie and a tall, thin black man wearing a white, double-breasted jacket and black slacks.

Greg grimaced after the introductions. *Her husband must be a lawyer or a doctor.* Jane was the type of woman who would run a credit report and background check before agreeing to a date. What would he have done if he hadn't met Amy in high school? Sure, he was retired from the military, but he never finished law school, and his résumé looked as checkered as a patchwork quilt. Why was he even thinking of Jane? Embarrassment flooded his body, and he glanced over at Maddy who helped herself to a spoonful of his vegan coleslaw salad.

Leaning against her, he pointed to the dishes. "The best dietary choices are the ham, coleslaw, and butternut squash. I'd skip the cornbread, mashed potatoes, and gravy."

"What about the pulled pork?" She nodded toward the last dish Remy delivered.

He shrugged. "I would only indulge if the sauce doesn't have any sugar."

Across the table, Jane waved a bottle of merlot. "Anyone want some wine?"

Clutching her napkin in her lap, Maddy widened her gaze then glanced at Greg.

He shook his head.

"No, thank you." Maddy turned toward her sister.

Frowning, Jane lowered the bottle. "But the wine is expensive. You liked the vintage the last time you were here. I said you can drink. Chris will drive you home." She patted the chair beside her.

Again, Greg shook his head. He didn't want to tell

Maddy what to do, but he wanted to encourage her in the right direction.

Maddy bit her lower lip. "I'll pass."

Leaning over, Greg squeezed her hand. "Good job."

She smiled and returned the squeeze before releasing his fingers. "I'm making better choices." She gazed at her sister.

Pursing her lips, Jane nodded. "I see." She glanced around the table. "Who would like to say grace?"

Collin shifted in his seat and raised a hand. As soon as his mother granted approval, he bowed his head and squeezed his hands together in a steeple. "Thank you, God, for all this food, and thank you for Aunty Maddy bringing the General. Please grant his new leg special powers so he can fight for good and destroy all evil. Amen."

Everyone at the table stared at Greg. Embarrassment colored his cheeks. Before meeting Collin, no one, except for Amy and his mother, prayed for him. No one, except for Amy and his mother, thanked God for him. Leaning over, he patted Collin on the head. "You'll be a great soldier someday."

Collin beamed with a smile. "I wish you were my uncle. I want to see you all the time."

A flash of pain darted across his chest. Greg thought of Amy wanting children for so long. Why did he deny her? Would he be a different person if he and Amy cared for a son like Collin? Years of regret clogged his mind, and he bowed his head, wondering how he could make things right.

****

After lunch, Maddy lifted her empty plate. "I'll help clean up." She stood, surprised by the feeling of satisfaction from eating healthier.

In the kitchen, Jane cornered Maddy by the sink. "Collin's really taken to your friend." Tilting her head, she grinned. "I don't care what Pete says. I like him."

Maddy turned on the hot water, rinsed the plates, and stacked them in the dishwasher. Jane never liked anyone who wasn't rich, famous, or important. Greg didn't fit that description. "You only like him because Collin likes him."

Jane placed glasses in the sink to be rinsed. "Actually, he's really cute and kind of charming." A wistful sigh escaped. "If I wasn't married, I might ask you to set us up."

Maddy gasped. "He's engaged."

Shrugging, Jane narrowed her gaze. "He's not married. Anything can happen."

Heat rushed to Maddy's face. "Nothing will happen."

"I think he likes you." Jane winked and nudged her.

Scooting away, Maddy focused on rinsing the glasses. "Of course, he likes me. We're friends."

"No, I mean he *likes* you."

Avoiding her sister's avid stare, Maddy shrugged. "I'm fat. He's not attracted to fatties."

"Trust me. I'm always right about love." Jane leaned a hip against the counter and crossed her arms over her chest. "So, when will you tell Darren about him?"

Maddy pinched together her lips. *Why won't you*

stop telling me what to do? I'm already practicing transparency, the second rule of friendship. "Darren knows everything."

"Good. He won't be surprised to see him during the video call."

Anxiety knotted in her lower back. *Video call?* "Who's calling him?"

"We are." She turned off the faucet. "Leave the rest for Remy. Let's go talk to Darren."

Tightness stretched across Maddy's chest. She didn't want to video call Darren. Not in front of her meddlesome family, but if she refused, she would need an excuse. What was a reasonable excuse?

Jane led her into the family room. Everyone gathered on the sofa in front of the big screen TV hooked to a laptop computer. Jane selected a button and, moments later, Darren's face loomed larger than life.

"Happy Easter." He leaned forward, filling the screen with his dark eyes and bright smile.

Caroline and Collin danced before the TV. "Happy Easter."

"How's Denver?" Chris sipped from his bottle of beer.

"Mild for spring. Not much snow on the mountains. Everyone has been saying we'll have a dry summer." He glanced around the room. "Hey, Jane. Hey, Pete. Hey, Maddy." He nodded. "Who's the guest?"

Jane shot Maddy a warning glance.

Frowning, Maddy focused on Darren. "This is Greg, my friend and boot camp partner."

"He's a superhero." Collin ran up to the TV. "Do you want to see his leg with special powers?" He bolted toward Greg and pointed. "Show him your leg."

Maddy scooped Collin into her arms and carried him away. "Not now."

"Superhero?"

Derisive laughter sputtered from Darren's mouth. With Collin in her arms, Maddy swung toward the TV. "Drop it. He's just a child. He doesn't know what he's saying."

"Ah, Maddy, we're just having fun." Darren swept his gaze across the room. "Aren't we having fun?"

Peter cleared his throat. "This call was a bad idea. Nice seeing you, Darren. We'll catch up when you get back." Standing, he kissed Jane's cheek. "Thanks for brunch."

She grasped his hand and frowned. "You're leaving?"

He nodded, glancing at Greg. "I have other things to do."

After he left, Chris stood. "I think I'll get another beer." He lifted his empty bottle and flashed a warm smile. "Good seeing you, Darren. We should schedule a round of golf after you get back."

"Definitely." Darren nodded. "I should return this week. I spoke to my boss on Friday and asked for a desk job." He tightened his smile, and his jaw twitched.

Maddy sank onto the sofa cushions with Collin in her lap. *Darren asked for a desk job.* Shock numbed her arms.

Collin slipped off her lap.

After blinking several times, Maddy skittered her

gaze around the room.

"Really?" Jane lifted her eyebrows. "But you love sales."

He nodded. "When I'm not home, Maddy gets lonely. She wants to start a family."

Jane nodded at Maddy. "Makes sense." Turning toward Darren, she lifted her palms. "I know you earn tons of money in sales. You could do what we do and hire a nanny."

Collin climbed onto the sofa next to the General.

Maddy registered his tinny voice as he talked to Greg, but she couldn't follow the conversation. She sat speechless. *Darren's coming home.*

"Maddy wants to raise the children herself," Darren said through the TV speakers.

Hearing her name, Maddy hitched her breath and gazed at Darren's grim face. He offered to quit his sales position to keep her by his side. Why did he think sacrifice would make her happy if that sacrifice made him miserable? She pinched her eyebrows together and clasped her hands tightly in her lap. "What about your territory?"

Darren narrowed his gaze at Greg. "My region will be reassigned to another sales representative. I'll process the orders at the main office in Atlanta." He shifted his gaze to Maddy. "No more travel."

A tingle of relief prickled her skin followed by a wave of anxiety. "When are you coming home?"

"Probably Tuesday or Wednesday." He shrugged. "As soon as the paperwork is processed and a new sale representative flies out to replace me, I'll come home." Leaning back, he exhaled. "I'll call and let you know.

Okay?"

Still stunned, she nodded. *He chose me*.

"I love you, Maddy." He held her gaze for a few seconds before he glanced at the others in the room.

"I love you, too." She swallowed, staring until the call ended and his image disappeared.

Smiling, Greg patted her knee. "Great news, right?"

She absently nodded. For the last year, she pined for a man who would stay around town and spend regular time with her. When all of her dreams had come true, she didn't understand why she ached with sadness.

****

Returning from brunch at Jane's house, Greg unlocked the door to his studio apartment and set his keys in a bowl on the kitchen counter. Unbuttoning his collar, he strolled over to the answering machine and pressed the Play button.

No messages.

Sinking onto the edge of the mattress, he clasped his hands between his knees. Was he blinded by Amy's perfection or too paralyzed by his fear of returning to New York to acknowledge the truth—that something was deeply wrong? With anxiety moistening his palms, he picked up the phone and called his mother. "Happy Easter."

"Oh, sonny, I'm so glad you called. I've been so lonely this holiday."

A prickle of anxiety crawled over his skin. He frowned. "Isn't Amy with you?"

She exhaled a heavy sigh. "Oh, sonny, she said she wanted to spend the holiday with her family. I understand, I really do, since she already gives me so much of her time the rest of the year, but I'm still lonely without either one of you."

Familiar guilt clutched his chest. "I'm sorry, Mom. Why didn't you go with Amy to see her family?"

"I didn't want to look like a pest and invite myself."

He lifted his eyebrows. "She didn't invite you?"

"Oh, no, she didn't. I wanted to go, but I couldn't bear to ask. You know how I feel about begging."

He rubbed his forehead, remembering how his mother hated the humiliation of asking for what she needed. "It's not begging. We're family."

She muttered something he couldn't decipher before she raised her voice. "I wish you'd stop holding your father's anger against us."

Leaning back, he raised an arm. "Mom, I don't blame you or—"

"Yes, you do," she snapped. "You put that poor girl through hell. She wants to move to the suburb and start a family. At fifty. I keep telling her we're not living in the Middle Ages. No woman needs to waste her life to be loved." She broke into a sob. "Sonny, you need to let Amy go."

"Mom, I'm coming home." The truth about Amy shattered his insides. He clawed through the wreckage, determined to right every wrong, and finally unite with the woman he loved. "As soon as I settle a few things here, I'll be on the first flight home."

After saying goodbye to his mother, he dialed Amy's number. The call switched over to voicemail. Although his hands trembled, he steadied his voice.

"Baby, I'm quitting my job. I'm moving back to New York. Let's sell the apartment. I don't care where we live. As long as I'm with you, I'm home." Ending the call, he fell back onto the mattress, wondering if his grand romantic gesture was too little too late.

Chapter 16

On Monday morning, Maddy's phone rang. *I can't move*. Muscular pain pinned her to the bedroom mattress. The sound of the phone aggravated the pounding sinus headache knocking against the backs of her eyes. She must be paralyzed with soreness from yesterday's three-mile run and clogged up from her allergies. Rolling over, she stretched an arm and wriggled her fingers until she curled the phone against her palm and placed it against her ear. "Hello?"

"Why aren't you at boot camp?" Peter asked.

"Oh, shit." Glancing at the clock on the nightstand, she read the time—six fifteen. She must have forgotten to set her alarm.

"Is he with you?"

He? She rubbed her forehead and squinted. "Who are you talking about?"

"Greg."

A prickle of fear rippled through her. "Isn't he at boot camp?"

"No."

"Oh, shit." She struggled to sit. *Why wasn't Greg at boot camp?* "Have you tried calling him at home?"

"I thought I'd call you first."

Anger flared her nostrils. "I can't believe you think I'm cheating on Darren. Greg and I are friends. He has his place, and I have my place. No reason exists why he would stay overnight here."

A moment of silence stretched between them.

"I'm not calling him. I'm calling his counselor," Peter said. "If they lock him up, then I won't have to worry about you and your so-called friendship."

"Don't punish him." Blood thumped in her ears. She dug an elbow into the mattress and propped herself up, wincing when painful muscles strained against hot skin. "He's done nothing wrong. If anyone should be locked up, that person should be you." She shifted her arm and collapsed onto the bed. Staring at the ceiling, she sighed. "You'll never stop worrying about me."

"You're right." He sniffed. "Things might look good right now, but give them time. You'll find a way to mess up things."

Oh, wonderful. She loved how much confidence her family had in her ability to change. Groaning, she clutched the sheet with her hand. "Why don't you leave me alone and go check on your class?" Without waiting for a response, she ended the call.

Silence echoed in the room.

A low groan emitted from her pursed lips. She thought about Greg. Why did he miss boot camp? Was he sick? Still sleeping? Out for a run? Chatting on the phone with Amy? Or stuck in traffic? She picked up her phone and typed.

—Where are you?—

After she sent the message, she placed the phone against her chest. She panted, the jagged breaths matching the worried march of fear beating against her ribs.

****

After booking a flight to New York for Tuesday morning, Greg stood in the kitchen frying three egg whites with chopped red and green bell peppers in coconut oil. Sizzling steam wafted through the studio apartment, filling the space with the scent of grease and pepper. As soon as the eggs hardened into golden brown firmness, he slipped the vegetable omelet onto a plate and carried it over to his bed where he sat on the mattress, feeling as strange and naughty as a child as he ate. He missed the mahogany dining table and upholstered chairs in his New York apartment. Sometimes, he wondered if Amy sold the ensemble for something less ostentatious since his last visit during the holidays.

Glancing at his to-do list, he read through the items to see if he missed anything: book flight, quit job, see Dr. Carter, ask to transfer case to doctor in New York, pack, cancel lease, return leased car to dealership, apply for marriage license online, and schedule wedding for tomorrow afternoon at city hall. He frowned. An odd sense of incompletion troubled him. What had he missed?

Setting aside the list, he continued eating. Halfway through breakfast, he picked up his cell phone and dialed Amy's number. At six-thirty, she should be awake, standing before the window in the living room with a fresh cup of coffee, and watching the sunlight struggle to poke its pink and gold fingers through the spaces between skyscrapers.

The call rolled over into voicemail. The electronic voice stated the mail box was full and could no longer accept any messages.

Damn it. He ended the call, tossed the phone on the mattress, and glared at the half-eaten omelet on his plate. *Why won't she take my calls?*

A shiver of panic snaked up his spine. *What if something's terribly wrong?* He shook off the negative thoughts, but a dense foreboding overwhelmed him.

A beep from his phone redirected his attention. He stared at the message on the screen from Maddy. She wanted to know where he was.

I forgot boot camp. Too preoccupied planning his return to New York, he neglected to send a message to Peter or Maddy. Quickly, he typed.

—*Sorry about missing boot camp. Too much to do. Moving to NY. Leaving tomorrow AM*—

A few moments later, Maddy responded with another text.

—*Can we talk?*—

He curled his hands into fists, blood throbbing against his skin. *No, I don't want to talk. I want to smash this phone against the wall. I want to toss over the desk and slam the chair through the window*. He heaved his chest, struggling to breathe his way through the weight of his thoughts.

Another text message beeped from his phone.

—*Are you okay?*—

Fuck, no, I'm not okay. Standing, he stalked into the kitchen and dumped his plate into the sink. The dish clattered but didn't break. He rinsed his hands with cold water until his fingers were numb.

His cell phone rang.

Tensing his jaw, he dried his hands on a dish towel.

Don't answer.

The trilling melody played.

Glancing at the screen, he confirmed the caller was Maddy. If he started talking, he might change his mind, soften, and let go of everything he held onto. *Don't answer.*

The ringing stopped. A few seconds later, the song jingled again.

Persistent, isn't she? Sweat beaded on his forehead. *She'll keep calling, won't she?* He swiped a hand across his brow. *Maybe she's the only person left who cares.* He grabbed the phone. "Hello?"

"What's going on?"

The angry tone of Maddy's voice caught him off guard.

"Why are you moving?"

He cringed. The sound of her voice escalated with each question.

"Why didn't you tell me anything?" She stumbled on a hitched breath. "I thought we told each other everything."

He scoffed. "I'm not your family, Strong. I have boundaries." What a mistake to pick up the phone. He should have ignored her like Amy ignored him. Guilt pinched his chest. No, Maddy was right. He should have called her, told her what was going on, and kept her informed. A general never abandoned his troop. By not telling her about his move back to New York, he deserted her. He softened his shoulders. "I'm sorry. I should have said something."

"Yes, you should have." She exhaled. "If I wasn't so damn sore from our run yesterday, I'd drive over to wherever you are and kick your butt. Right now, I can't get out of bed."

He snickered. "So, you missed boot camp, too."

"My brother called." She groaned. "He assumed we were spending the night together and missed class on purpose."

Shaking his head, he sighed. "I can't believe your family."

"I warned you."

Stopping in front of the window, he chuckled. "Yes, you did. I'll call him after we're through here and let him know. I'm transferring to a boot camp in New York once I get reestablished with the local VA office." He thought about her overworked body, remembering the early days after losing his foot. Every morning he would roll out of bed, collapse into a heap on the floor, crawl to the bathroom, and, with his arms, hoist himself onto the toilet. Closing his eyes, he groaned. "If you can combat-crawl to the shower, turn the water on as hot as you can tolerate, and climb in until your muscles soften."

"Sounds like you've done this maneuver before."

"More than once."

"Okay, I'll try it, but not until you tell me what's going on."

With open eyes, he clutched the phone tighter and swallowed the fear in his throat. "I haven't heard from Amy since last week. I've called and left messages, but this morning her personal voicemail was full. She didn't celebrate Easter with my mother. I talked with my mother yesterday, who told me I need to let Amy go." He gulped. "I'm afraid she's avoiding me since I asked her to consider a move to Atlanta. I left her a message last night, telling her I'm quitting my job and moving home. I thought she'd call back or send a text, but I've received nothing. The behavior is not like her. She has always stayed in communication, even during the times we broke up." He shuddered. "I'm scared something's wrong, and I'm not quite sure what it is."

"I can speculate," Maddy said. "But we won't know for sure unless you both speak."

"How can we speak if she's not returning any of my calls? Not at home or at work." He sighed. "I'm moving back to New York, because I need to marry her as soon as possible."

"Do you think she still wants to marry you?"

Coldness shuddered through him. He gulped. "I...don't...know." Switching the phone to his other ear, he placed a hand against his waist. "Sometimes I wonder if it's worth it."

"What's worth it?"

"Life." As he paced back and forth across the length of the room, he exhaled and shook his head. "My dad was right. I should have given up long ago."

"No, your dad was wrong. You should never give up. You should keep fighting."

He clenched a hand into a fist and banged it against the wall. The photograph of Amy clattered to the floor, and the glass fractured.

Maddy yelped. "Are you okay?"

Kicking the picture until it turned upside down, he breathed in deeply through his nose and exhaled slowly from his mouth. *One thousand one, one thousand two, one thousand three...*

"General? Are you there?"

One thousand four, one thousand five, one thousand six…

"Hello? Greg?"

"I'm here." *One thousand seven, one thousand eight, one thousand nine, one thousand ten…* He sank into the mattress. Darkness loomed on the horizon of his thoughts. He needed something to distract him. "I'm okay. That loud sound was just a falling picture." He stared at the camera packed on top of his suitcase. "I used to take pictures. The day after our fight, Amy sent my old camera. Amy offered to show some of my old photographs at the gallery where she works. She was always proud of them. She was always proud of me." Silent tears streamed down his cheeks. "I should go on a photo shoot in the botanical gardens before I move, but I just don't feel like doing anything."

She groaned. "If you're not doing anything, you can drive me to work. I have a merger/acquisition meeting this morning, and I don't think my legs are fit for driving."

Helping her might help him. He arched his eyebrows. "Where do you work?"

"Downtown…in the Peachtree Offices. Do you know it?"

That location is three blocks from my office. He glanced at the clock. *If I leave now, I can arrive at her place before the Clifton Crunch and get back here within forty-five minutes.* "Okay. I'll take you to work. What's your apartment number?"

"4L."

Standing, he scooped his keys out of the kitchen

bowl and headed for the door. "I'll see you in twenty minutes." *What good is lying about being a general if I can't come to the rescue?*

Chapter 17

Maddy lay in bed with the phone against her chest after speaking with the General. *I can't believe he's leaving for New York.* A wave of sadness washed over her. *Darren will be home again soon.* A flutter of anticipation stirred in her stomach. *My life is changing.* A fistful of fear punched her deep in the gut. *Even my job is at stake.* A worse thought lodged in her mind. *Nothing is stable.*

Since she was a child, she doubted her judgment. Everyone around her criticized her when she was wrong, which was only most of the time. Now, as she lay in bed, she questioned herself. *What if Pete's right and Greg is a psychotic mess? If he has a breakdown at my apartment, I could end up dead like those poor women who were doing the right thing by helping those vets suffering from PTSD.*

Rolling over, she moaned from the pain searing her legs and cramping her lower back. If she didn't get up soon, she would be lying in bed by the time the General arrived to drive her to work. A seed of confidence sprouted within her. *I'll be safe.*

A moment later, a sense of peacefulness blanketed her. *He's never hurt me before. Why would he hurt me now?*

Releasing the phone, she scooted to the edge of the

mattress. With outstretched arms, she plunged headfirst toward the floor. From a pushup position, she lowered into a combat crawl. Carpet burned her elbows as she maneuvered across the bedroom floor. Cool tiles slipped beneath her palms when she dropped into the bathroom. Gripping the edge of the toilet, she hoisted her body into a kneeling position. She shifted her grasp to the sink and hoisted her legs to a stand. Panting, she leaned over and turned the shower faucets until steam floated through the room, fogging the mirror. She yanked off her clothes and slowly lowered her body into the tub, letting hot water pelt her sore muscles until they softened like butter.

Afterward, she toweled dried her body and shuffled into the bedroom. She tugged a purple dress over her bra and panties and shoved her feet into flats. By the time she hobbled into the kitchen to prepare breakfast, she heard the doorbell ring. She clutched the cereal box against her chest, her heartbeat stuttering in her chest. She could almost smell the fear and anticipation beneath her floral perfume.

He's here.

****

Greg stood outside Maddy's apartment, cradling the camera in his hands. He wanted to take Maddy's photograph to remind him of his time in Georgia. Adjusting the aperture, he hoped for a candid moment.

When Maddy opened the door, he snapped a picture. The flash illuminated the space between them for a moment.

Gasping, she jumped. "Oh, my God, you scared me. I thought you had a bomb or something."

Lowering the camera, he frowned. "Why would I have a bomb?"

Placing a hand over her heart, she shook her head. "Because you have PTSD, and you're leaving for New York, and no one will ever see you again."

"Don't be melodramatic." He let the camera dangle from a strap around his neck. "I'm only taking you to work." Lifting the camera, he clicked the shutter again.

"Stop." She covered her face with her hands. "No more pictures."

He studied the curves of her body straining against the purple dress she wore. She wasn't slender like Amy, but underneath the rolls of fat, she was strong like a soldier. When she lowered her hands from her face, her blue eyes reflected a desperate wilderness. Excitement seeped through him, and he smiled. "You're beautiful."

"Don't lie. The second rule of friendship is transparency." She grabbed her purse, stepped out of the apartment, and locked the door. "Thank goodness we have an elevator. I don't think I could walk a flight of stairs." She shuffled along the hallway in short, jerky movements.

"I wasn't lying." He pushed the button for the elevator and waited beside her. "I should have never given us rules." With a sidelong glance, he arched his eyebrow. "Let's forget the rules and just be friends."

"Okay." She narrowed her gaze. "No flirting."

"I wasn't flirting." He sighed and shook his head. "You can't take a compliment."

"You're flattering me." She curled her hands into fists. "Guys only flatter women when they want something. What do you want?"

Lifting his palms, he grimaced. "Nothing, I swear."

The elevator doors parted, and they stepped inside.

As the elevator descended, she leaned back against the wall and closed her eyes.

Lifting the camera to his face, he snapped another picture.

She sprang open her eyes and frowned. "Put away that thing, or I'll break it."

Remembering how she almost pummeled his face during boot camp, he shoved the camera into the leather case. Oh, how he missed Amy. She always welcomed having her picture taken. She would toss back her head and laugh, showcasing the graceful curve of her supple neck. A dark cloud of worry descended. *Where was she? Why wasn't she accepting any calls? Or returning any messages?*

The elevator stopped moving, and the doors parted.

Offering her his arm, he helped her hobble into the lobby.

"Why don't you like your picture taken?" he asked.

Shaking her head, she sniggered. "Only children do."

"Amy likes her picture taken."

She stiffened against his arm. "I'm not Amy."

Sadness enveloped him. He nodded. "You're right. You're Maddy."

The sliding glass doors parted. Bright sunlight reflected off puddles from overnight rainfall. The air still smelled thick with moisture. He slid a pair of sunglasses over the bridge of his nose and pointed. "I'm parked over there." After releasing her arm, he hustled to the car and opened the passenger door.

Grabbing the door frame, she slowly lowered her body into the seat.

She looked like an elephant curling into a tight spot during a circus act. Too bad he couldn't capture *that* picture.

Glancing up, she smiled. "Thanks for driving me to work."

"You're welcome." Something softened in his chest. All morning, he focused on what he needed to do to return to New York. All his thoughts centered around Amy, and nothing else. He agreed to drive Maddy to work as a distraction from the thunderstorm of guilt and depression threatening to eclipse his grand plans of reuniting with the love of his life. Seeing Maddy here, in his car, with the sunlight slanting through the windshield and illuminating her pale face and light hair, he realized Maddy was anything but a distraction. She was real, and she needed him as much as he needed her. Shutting the door, he strode around the vehicle to the driver's side. Slipping into the front seat, he started the engine and drove away from his fears.

****

Ten minutes later, during bumper-to-bumper traffic, a knot tightened in Maddy's stomach. She took a deep breath. *I need to tell Greg how I feel. I can't keep eating my feelings*. She glanced at his profile. "Why didn't you discuss moving to New York? I told you to visit Amy, not move. What if you both reconcile and decide Georgia is the best location for you to live? Then you've quit your job and exited this opportunity." She stared at her hands, afraid of the feelings swirling inside. "I'm hurt you didn't tell me. If I didn't call, then you would have left, and I wouldn't have known anything." A rush of grief overpowered her, but she pushed back her shoulders and ploughed forward. "Not knowing would have devastated me. The shock is what's unbearable. You never get over it."

Greg lifted his eyebrows. "I already told you I'm sorry."

She glanced out the window. "I was twenty when my parents died in an auto accident. No one expected their deaths. Shortly thereafter, I started binge eating and later binge drinking. Peter did his best to help us, but he was only twenty-three." She gulped. "When I learned about your move, I panicked. Everything I should have dealt with long ago surfaced."

"You're not the only one dealing with things you should have previously resolved." He coughed and clutched the steering wheel until his knuckles whitened. "Two weeks ago, Amy sounded really excited about a new artist for the gallery, some guy named Robert McKenzie, who makes blue saffron eggs. I thought nothing of her attitude since she's always enthusiastic about discovering talent. She wanted me to come up for opening night on Thursday, but I couldn't because of boot camp. Then I mentioned the job situation down here and suggested she come and visit, and she became upset. We haven't spoken since." He glanced over. "She's always responded before, so I don't know why she would stop communicating now, but some part of me thinks she might be cheating."

What a hypocrite. Maddy swatted his arm. *Why could he sleep with whomever he chose, but Amy couldn't?*

"Ouch." He winced from the slap.

She narrowed her gaze. "You said seeing another person wasn't cheating if you weren't married."

Shrugging, he breathed in. "I guess I was wrong."

Traffic clotted around an intersection. He slowed to a stop.

With a sidelong glance, she studied him. He stared straight out the window with a dark, vacant gaze. He looked tired and pale. A sour smell seeped from his pores. Why was she so hard on him? He was her friend. She should show a little compassion, whether or not she agreed with his actions or Amy's behavior. Leaning over, she rubbed his cold and clammy arm. "I'm sorry."

As soon as the light turned green, he accelerated through the intersection. "My mother blames me for not marrying Amy years ago."

"She might be correct, but you can't change the past. You can only change the future."

Shaking his head, he sighed. "I only want to change the now."

As the car moved through downtown traffic, she thought. "Is her relationship serious with this new guy?"

"I don't know." He shrugged. "How serious can you get in two weeks?"

Very serious, if one follows the thrilling impulse of attraction full of possibilities. She dealt with the exact situation at work on a daily basis, only discovering the rare transformation of infatuation to love when she received the occasional wedding invitation from a customer she helped. The majority of the time, from her experience helping hundreds of repeat customers, the blush of newness faded and disappeared as quickly as it arrived. She patted his shoulder. "You have a chance. You just need a plan."

He steered into a parking space outside the office building where Maddy worked. Turning off the engine, he shifted in his seat. "I'm flying home tomorrow to tell her I love her and want to marry her at city hall. I already filled out the online application and am waiting to confirm our appointment time. We could still have the other wedding in the fall, if she wants, but we can make our marriage official immediately. No more waiting." He stared at his hands. "I just need to say, 'I do,' this time. I'll ask Dr. Carter for help. She's been successful treating my anxiety so far. I trust she'll have some suggestions." Lifting his head, he met her gaze. "Do you think my plan will work?"

In the two weeks since they met, she never witnessed him looking so scared and frail. Would offering to marry Amy immediately win back her heart from the new man in her life? "I don't know, but if you love her, anything is worth a try."

He swallowed. "I love her with all of my might. I've just been running from her love for thirty years."

"Why?"

"Because of my PTSD." He rubbed the moisture from his eyes.

Tenderness pinched far down in her chest. Did Darren love her with the depth of Greg's love for Amy? Or was his love different? She thought about his behavior. He either smothered her with his presence or abandoned her to a loneliness which triggered her deepest fears. Would the dynamics of their relationship change when he worked a desk job?

"Don't worry." She squeezed his hand. "If it's meant to be, it will happen, all right? Just let me know if I can do anything to help you win her back."

He cupped her hand with both of his. "What if she doesn't take me back?"

Deep lines carved around his tense mouth. "You can't do anything if she chooses the other man. You can just let go graciously and fly back to Atlanta. I'll be here. You're not alone."

Releasing her hands, he collapsed against the seat and stared out the window. "She's everything." Glancing at the clock on the dash, he widened his gaze. "It's almost eight. You better go. I don't want you to be late for work on the big acquisition/merger day."

She inhaled and sighed. *Work.* The one thing she always felt confident about suddenly became as perilous as the rest of her life. "Will you pick me up and take me home tonight?"

"Sure." He nodded. "I have to return the car to the dealership by five. Will that schedule be a problem?"

Maybe Rick can cover, and I can leave an hour early. If either of us has a job. "Should be fine. You can drop me off at home, and I can follow you to the dealership, and drive you back to your place."

He smiled. "Sounds like a plan."

After opening the car door, she stood. Pain shot through her legs. She placed one foot before the other, climbing the stairs to the office building. She winced. A grumble erupted from her stomach. *No stress eating.* She needed to stick with the diet, lose the weight, and focus on the future.

Chapter 18

Chilly air blew through the vents in the conference room. Maddy shivered. She wished she grabbed the sweater off the back of her chair before arriving, but if she hobbled down the hall now, the meeting would probably start by the time she returned. Already most of the fifty-three employees of PerfectFit.com milled about the room, sipping coffee, nibbling on pastries, and chatting in a low mumble about the impending takeover. After a few moments, people dispersed to select their chairs from the rows assembled before a podium at the front.

Maddy grabbed a cup of coffee from the serving table, skipped the breakfast choices of croissants and donuts, and opted for a slice of cantaloupe and a handful of strawberries. Shambling up the aisle, she found a seat at the end of the row and perched with her breakfast in her lap. Maybe she should have stopped at her desk and grabbed a pen and a pad of paper to take notes.

The company's president, Nick Malone, strode to the podium. He smoothed his tie with the palm of his dark hand and cleared his throat before leaning toward the microphone. "Good morning, good morning, good morning." He flashed a smile. "I'm here today to explain the announcement sent out last Friday about the exciting opportunity to become one with Global Dating Conglomerate in an effort to improve our product and enhance our customer relations. I'm proud to introduce our speaker, Mr. Joe Villay, Chief Strategist at GDC, who will talk about the details of this company marriage. Please give a warm welcome to Mr. Villay."

The employees half-heartedly clapped.

Mr. Villay strode to the front of the room. He wore an expensive suit and carried a stack of papers in his chubby hand. He looked more like an overweight, overpaid politician than a corporate executive.

"Thank you." Mr. Villay set his papers on the podium and adjusted the microphone downward. "I'm here from our corporate headquarters in New York City to discuss the next thirty days of our union. The sale of PerfectFit.com finalized as of Friday. In an effort to eliminate duplication of responsibilities, we will consolidate our resources. We anticipate keeping the Atlanta office open through the second quarter and beyond, if profits justify its continued operation. In the meantime, we are researching alternatives, such as outsourcing the call center and relocating accounting to headquarters. Research and development will continue at this location until further notice. In the event a position is outsourced, relocated, or eliminated, our human resources staff will work to find the best transition for your career." He glanced around the room. "Any questions?"

Call center outsourced. Fear plummeted into her stomach. She raised a hand.

Mr. Villay pointed. "Yes, ma'am?"

Maddy placed her plate of food on the chair beside

her and stood, fighting back a groan from her tight thighs. With shoulders back, she cleared her throat and employed her customer service voice. "Sir, how will you know if the call center is profitable?"

Mr. Villay crossed his hands in front of his body and rocked back on his heels. "The board of directors will examine the sales numbers."

With her heartbeat stuttering in her chest, Maddy lifted her voice. "But the majority of my staff doesn't up-sell services. We solve our customers' problems in five minutes or less."

A tense smile creased Mr. Villay's face. "Well, I'm sure a tracking mechanism built into the software tallies any residual sales your department makes." He glanced around the room. "Any other questions?"

Shaking her head, Maddy sank into her seat. Even if the call center remained open in Atlanta, the majority of the company would relocate to New York. The remaining staff might move into a smaller, more affordable location. Imagining how the corporate culture would change, she witnessed a dark cloud of foreboding overshadow her thoughts.

Tina raised a hand. "Any severance packages?"

Frowning, Mr. Villay shook his head. "Not at this time."

Someone in the back of the room stood. "Will you pay for relocation expenses?"

Again, Mr. Villay frowned. "We will reimburse for travel. The employee will be responsible for housing."

From the front of the room, someone waved a hand. "Will any of our benefits change?"

"Not at this time."

A long moment of silence followed.

"Any more questions?"

Maddy glanced around the room. Everyone appeared too stunned to formulate additional questions.

Mr. Villay bowed. "Thank you for your time. And welcome to GDC. We anticipate great things by the addition of PerfectFit.com to our portfolio of companies. I'll be back next month to discuss the execution of our action plan. Good day."

Weak applause filled the room.

Waiting until Mr. Villay exited the conference room, Maddy rose and gathered her cup of coffee and plate of fruit. She didn't feel hungry anymore. Emptiness filled her. Should she call Darren and tell him the details as she agreed yesterday during the video call? Would he even care? Or would he start worrying about her employment? With trembling hands, she set her cup and plate on the serving table and hobbled down the hall to her desk.

Oh, what would she do?

****

At the law office, Greg knocked on Larry Jackson's door. He had not spoken to the firm's owner since he left the after-work party earlier than expected.

The door opened, and Jackson smiled and extended his hand. "Good morning, Power. Good to see you. Come in. Have a seat." He gestured to the two chairs facing his cluttered desk. "I'd offer you coffee, but I don't know how to work the machine." Laughing, he reclined in the executive leather chair and steepled his fingers against his chest. "Have you decided on whether or not you'll accept the permanent position?"

"Yes, I have." Folding his hands between his knees, Greg perched on the edge of the chair nearest the desk. "I appreciate how highly you value my work, but I must decline the offer." He exhaled sharply and glanced toward the window where the Atlanta skyline reminded him of the view from his living room window in New York. A sharp pain clutched his chest. *Amy.* Where was she? Was she even thinking of him? Why risk his life here to return to the life he abandoned? Swallowing, he directed his gaze toward Jackson. "I'm here because I wanted to know if I could cancel my contract early, sir."

Frowning, Jackson leaned forward and crossed his arms on the desk. "How early?"

"Today, sir. I'm in the midst of a family emergency. I need to leave for New York immediately."

Jackson deepened his frown. "What type of family emergency?"

Greg thought about how to describe the unfolding tragedy, having nothing concrete to define the situation. Amy wasn't dying. She wasn't even sick. She was just not returning any of his texts or phone calls because she might be seeing another man. How could a lack of communication be considered an emergency when he dated other women throughout his entire time in Atlanta? Tightness closed his throat. Tears inched closer to the edges of his eyes. Remembering how the soldiers in his troop described the catastrophe in the field, he swallowed again. "My fiancée is missing."

Jackson leaned back and raised his eyebrows. "I didn't even know you had a girlfriend. You always struck me as a man with a single purpose."

A single purpose? Did Amy disappear because she viewed him as having only room for work and no space for her? He would have to change her perception immediately. Releasing his tightly clasped hands, he straightened his spine. "Right now, my sole purpose is to get to New York as soon as possible."

Jackson sat forward and crossed his arms on a stack of papers on the table. "I was really hoping to keep you here. Finding good help is hard. You always recognize the value in the paperwork. You know if you prepare a contract correctly, nine times out of ten you will never go to court, regardless of the circumstances. Words bind. They mean something. You're one of the few assistants I've met who can devote his life to crafting the right words for the right reasons."

The recognition stunned him. Bowing his head, he murmured. "Thank you, sir, for the compliments."

"I don't want to pry, but a part of me wants to know if you find your fiancée, is there any chance you might convince her to join you here in Atlanta? We could help pay for the relocation costs."

"I appreciate the generous offer, sir, but my fiancée doesn't want to relocate." If he and Amy had married during his service, the military would have paid for food and housing at whatever base he was stationed. But those days were over. He lifted his head. "New York has been and always will be her home. I hope you understand."

Standing, Jackson extended his hand. "Great working with you, Power. I hope you find your fiancée and start a new life together. I never married, so I don't know what it feels like to leave an opportunity for another person."

Greg stood and shook his hand. "I'm sure she'll appreciate the sacrifice."

"If she doesn't, you have a job here." He deepened his smile. "I'd take you back any time."

A wave of relief washed over him. Greg smiled. "I appreciate the offer, sir. Pleasure working with you." He turned and strode toward the door.

"Oh, one more thing," Jackson said.

Greg glanced over his shoulder. "Yes?"

"I hope you find her."

Suddenly, a tidal wave of fear crashed into him. He clutched the door handle to keep his balance. "Thank you, sir. I hope I find her, too."

Chapter 19

After the company meeting, Maddy glanced at a few of her staff members huddled in the center of the room, gossiping about the meeting. A knot of impatience tightened in her stomach, and she hobbled toward the group. "No more chatting. Let's get to work."

The group disbanded. People scattered toward their desks.

All the calls received during the meeting had gone to a pre-recorded voicemail message. When Maddy took a seat, she noticed the blinking light on the queue and wondered how many calls needed to be returned. Before putting on her headset, she typed a brief text to Darren.

—Merger finalized last Friday. Most of operations will move to NY. R & D and call center will remain in Atlanta until further notice—

Before sending the text, she considered mentioning the profitability speech Mr. Villay spouted during the meeting but decided to save that tidbit for when Darren called.

After she sent the message, she glanced around the room again. The morale in the call center plunged from productive to self-preservation. Instead of logging into the queue to respond to customers, the staff called their family and friends to share the news. Afterward, they logged into their computers and searched job sites or emailed headhunters. Maddy stiffened her shoulders and tensed her jaw. How could she regain their focus on work?

Rick nudged Maddy's shoulder. "I can't take the stress. I'll be on the roof for a fifteen-minute smoke break, okay?" Without waiting for a reply, he grabbed his jacket and left.

Maddy studied the chaos. A familiar prickle of anxiety inched across her scalp. She opened her bottom desk drawer and ruffled through pens and sticky notes, searching for the bag of chocolate-flavored almonds. Finding it, she emptied the contents into the candy dish. Three almonds bounced out. After crumpling the bag, she tossed it into the trash. *Why am I panicking? We still have our jobs, and if we can somehow prove the call center is profitable, then none of us will lose our jobs.* Straightening her spine, she rose. *We have jobs to do. Why aren't we doing them?*

"May I have everyone's attention?" Maddy waved her arms overhead. "I'm calling a department meeting."

Everyone stopped typing and craned their necks to listen.

Despite the stiffness plaguing her thighs, Maddy waddled up and down the aisles, gazing into each staff member's eyes. "I know we've been dealt unexpected news today. We might not have any say in what direction the company takes, but we do have control over our own thoughts and actions." Breathing in deeply, she nodded. "As long as we're employed by PerfectFit.com, we owe the company our very best work ethic."

She pointed toward the phones and monitors. "I want only to see people talking to customers while seated at their desks. The only website I want to see on anyone's monitor is PerfectFit.com. I need you to respond to emails from our customers or to other employees regarding concerns our customers might have." She thrust a fist into the palm of her open hand. "If I witness anyone violating these rules, I will file a formal complaint with human resources. Understand?"

Tina pouted. "When the company no longer cares about us, why should we care about the company?"

A grumble of agreement murmured throughout the room.

Thinking, Maddy shifted her weight from one foot to the other. How could she address her staff's concerns when she didn't have an answer? She raised her gaze toward the ceiling. Inspiration sparked her voice. "We care about our jobs because we care about our customers. They are the reason why we are here. If we stop caring, our customers will go to another dating website."

Roberto raised a hand. "But customers can't save our jobs."

Silence rippled throughout the room.

"Maybe they can." Chad stood, holding a stack of papers. "I've been reviewing the customer satisfaction surveys. Every single one rates our customer service as the best aspect of their experience. The only negative comments concern our hours of operation. They would prefer our call center be open twenty-four hours a day, three hundred sixty-five days a year." He lifted his face and smiled. "If being a bigger company means more resources, then we can double our hours at this location to meet our customers' needs."

Everyone murmured.

Hope fluttered in her chest. She always knew Chad went above and beyond. He proved her right again. From across the room, Maddy summoned him. "Why don't you present that information to Mr. Villay next month?"

Chad widened his gaze. "You'll let me?"

Relief flooded through her. She nodded. "Of course, the idea is yours. I'll do whatever I can to secure the time you need to speak. Okay?" She would have to discuss the proposal with upper management, but she was confident the response would be favorable.

Lifting an arm, Chad punched the air with a fist. "Let's save our jobs."

Applause thundered.

Rick opened the door and stepped inside. As he scanned the room, he crinkled his forehead. "What's happening?"

Maddy waved toward the staff who logged into the queue to take calls. "We're not letting Global Dating Conglomerate defeat us. We're taking control of our company one customer at a time."

Exhaling, he shook his head. "I don't know how you do it. I smoked three cigarettes before I could stop feeling like my heart raced a mile a minute, and you're here taking charge and making things happen." He pointed toward the hall. "I thought you'd be at the vending machine by now buying all the M & M's."

"Me, too." She smiled and patted Rick on the

shoulder. "But Chad found a possible solution." Leaning forward, she told him the plan. She hoped she could find an idea as strong as the proposal to restore her relationship with Darren.

****

Untangling a life took longer than Greg imagined.

After he packed his belongings from his desk at work, he arrived at his studio apartment and logged into the laptop computer to confirm his six-fifteen flight tomorrow. He would arrive in New York at eight-thirty, stop by city hall to verify both the status of the marriage license and the one o'clock appointment to be wed, and buy a bouquet of lilies from Amy's favorite florist before he surprised her at the art gallery at ten.

Glancing at the clock, he registered the time—eleven-thirty. *Perfect*. Three hours was enough time to pack, clean the apartment, and request a refund from his landlord for the prepaid rent before meeting Dr. Carter at three, picking up Maddy from work at four, and returning the leased vehicle to the dealership by five.

Without thinking, he worked through the morning and early afternoon until his stomach grumbled. Stopping, he grabbed the remaining loaf of bread on the counter and made a hummus, sprout, tomato, avocado, and cucumber sandwich. Halfway through eating, he heard an alarm on his phone beep. After picking up the phone, he swiped the screen. A reminder about his three o'clock therapy appointment glowed.

A bit of anxiety trickled through him. He swallowed the mouthful of mushy avocado and crisp cucumber and thought about what he would tell Dr. Carter. *I'm leaving my life here to return to New York.*

251

No word from Amy. A part of him feared he might not hear from her again. Worse, when he arrived at the gallery tomorrow, she might be out on an appointment. What would he do?

Setting aside his nervousness, he focused on what he had control over—his thoughts and his actions. He could strategize a plan of attack, even if the execution needed to be improvised.

After finishing his sandwich, he grabbed a light jacket and the keys off the counter. Before locking the door, he stepped back into the apartment. Clutching the camera to his chest, he glimpsed the sunlight against a skyscraper through the window, and another flashback collided with his thoughts. He staggered back, blinking, but the memory crashed, scattering his focus. He was eighteen, with Amy during the senior prom, at the top of the Empire State Building. As he framed the shot of her standing against the setting sun, the wind gusted, blowing Amy's hair across her face. "Can we get married here before you leave for basic training?" She angled her chin toward the horizon, and the city below them burst into flames with the reflection of the sunlight against the windows of a thousand buildings. "I want to be your wife before you're a lieutenant." He didn't answer her, hadn't even asked her to marry him, and yet, he always knew she was the one just as she had known.

Why didn't I marry her before I left? Why did I wait?

Turning, he set the camera on the bed and left the apartment, feeling like he might be too late to marry her now.

Chapter 20

During her break, Maddy sat in the lunch room and listened to Darren's sweet message before she returned his call. The phone rang and rang before it clicked over to voicemail. She sighed. Why was her timing always off?

"Hey, Dare, it's me." She cradled the phone against her ear and stood then paced. The stench of burned microwave popcorn filled the room. The smell left her with no appetite, although she hadn't eaten since breakfast. "The company meeting turned out better than I thought. One of my staff has a plan to expand our department here, even if the rest of the company gets outsourced overseas or relocated to New York." She stopped before the window and glanced from the busy street to the crowded skyline. "When you get a chance, please call me, okay? Love you. Bye." She thought about heading over to the deli across the street and grabbing a sandwich to eat at her desk, but the effort to walk with sore legs discouraged her. Maybe she would lose another pound from starvation and worry.

After pressing the red button to end the call, she hobbled out of the lunchroom. When would her legs stop feeling like rubber? She sank into the chair, placed the headphones over her ears, and logged into the queue to wait for the next escalated phone call. Since the R &

D department finally fixed the ability to self-edit profiles, the number of calls she fielded each day declined significantly.

A half hour later, someone stopped by her desk to drop off an overnight package. As soon as she glimpsed the return address, a zip of excitement rocketed through her. *My wedding dress.* Should she slip into the restroom to try on the gown or wait until she was home?

After several minutes of sneaking glances at the package, she logged out of the queue and lumbered into the restroom's handicap stall to change into her dress. A spray of floral air freshener misted overhead, masking the stink from the adjacent stall. She tore open the cardboard box and caressed the fabric. The material was softer than she imagined with a built-in bra in the tight bodice and lots of light layers making up the long skirt.

Carefully, she placed the cardboard box on the dirty tile floor to protect the gown before she wiggled into the flowing fabric. She slipped her arms through the holes in the bodice and yanked the zipper. Halfway up her back, the movement stopped. She tugged harder, but the zipper refused to budge. Lifting the skirt, she stepped out of the stall and hobbled over to the mirror. Frowning, she tried one last time to tug the material across the span of her broad back, but her efforts were useless.

The dress was too small.

Disappointment shot through her. Would the gown fit if she was sober when she bought it? Or was she simply just too big to be a bride? With trembling hands, she slipped back into her work clothes. When she folded the dress, the layers of material didn't fit into the box. Finally, she draped the dress over the crook of her elbow and limped toward her desk.

Tina pointed and gasped. "Is that your wedding dress?"

Heat flamed her face. She bit her lower lip and nodded. "I'd have to lose two bra-sizes and grow six inches for the gown to fit." She stared at the dress and sighed.

"That's terrible. If the dress was too big, you could get it tailored."

"I bought it online."

"Return it."

Hanging the dress over the back of her chair, she rifled inside the box for the invoice. On the desk, her cell phone vibrated. "Hey, Dare."

"Got your message, sweetheart," he said. "I'm sorry to hear about work, but you sound hopeful."

She groaned. "Yes, I am. But you never know how things will go with these situations."

"Don't worry. Everything will work out. Even if they ship your department overseas and relocate the rest of the company to New York, I'm confident you'll find a better job right where we are. Atlanta isn't a small city anymore."

Not wanting to dwell any longer on work, she fingered the edge of the invoice. "How are you doing? Have you heard anything about when your replacement might arrive or when you'll fly home?" She scanned the invoice for the company's return policy.

"I'm fine," he said. "No news yet, but I'll call as

soon as I know."

"Okay." She studied the fine print at the bottom of the invoice. *We offer full refunds for faulty or damaged items only. All other items must be exchanged. Customers are responsible for shipping costs to our facility in China.* A blanket of depression descended over her shoulders. What was the cost to ship the dress to China? She logged into her computer and searched for the answer.

"One more thing before I go." He inhaled. "I feel really uncomfortable with you hanging out with Greg." He exhaled. "Peter said you both missed boot camp this morning. Are you cheating on me?"

Why doesn't he trust me? She dropped the invoice on the desk. "No, I'm not." Anger burned her face. "You have nothing to worry about. Greg's leaving for New York."

"How long will he be gone?"

Why did Darren assume Greg traveled for work? "He's going home to marry his fiancée. I'll probably never see him again." The finality of the statement shocked her, and she sank back against the chair with a knot in her chest.

"Hold on a second. I just received a text."

With a tight throat, Maddy stared at the blinking light on the queue and hoped Rick might answer the escalated call. Why should she give Darren another chance to prove he loved her more than he loved work and her family? Why should she constantly change who she was to please him?

"That message was work-related. My replacement is coming this evening. I have to brief him on the list of clients tomorrow morning before I can leave." He sighed. "Listen. I don't want to get into a fight. Why don't we finish talking tomorrow night after I get home?"

She tasted bile at the back of her throat. "Sure."

"I love you, Maddy."

Bitterness clung to her tongue. She opened her mouth and closed it again. How could she say she loved him when he left her feeling unloved by doubting her fidelity? Didn't all the time she invested in the relationship matter?

"Maddy?"

Why didn't he focus on her efforts to lose weight as a testimony to how much she loved him? Couldn't he say something positive and life-affirming for once? Chewing on her lower lip, she concentrated on the computer screen. To ship the dress to China cost as much as the dress was worth.

"Maddy, are you there?"

"Yes, I'm here." One hundred dollars to return the dress for the correct size. Twice the amount she wanted to spend for a dress she might no longer wear. A fresh wave of anger crashed through her. "I have to get back to work. Have a safe flight." Ending the call, she crumbled the invoice in her fist. *What a waste of money*. She stared at her engagement ring. *Where will I go if we break up? What if I lose my job? What if my family hates me for what they view as another mistake?*

Picking up her phone, she sent Greg a text.

—Darren called. He's coming home tomorrow night. He's suspicious of our friendship. Not sure if I should call off wedding—

A few seconds later, Greg responded.

—*Don't break up. He quit his job. For a guy, work is identity. He surrendered his identity for the sake of the relationship. Be patient. Let it all play out. Don't let your anger blindside you. See you at four—*

Holding the phone against her chest, she closed her eyes and, for the first time since her parents died, she prayed. *Please, God, may Greg be right about Darren.*

****

At the Atlanta VA Medical Center, Greg paced back and forth across the linoleum floors while he waited for Dr. Carter.

A flurry of artillery fired down the hallway.

"Rat-a-tat-tat. Rat-a-tat-tat."

Greg did not jump or startle. He smiled, registering his progress.

"Mr. Power?"

Dr. Carter stood before him with her severe face, white lab coat, and stiletto heels.

Why won't she call me Greg? Irritation bristled against his shoulders. *Let it go.* He forced a smile. "Yes?"

She waved toward her office. "Follow me."

He entered the tiny office and perched on the edge of the leather recliner. The room still stank of day-old coffee. He clasped his hands between his knees, staring at the carpet, hoping the meeting would be over sooner than the scheduled fifty minutes.

Dr. Carter leaned back in her swivel chair and crossed her legs. She dangled a heel out of a stiletto. She tapped the blunt end of a pencil against his chart. "So, tell me about your week. What happened in boot camp?"

He sighed. What was there to tell? "I've been working out harder, lifting heavier, and supplementing my meals with the occasional protein shake. But I don't think I've put on any muscle." He rolled up his sleeve and flexed a bicep.

Narrowing her gaze, she nodded. "Well, it's early. Maybe after four more weeks, you'll notice a difference." She examined the chart. "I did receive a call from Peter Strong this week. He voiced his concerns about your friendship with his sister, Maddy." Lifting her face, she squinted. "He thought you might be endangering his sister's life. Did you invite her over to your apartment and almost strangle her like the last woman you met?"

A bolt of frustration shot through him. He unclasped his hands and rolled back his shoulders. "Don't you listen? I didn't *almost* strangle the other woman. The night terrors controlled my actions." Standing, he paced the length of the room with jerky movements. "Maddy doesn't even know where I live. She's never been to my apartment."

She arched an eyebrow. "Have you been to hers?"

Sighing, he glanced away. "Once. To pick her up and drive her to work." He met her gaze. "I didn't go inside. She wouldn't let me. We're not romantically involved."

"But you want to be?"

"No." The word spat out of his mouth with such quick ferocity he questioned his motives. When he first met Maddy, he was disgusted by her weight. But as he came to know her, his opinion changed. She softened all of his hard edges and brought to surface every bit of himself he tried so hard to erase. Even running with her wasn't the same as running alone. When he ran, he always tried to escape. With her, he ran toward a common goal. *Why don't you run with Amy?* Maddy asked. Why didn't he? He raised his eyebrows and shook his head. "She's my best friend. She understands me better than I understand myself."

"Sit down and take a deep breath, Mr. Power. I need to know what's happening in your life, so I can offer suggestions."

He sank on the ratty sofa and sighed. "I missed boot camp this morning. Maddy did, too. But we weren't together." Lifting his face, he shook a finger. "I bet you forty dollars her brother will call you later today. I swear he thinks we're having an affair. *He* is the problem, not us."

A faint smile played at the corner of her lips. "He already called. But I didn't accept your bet, so I don't owe you forty dollars."

Chuckling, he lifted his palms. "Her sister doesn't seem to mind our friendship. She invited me over to celebrate Easter. Why would she include me if she thought I endangered Maddy's life?"

Dr. Carter uncrossed her legs. "I don't know anything about the sister."

"She's pretty." Embarrassment flamed his cheeks. "She's smart, married to a doctor, and lives in Druid Hills with a full-house staff and two children." Mist clouded his vision, and his throat tightened with an unidentified emotion. "Her son, Collin, really liked me. He kept calling me a hero, but I told him heroes save others. I didn't save anyone."

She lifted her eyebrows. "Are you sure?"

Nodding, he rubbed his eyes with his fists. "I was the only one hurt."

Leaning forward, she clasped her hands over his chart. "What if you disobeyed orders and stayed on base? Whom would they have sent? Would the operation have played out the same way?"

"You're speculating." He asked himself the same questions over and over during his rehabilitation, but he didn't have any answers. "No one knows." He raised his empty palms. "What happened is what happened, and nothing either of us thinks will change anything." He leaned back and slapped his thighs. "I need to tell you I quit my job. This therapy session will be my last. Please transfer my case to another doctor and find me another boot camp." He blinked. "I'm leaving for New York tomorrow morning. I'm going home to marry Amy."

Dr. Carter lifted her eyebrows and scribbled something in his chart. "Those choices aren't small decisions. What made you change your life so dramatically?"

"For the last few days, Amy won't return my phone calls or messages." He choked on a sob. "I think she's cheating. My mom told me to let her go, but I can't. I need to win her back." He covered his face with his hands and curled forward, shaking with tears.

"I'm sorry to hear the news about Amy. Can I help you with anything before you go home?"

Home. The word felt like a sucker punch to the gut. He stopped crying and dried his face with a tissue. For some reason, he thought Dr. Carter would parrot his mother and lecture him about wasting his effort on wooing a woman who had every right to walk away. He stared at the crumpled tissue in his trembling hands. Could Amy leave him after more than three decades together? Acid roiled in his stomach. Somehow, he knew if she refused to reconcile, he would never see her again. When he imagined the future without her, he only saw a vast wasteland. How could he live without her? He balled up the tissue in his fist. She was his everything.

Sniffing, he lifted his head. "I've spent most of my adult life running. I ran away from my family and joined the military. When I returned, I ran away from Amy by refusing to marry her. I ran away from New York by taking temporary jobs in other states." He gulped with a moment of hesitation. He wanted to be like Maddy, stopping and confronting the situation directly, instead of running away and hiding like a coward, so he pushed forward. "Each time, I thought I ran to something better: a career, independence, or an opportunity. But I really ran away from the most important things: my family, my true love, and my home." He thumped a fist against his chest. "I need to go back and fight for what matters. Or I'll end up bitter and alone."

"How do you plan on winning back Amy?"

He recalled Maddy explaining the grand romantic gesture. "I'm surprising her at the gallery where she works and asking her to marry me at city hall that same day. I already have the marriage license and the appointment. I just need her to say yes."

"What if she says no?" She puckered her lips, her forehead furrowed.

Pain knotted his chest. What would he do? If he sold the apartment, would he move into his mother's home? He laced together his hands. Or would he move back to Georgia and accept a permanent position with the firm he just left? Breathing in deeply, he thought of Maddy, and the knot loosened in his chest. What if things fell apart with her and Darren? Could he start over with her? Or was that idea just an idle fantasy? "I...don't...know."

"Well, I think you should prepare for both situations." She set the clipboard on the desk and lifted her palms. "Do you want to role play? I can pretend to be Amy."

With her severe looks and stern face, he could not imagine acting out the scenario. He needed to practice with someone softer, gentler, and more yielding. "Can I ask someone else to help me?"

"Who do you have in mind?"

"Maddy."

"Is she a licensed therapist?"

"No, she's a tech support manager for an online dating company. But she's an expert on romance."

"You need to practice with a professional." Dr. Carter pursed her lips. "Maddy is your friend. She isn't trained on how to role play."

She doesn't trust us just like Maddy's brother. He waved his hand. "Don't worry. Everything will work out."

Staring, she shook her head. "You need to be prepared."

He sat straight and pushed back his shoulders. "I am."

She softened her gaze. "When are you leaving?"

"Tomorrow a little after 0600 hours."

Standing, she shook his hand. "Good luck."

"Thank you, Doctor." Releasing her hand, he smiled. "You were right about boot camp. The training hasn't fixed everything, but the opportunity certainly helped."

"I'm glad I was able to serve you." She opened the door. "Now, go marry Amy."

"I will." He stepped into the silent hallway and strode toward the nearest exit. With each step, he practiced. "I do, I do, I do…" His footfalls echoed with his worries. *What if she says, I don't?*

Chapter 21

"Thank you for calling PerfectFit.com where romantic dreams come true." Maddy sat in the work cubicle later that afternoon. "This is Maddy. How may I help you?"

"What's that banner on your website?" a woman caller asked. "Are you really selling to the Global Dating Conglomerate? How will that change affect the service I receive and the monthly subscription I pay?"

Maddy placed the caller on mute and groaned. Instead of fixing profile text, she fielded several inquiries about the acquisition/merger. The corporate office prepared and emailed a standard statement to be read by all members of the call center, but Maddy soon discovered the answers left her callers with more questions. She released the caller from mute and smiled. "Your service and subscription fees will remain the same."

"What about content, style, and delivery? I don't want to wake up one morning and not recognize the site. That's what happened to my account on Find-a-Mate. That's how I ended up here. I liked the locally-owned, locally-sourced singles. Now I don't know what to think."

How many of these similar calls would she have to take today? Ten? Twenty? Thirty or more? She sighed.

"I understand your frustration. Believe me, I've felt it, too. From what I've been told, nothing about our services is changing."

"Y'all aren't getting laid off, are you?" the woman asked. "Because I don't want to call someone in India who doesn't understand my Southern twang, you hear?"

Maddy's cell phone vibrated on her desk. She focused on the caller. "I reassure you the content, style, and delivery will remain the same, ma'am."

"Okay, well, thank you for answering my questions."

"And thank you for calling PerfectFit.com where romantic dreams come true." Maddy logged out of the queue, picked up her phone, and read the text message from Darren.

—Tomorrow's plans finalized. Leave Denver at twelve-thirty. Arrive in Atlanta at six. Will meet you at home. XOXO—

Dark clouds of sadness roiled within her, and she tucked her phone next to her monitor to focus on work. Greg left and Darren returned on the same day. Why did she suddenly feel like running away? Beads of sweat dampened the back of her neck. Rummaging in her drawer for something to eat and finding nothing, she crossed her arms on her desk and buried her head in the dark triangle. Breathing deeply, she thought about the past two weeks. So much happened, and yet nothing changed.

Bzzz…bzzz…bzzz.

Lifting her head, she stared at her cell phone. The caller ID read Greg Power. She swiped a finger across the screen and held the phone against her ear. "Hey,

General."

"Are you ready to leave work?"

Sighing, she connected her gaze with Rick who nodded. "Sure. I'm on the second floor."

"I'll meet you in the lobby. No need to cause any more drama. You've got enough on your plate."

His voice sounded purposeful, strong, and confident. The tension melted from her shoulders, and the sweat dried from the back of her neck. Hope expanded, and the dark clouds of sadness scuttled away. "Thanks, General." She logged off of her computer. "See you soon." After ending the call, she slung her purse over her shoulder and tucked the wedding dress in the crook of her arm. Bittersweet longing filled her. Why did she suddenly want Darren to go away and Greg to stay?

****

Greg paced across the squeaky linoleum floors of the lobby of Maddy's building. Each time the bank of elevator doors opened, he glanced at the people striding out. Finally, a short blonde in a tight purple dress shuffled out of the elevator, carrying a wedding dress.

With his heartbeat drumming in his chest, he hustled over. "Is Darren back? Did you guys get married?"

Tossing back her head, she laughed. "No, silly, he's arriving tomorrow night. We're meeting after work." She lifted her arm. "I bought this wedding gown online over two weeks ago. It arrived today." She narrowed her gaze. "The dress is at least two sizes too small and a foot too long."

She's not married. He frowned. *Why do I care*

whether or not she's married? He shook his head, unloosening the absurdity of his thoughts. He relaxed his shoulders, and his heartbeat slowed then sped again. "Sounds like the dress would fit Amy."

She arched her eyebrows. "Does she have a gown for the wedding?"

He shrugged. How many dresses did she purchase and return over the years? Two or three? He couldn't remember. "I don't know. She might. She might not. If she would only return my calls, I could ask."

"Well, the return shipping costs one hundred dollars. I'd rather give the dress to you if she might wear it."

He held out his hands. "Let's see."

She pressed the gown against her body, and the skirt pooled at her feet.

The shock of white gossamer propelled him back to the months before his father died. He and Amy stood beneath an arch of ivy in his parents' backyard. Amy's white summer dress floated around her legs like a cloud. Kicking off her slip-on sandals, she grabbed his hand. "Let's run on the beach." Without changing into his running blade, he grabbed her hand and jogged beside her, keeping the rhythm of her hop, skip, and jump pace.

A cloud of sand kicked by the wind caught in his eyes, triggering a memory of the dark morning in which he combat-crawled through the desert before the land mine exploded, severing his foot from his leg. Releasing Amy's hand, he turned and ran up the beach toward his parents' backyard, chased by the memory of defeat and loss.

Now, he stood in the lobby of an office building gazing at a frothy white gown, choking back fear. *Am I leaving the one person who needs me to return to a woman who might no longer care to have me around?* An ocean of grief overwhelmed him, and he turned away, unwilling to let Maddy see the doubt and panic in his gaze.

"What's wrong?" She touched his shoulder.

Shaking his head, he rubbed his eyes and sniffed. "You'll be a beautiful bride."

"Take the dress." She scoffed and thrust the white bundle toward him. "If Amy doesn't like the gown, she can donate it to her favorite charity or sell it on consignment."

Turning, he clutched the dress against his chest, his soft fingertips brushing against her hard knuckles. A bullet of excitement shot through him. Did she recognize the energy between them, or was he the only one terrified of letting go? "Are you sure?"

With wide eyes, she nodded. "I don't think I'm getting married anymore."

The ammunition of her words blasted through his heart. He tightened his grip on the gown. "What happened now?"

"Nothing happened." She shrugged. "I just feel differently. I'll tell you on the drive back."

With one hand, he held open the door. A breeze blew against him, and tiny sprinkles of rain dusted his head. "I parked in the lot in a visitor spot." Silently, he walked beside her in the light rain. Holding open the passenger door, he waited while Maddy slid inside. He strode around the vehicle and placed the wedding dress on the backseat before he sat and started the engine. Turning on the windshield wipers, he shifted into Reverse. "Want to start talking now?"

"Not really." She sighed. "I just don't know how much a person can change."

A thought occurred, something Maddy said not too long ago. He glanced at her profile, but her hair shielded her face. "What if Darren's desk job is his idea of a grand romantic gesture?"

Lifting her head, she turned, and her mouth twitched. "Why did he take so long?"

Another thought drifted through his mind. "Because nothing threatened the status quo until I arrived. He sees me as a threat, even though nothing is between us."

She tilted her head. "Really? You think our friendship is nothing?"

Tension knotted his shoulders. Between the look of confusion on her face and the harshness of her words, he couldn't tell if she felt the energy between them as something more than the camaraderie between friends. He sighed. "Doesn't matter how we feel about each other, does it? The reality is you live here with your family, and I belong in New York. Long-distance relationships don't work. You need to be with the one you love, in person, not communicating through video calls and texts. Love thrives on touch and intimacy."

She placed a hand on his thigh. "Don't go."

The jolt of electricity from her fingertips distracted him, and he swerved to a stop merely inches from the luxury vehicle in front of them. With his heartbeat hammering in his chest and sweat beading at the back of his neck, he brushed aside her fingers. "Don't ruin our friendship."

Swallowing, she folded her hands in her lap and gazed out the window. "How do you feel about me?"

Why lie? He couldn't lie. But he couldn't speak the truth. Not now while he drove. Lifting his foot off the brake, he maneuvered through traffic. "I—care—about you—a lot."

For a long moment, she sat in silence. Finally, she heaved a sigh. "I care about you, too."

Feeling like he escaped from an emotional battle, he focused on the road, the unspoken love for her knotted in his chest.

****

Through heavy rainfall, Maddy drove Greg to his apartment after he returned his leased vehicle to the dealership. Several times, she thought about what he said about caring a lot about her. How much more did he need to care to stay in Georgia?

Following his directions, she drove into an underground parking garage three blocks from where she worked. Marveling at the coincidence, she wondered how many times he walked past her building aware she was there, working, while he was going home, alone. She steered into his parking space, letting the engine idle.

"Do you want to come up? I could make you dinner." He released the seatbelt and turned toward her. "I have a fair amount of food in my refrigerator. You can take home whatever you'd like. I hate waste."

The invitation sounded like a pickup line, but Maddy didn't care anymore. He was leaving. She was staying. Why not go up to share a last meal? Shrugging, she turned off the engine. "Sure." She followed him to the elevator and waited.

He glanced at her feet. "How are your legs doing?"

She grumbled. "Better than this morning, but they're still sore. Are you ready for your trip tomorrow?"

"I guess about as ready as I'll ever be." He shoved his hands into his pockets and stared at the ground. "How did the acquisition/merger meeting go?"

The elevator doors parted.

He held an arm against the door's sensor.

She stepped inside and leaned against the wall. "Fine." The space smelled like sandalwood and pepperoni. A growl erupted from the bottom of her stomach. In the midst of worry, she neglected to eat lunch. "The new corporation is keeping everything the same for now. But if we lose business, I wouldn't be surprised if they closed the Atlanta office, shipped the call center overseas, and relocated the important players to New York."

"You can visit me and Amy. We'll help you find a place to live." Nudging her arm, he winked.

"I'm not important." She laughed. "I'm just a tech support manager. If the call center isn't profitable, I'll be out of work."

He stared into her eyes. "You're important to me."

Shivering from the stark tenderness in his gaze, she stretched up on her tiptoes.

The doors parted. He ducked into the hall and waved. "Are you coming?"

Nodding, she sank back onto her heels and hobbled

out of the elevator. Disappointment sagged against her shoulders. Why didn't she kiss him?

He walked halfway down the corridor before jangling a set of keys from his pocket. "Welcome to my humble abode." He opened the door.

She lumbered into the furnished studio apartment and gasped. "Look at that view." Wandering past the kitchen, the desk, and the queen-sized bed, she stood before the window overlooking downtown. The sun sank below the horizon, and streaks of purple and orange colored the sky. Lights from skyscrapers twinkled like stars. She leaned her forehead against the window and exhaled, her breath fogging the glass. "I wish I lived downtown. No more Clifton Crunch. Just three blocks to work. I could eat at home instead of buying an overpriced burger from a greasy restaurant chain. Maybe even lose a few pounds." She sighed before turning away from the view.

He set the wedding dress on top of his suitcase by the front door and strode into the kitchen. "Take a look in the refrigerator and let me know what you want me to bag up."

"Are you shipping your furniture to New York?" She stroked the bedspread with her fingertips and ran her hand across a lampshade.

"The furniture isn't mine. The studio came furnished."

Thoughtfully, she nodded. "When I moved into Darren's apartment, I only purchased lace curtains for the windows. I didn't like the plastic-looking blinds." She peered into the refrigerator and frowned. "What's this thing?" She picked up a green, spiky, oval-shaped object.

Plucking the odd-shaped fruit from her hand, he smiled. "It's a jackfruit. I shred and grill it like chicken. Would you like me to show you how to prepare it?"

A song chimed from the bottom of her purse. She rummaged for her phone. When she glimpsed the caller ID, she tensed her shoulders. Turning her back toward Greg, she swiped her finger across the screen. "Hi, Darren." As she kept talking, she stepped farther away and lowered her voice.

Darren babbled on and on about his flight itinerary and their plan to have dinner with her sister and brother-in-law after he returned. "The kids will be asleep," he said, "so you don't have to worry about having a glass of wine."

Remembering that night, she cringed. When would she tell him that she wanted to live a healthier lifestyle, and not on her own? With Greg, she could skip booze and french fries without missing out on all of the fun. When she shared the experience with someone, eating clean and drinking water wasn't as painful as she imagined. When she didn't drink alcohol, she slept better and woke refreshed.

A stab of guilt pierced her chest. She already asked him to give up his job. How could she ask him to give up something else? As the call dragged on and on, she glanced over her shoulder and glimpsed fierce concern in Greg's brown eyes. Quickly, she turned her back toward him and hobbled over to the window. A couple of minutes later, she ended the call. "Sorry about the interruption." She tucked her phone in her purse. "Darren wanted to coordinate plans for tomorrow night."

"You don't look too happy." He dragged a bar stool toward the counter and poured two glasses of distilled water. "Want to talk about what's upsetting you while I make us dinner?" He grabbed a cutting board and a chef knife. "I hope you like vegan tacos."

"I'm so hungry, I'll eat anything." Sitting on the bar stool, she sipped from the glass of water. "I was too preoccupied to eat lunch."

"Are you and Darren all right?" He peeled the skin from the jackfruit and shredded the meat.

Moaning, she rubbed her face with her hands. "I don't want Darren to come home and blame me for everything. The house is never clean enough. I'm not thin enough." She glanced up at the ceiling and shook her head. "I don't want to always go out with my family. Sometimes, I just like the two of us being alone." She met his gaze. "Once Darren returns home and we resume our old lifestyle, I'm afraid I'll slip into old habits and regain the weight I've lost."

As he shredded carrots and cabbage into a bowl, he nodded. "I hear you."

She twirled the engagement ring around her finger. "Once I find a place to live, I'm breaking up with Darren."

"Don't." He wiped his hands on a dishtowel. "You haven't given him a chance to prove himself."

She shrugged. "What's there to prove?"

"Everything." He lifted his arms, palms up. "How unfair to give him an ultimatum and then leave once he chooses you?" Striding around the island, he braced his hands against her shoulders and glowered. "What would you say if Amy said she can't marry me tomorrow?"

Tension twitched in her jaw. "I'd say it's about time she stood up for herself."

Bowing his head, he sighed. "Returning to New York *is* too little too late." He released his arms from her shoulders and stepped around the island to resume cooking.

"I'm not Amy." She pointed to her chest. "She might be absolutely thrilled to have you back."

He harrumphed, sliding the shredded jackfruit into a sizzling skillet.

Watching him cook, she wondered if she overstepped her bounds by harshly speaking, knowing her words were partly colored by the intensity of her feelings. Intense feelings he would not acknowledge he returned, although she suspected those feelings might exist, lingering beneath his love for Amy. "I'm sorry." She finished the glass of water. "I shouldn't have said what I did about Amy."

He slid the jackfruit onto a plate and heated tortillas, one at a time. "I wish I processed the war differently."

"How differently?" She crossed her arms on the counter and leaned forward.

Placing aside the tortillas, he grabbed two plates. "I'm proud of serving my country, but I don't think I would have enlisted if I knew the cost." He swallowed. "I left because I hated my father. I didn't want to be indebted for anything, although I probably could have taken the opportunity to go to college like he wanted. Maybe I would be an attorney by now and not an assistant. Maybe I would have married Amy, and we would be celebrating our thirtieth anniversary. Maybe I would have children and grandchildren. Maybe, maybe, maybe…" He shook his head. "I can't change the past. I can only hope to change the future." Pointing, he focused on Maddy. "Same applies to you. Sure, you've made mistakes, and you wish you could change a few things, but you can only work with what you have right now. I've seen how your family interacts. No wonder you chose a man like Darren."

Frowning, she leaned closer. "What does that statement mean?"

"Darren is as controlling, demanding, and judgmental as your siblings. You're comfortable with the familiarity of those personality traits. That's why you chose him." He lifted his palms. "You have to work with what you've chosen. You just can't walk away. You have to do what's right—stay and fight for your relationship."

She snickered. "Like you did with Amy?"

Narrowing his gaze, he shook his finger. "I'm sharing the lessons I've learned from my mistakes, so you won't make them."

She stared at her hands. "What if leaving is not a mistake?"

"Give him a chance before you walk away. He might surprise you." He placed a plate with two jackfruit tacos before her. "Bon appétit."

Sniffing the spicy jalapeno sauce, she smiled. "Smells good."

"Taste it." He waved a hand at the food.

She scooped up a soft taco shell and bit into the

juicy jackfruit, crispy carrots, and tangy cabbage. "Mmm…tastes better than the Pig-N-Chik."

Smiling, he took a seat beside her. "Glad you like it."

She took another bite and closed her eyes, savoring the texture and flavors. Could she learn how to cook healthy foods Darren might enjoy? Could she somehow figure out how to manage her weight while in a relationship instead of severing ties with someone she loved?

"Maddy?"

Opening her eyes, she met his gaze. "Yes?"

"I can't leave tomorrow morning without knowing if I'm through with the night terrors. Would you mind staying the night and holding me, just so I know I won't strangle Amy in my sleep?"

She gulped. Didn't he know the danger in that proposition? Couldn't he feel the magnetic pull she struggled against whenever she was near him? Hoping to sidestep the issue without hurting his feelings, she widened her gaze. "Why not use a pillow?"

He shook his head. "I want a person."

Any person or her? Daring him to admit the truth, she narrowed her gaze. "Hire someone." Was he ashamed of finding an overweight woman attractive? Pressing again, she swiveled toward him on the bar stool. "Why the last ditch attempt to have sex?"

Staring, he shook his head again. "If I wanted to have sex, I would have left a long time ago." A muscle in his jaw twitched. "I need your help. That incident with the girl I almost strangled really frightened me. I can't go back and marry Amy if I think I'll kill her while she sleeps."

A cynical bark of laughter escaped her open mouth. "But it's okay to strangle me?"

"You're the only one I know who is strong enough to fight back and win."

Shaking her head, she chuckled until her sides ached. When she glanced over, she witnessed dark concern haunting his gaze. The laughter trailed away, and a prickle of apprehension crawled across her skin. The gravity of the situation swirled her thoughts. *He's dangerous. I could die. He's never hurt me. I'm strong. He can't lift a hundred pounds. I can slip out of a choke hold, kick his groin, and toss him out of the bed.* Nothing changed in his expression. Resistance yielded in her tight jaw. He needed her reassurance. Leaning over, she grabbed his hand. "Okay. I'll do it. For Amy."

"Thank you." He squeezed her fingers.

After dinner, Maddy helped clean the kitchen. She bagged the food she wanted to take with her tomorrow and placed it on the top shelf in the refrigerator. After closing the door, she glanced around the studio. "Now what?"

The bright lights from the skyscrapers filled the room like stars. He withdrew his phone. "I'm setting the alarm for four-thirty. You'll have time to go home and change for boot camp after you drop me off at the airport."

Boot camp. She shuddered, wondering how lonely she would feel without him.

He set the cell phone on the nightstand. "Are you sleeping in your dress?"

Oh, why did she remove the overnight bag from

her trunk? "I guess I could strip down to my bra and underwear."

"I have a T-shirt you can borrow." He tossed her a man's medium white undershirt.

Holding the material against her body, she smirked. "Two sizes too small." She tossed aside the T-shirt and sank on the edge of the mattress. Clutching her hair in her hands, she mumbled. "I'll never lose this weight."

"A soldier never surrenders unless his general does." He sat beside her. "I haven't surrendered."

"But you're leaving, and I'll be alone." She gulped, feeling the impending loss circle like a vulture. "I'll be a soldier without a general."

Clasping his hands between his knees, he bowed his head. "I have a confession to make. I was never a general. Just a captain. Maybe if I served thirty years, I would have ranked higher, but then again the Army holds no guarantees."

Releasing her hair, she lifted her head and clenched her fists. "Why did you lie?"

He inhaled. "Changing is hard when people know you a certain way. Becoming who you yearn to be is easier when someone doesn't know you." He met her gaze. "I wanted to change."

Recognizing the desire, she nodded. "Me, too." She narrowed her gaze and shook a fist. "But I didn't lie about who I am."

"I'm sorry."

The whites of his eyes glowed.

"Please, forgive me."

She held her breath. He was leaving anyway. Why did it matter whether or not he told the truth?

Resistance crumbled inside, and she unclenched her fists. If she could rewind the clock, she would have added a third rule of friendship—never fall in love. She hated how he lied, but she didn't hate him. "Apology accepted." She touched his hand. "I don't care if you were a captain. You'll always be my general."

He flashed a brief smile. "Thanks." Yawning, he stood. "I'm getting ready for bed."

After he closed the bathroom door, she rose and padded toward the window. Gazing at the skyline, she wondered how many other hearts had broken tonight throughout the city.

"Your turn." He left open the bathroom door while he strode over to the bed in a T-shirt and boxer shorts. Perched on the edge of the mattress, he unfastened his prosthetic.

Turning, she ducked into the bathroom and shut the door. Staring at her reflection, she longed for makeup wipes and a toothbrush. Using hand soap and warm water, she scrubbed her face and blotted her skin dry with a hand towel. After squeezing toothpaste on her index finger, she massaged her teeth and gums.

Staring at her reflection, she knotted her shoulders. What if Darren crawled into bed with another woman, not to have sex, but to sleep? Would she care? She shrugged, releasing the tension. She shared a bed with her brother while she was vacationing with her parents. The hotel room had two king beds—her parents shared one bed, and the children shared the other. She remembered the staking out of territory, the kicking feet, and the tug of war for blankets before settling into sleep. She wondered how sleeping with someone with

PTSD would affect her. Mostly, she dreaded the possibility of waking in a choke hold, kneeing him in the groin, and tossing him out of the bed in the middle of the night.

Another set of thoughts rushed through her, and she blushed, feeling the tingle of lust and desire. She yearned to be touched as a woman again. Stripping out of her dress and nylons, she turned off the bathroom light and padded back into the moonlit room.

Beneath the covers, Greg curled on his side. He patted the pillow. "Face the wall. I'll wrap my arms above your chest."

Nervous, she turned and slid across the mattress, jerked the sheet over her shoulder, and tucked it under her chin. He wrapped an arm around her. She felt his body heat against her back. For a while, she lay against him, eyes open, listening to her nervous breathing. Every muscle fiber tensed from the awkward and defenseless position. "I'm uncomfortable." She wriggled out of his embrace.

"Are you leaving?"

Panic seized his voice. Rolling over, she scooted across the mattress. With her knee, she nudged the space where his leg ended. With her foot, she ran her toes along his other calf, feeling the rough hairs against her skin. Draping an arm around his body, she inched closer, breathing in the smell of his musky skin, relaxing into the satisfying intimacy of touch. She rested her cheek against the hollow of his hummingbird chest and closed her eyes. "I'm not going anywhere."

"Promise?"

The yearning in his voice melted any remaining

trepidation.

She snuggled against him. "I promise." Only one worry occupied her mind. How she would say goodbye when she never wanted to let him go?

Chapter 22

Beep. Beep. Beep.

From the depths of sleep, Greg surfaced. Bobbing his head, he brushed his lips against a nest of soft hair. A firm body nestled against his chest. Warmth invaded him. A flicker of lust stirred. Remembering whom he was with, he moved away, untangling arms and legs from the comfort of Maddy's body.

Beep. Beep. Beep.

Sitting, he grabbed the cell phone and swiped the alarm into silence. Running his fingers through his hair, he marveled at the miracle of a dreamless slumber. Shifting on the mattress, he glimpsed Maddy's body rustle beneath the covers in the predawn light. He touched her shoulder.

Opening her eyes, she stretched and yawned. "Time to go already?"

He nodded, smiling as she lolled in the sheets. Part of him wanted to capture her on film, titling the photograph "Before Sunrise."

She propped herself with an elbow and squinted. "How did you sleep?"

"I can't remember anything."

"Your experiment worked."

The lightness of relief flooded his body. *I can marry Amy*. The peacefulness flitted away like a shadow. Being with Amy meant leaving Maddy. Oh, why did he want to stay?

A slow smile dawned on her face, her teeth glowing in the faint light from the twinkling skyscrapers.

"You're cured of your night terrors."

He chuckled, bending to retrieve his prosthetic. "Are you showering?"

"No, you go ahead. I'll wait until after boot camp."

In the bathroom, he turned on the cold water and rinsed away his feelings. Dressed, he cracked open the bathroom door and brought a shaving kit to pack into a suitcase. As she stood before the window, a puddle of light illuminated her. He stared, wishing again for his camera, longing to frame the image of her Rubenesque figure against the city's lights.

A pang of loss pinched his chest. Oh, God, why was he leaving her? For a moment, he considered taking her to New York, far away from the chaos of her family, but the thought was just an idle fantasy. Her whole life was here.

She turned. A pink flush invaded her face. She crossed her arms over her bra and underwear.

"You're beautiful." He smiled. "If circumstances were different, I'd make love to you."

Narrowing her gaze, she dropped her arms to her sides. "You'd make love to *any* woman."

He snickered, shaking his head. "I'd have sex with any woman. I only want to make love to you. Don't you know the difference? Sex is physical. Making love is caring." Pivoting, he strode toward the kitchen. "Want something to eat or drink?"

"No, thank you."

The bathroom door shut, and the lock clicked. A few minutes later, she stepped out of the bathroom wearing yesterday's purple dress. She fluffed her hair with her fingers.

Smiling, he touched a stray hair and tucked it behind her ear.

She grimaced and stepped back. "I look terrible."

Why didn't she believe him when he said she was beautiful? An idea blossomed, and he grabbed her hand and directed her to the full-length mirror. He placed his hands on her waist. "You need to see what I see." He shook his head when she met his gaze. "Don't look at me. Look at you." He touched the tops of her shoulders. "See the power in your arms, the curves in your body, and the strength in your hips and legs."

With her gaze, she followed the terrain of her body. "I'm as fat and lumpy as a bad pillow."

He ran his hands down the length of her arms. "All I feel is strength." He pointed to her chest. "Look at that hour-glass figure. You're as voluptuous as Marilyn Monroe." He cupped his hands on the curve of her hips. "Don't you see you're beautiful?"

After a long moment, she softened her gaze and nodded. "I'm very feminine, that's for sure."

He placed his hands on her shoulders and sighed. *Oh, why can't I forget about Amy and just be with Maddy? I could rescue her from Darren, and we could build a future together here.* He tugged her back against his chest and breathed in the floral scent of her shampoo. "Darren's a lucky man. If he can't appreciate you as you are, then he's not worth your time. You deserve someone who loves you, no matter how much you weigh."

Wringing out of his embrace, she stepped away from the mirror. "Let's go before I ask you to change your mind."

Nodding, he grabbed the bag of food from the refrigerator. He left the keys in the bowl on the kitchen counter. Holding open the front door, he watched Maddy step outside. He handed her the bag of food and retrieved his belongings in two suitcases. Glancing around the room, a silent witness, he felt the pain and loneliness of the last six months fade away.

At the airport, he wove through clots of strangers toward the flight terminal with Maddy trailing behind him. The brisk clip of heels against linoleum and the scuff of wheels and random conversations floated around him. Jostling a few people with arms and legs, he wheeled one of the two suitcases past the crowds to the checkout counter. He sniffed a whiff of coffee from someone's travel mug and imagined Amy standing at the full-length window of their apartment, sipping her special dark brew. In a few hours, he hoped to be beside her again.

After he checked his bags, he strolled over to the security line. He stopped before the TSA checkpoint and pivoted toward Maddy. "Goodbye."

Shaking her head, she clutched his shirt with a fist. "Don't go."

For a long moment, he gazed into her misty blue eyes. "Why don't you want me to leave?"

"Because I love you." Widening her eyes, she released his dress shirt and clasped a hand over her mouth.

She looked like a little girl caught revealing a secret. "Don't worry." He peeled away her fingers and cupped her face with his hands. "I love you, too." He bent and kissed her. All at once, he felt everything—her parting lips, her soft and yielding tongue, and every curve of her body igniting all the nerves in his skin. Finally, he released her and rifled in his shirt pocket for his ID and ticket.

She seized his arm. "How can you leave after *that kiss*?"

He stared into her wild eyes and imagined pioneering a new territory of love before he realized he had no right to make that decision. "Long before we met, we belonged to other people." He steeled his back. "Yes, I've made tons of mistakes. So have you. But we can fix things and make them better. We don't have to go forward with our lives as broken people." He pursed his lips and braced her shoulders with his hands. "I'm marrying Amy. You're making things right with Darren. But we'll always have our friendship." The fear and longing in her eyes mirrored the uncertainty in his heart.

"Oh, why are you faithful now?" She moaned. "If you love me, then why did you choose her instead of me?"

"I have chosen you." He smiled. "I've chosen our friendship. Isn't that type of love enough?"

"I suppose." She shrugged.

The desperation in her eyes faded to wistfulness. *Oh, how I'll miss her*. He kissed her again. "We'll keep in touch."

She clenched a fist over her chest. "Promise?"

"Promise." Turning, he strode through the TSA line. At the end of the conveyor belt, he tucked his ID and ticket into his back pocket. Standing tall, he saluted her. "Be strong."

Smiling, she braced her legs and returned the salute. "Yes, sir, General."

He lowered his arm and strode into the crowd. If he was going home to be with the love of his life, why did his heart feel like it burst into a million pieces?

Chapter 23

At six o'clock, Maddy arrived at boot camp. A drizzle of rain dampened her shoulders, and she tugged the hood of her running jacket over her head. She jogged over to the entrance of the gym, placed her hands against the wall, and leaned into a hamstring stretch. The soreness in her legs wasn't as bad as yesterday, but tightness lingered.

Peter nodded. "Looks like your partner left you stranded."

A general never abandons his troop. Frowning, Maddy grabbed her left ankle and lifted a foot toward her buttocks, feeling a tug in her left quadriceps. "He didn't leave me. He moved back to New York to marry his fiancée."

"Good riddance." As more raindrops fell, Peter gripped the clipboard to his chest. "I feel better now he's gone. I should have never paired you together."

Releasing her left foot, she grabbed her right foot and repeated the quadriceps stretch. "Actually, I'm glad I was Greg's partner." Before changing into her workout gear, she stepped on the scale and noticed she lost another five pounds. "I'm in the best shape of my life, thanks to him."

Peter gaped. "What about me? You didn't do anything except follow my diet and exercise plans."

A slow smile spread across her face. "You didn't provide the motivation or the encouragement." She narrowed her gaze. "You only provided doubt and ridicule." She stalked toward the other recruits milling about the gym entrance, waiting for the whistle to signal the beginning of four laps. The rain pounded heavier now, splattering against the slick nylon jacket and rolling off like tears.

After the whistle blew, she bolted into the crowd. She missed Greg's warm, firm hand guiding her at the beginning of the run. Later, she missed the camaraderie of conversation, as they discussed the relevant topics affecting their lives. Focusing on her body, she remembered to practice what Greg taught her, swinging her arms forward and backward to match an alternating stride. Breathing in through her nose, she exhaled through her mouth.

When a stitch pinched her side, she slowed to a walk, keeping her body moving as oxygen pumped to her tired muscles, infusing her with the energy to try again. With a tight chest, short breaths, aching legs, and sore feet, she rounded the final lap around the gym. As she thought about the remaining four weeks of boot camp, she lifted her face toward the rain, letting the cold pellets wipe away the warm sweat on her flaming cheeks. Turning toward the gym, she entered the weight room and powdered her hands, wanting to lift heavy, wanting to prove she was strong.

****

Stopping at a florist, Greg leaped out of the taxi and asked the driver to wait five minutes. He opened the door and stepped inside a botanical oven of greenery. Dipping his head, he smelled Maddy's shampoo in a spring bouquet of wild flowers. A pang of longing squeezed his chest, and he wandered toward a bucket of white lilies, plucking the best bunch and handing it to the cashier. Sliding into the backseat of the taxi, Greg slammed the door. "Chelsea Mar Gallery."

The driver glanced up into the rearview mirror and nodded. "Are you picking up someone for a funeral?"

Greg clutched the lilies tighter. The question's dark insinuation did not dampen his mood. "No, they're bridal flowers." Smiling, he thought of Amy. She always loved lilies better than roses.

Leaning into the horn, the driver merged into the clot of New York City traffic. The honking blasted around them like dynamite, but the cars did not move.

Welcome home. Greg slumped against the seat and sighed.

During the flight, he felt overdressed in his suit and tie, but he didn't feel comfortable changing in the airport restroom. He wanted to surprise Amy, who often witnessed him in his running shirt and shorts. As they drove past a bridal store, he wondered if he should have rented a tux instead.

Setting the bouquet on the seat beside him, he removed his cell phone from his jacket pocket and sent a text to Maddy.

—Landed safely. On my way to gallery. Nervous. Wish me luck—

As the car inched through traffic, he slipped the phone back into his pocket, folded his hands in his lap, and gazed out the window. The towering skyscrapers and the scurrying people should have increased his anxiety, but all of his attention was focused on his mission.

A few moments later, his cell phone beeped. Glancing at the message, he read Maddy's response.

—Glad you're safe. No luck needed. Every woman loves a grand romantic gesture—

Smiling, he tucked the phone into his pocket and took a deep breath. He didn't want to invite anyone to witness the civil ceremony until he knew Amy said, "Yes." Panic seized his chest. What if she didn't say yes? Would he move out of their apartment and back into his mother's house on Long Island? Or would he return to Georgia and take a permanent position with LJ's law firm? Breathing into his worry, he relaxed his shoulders and remembered Maddy's encouraging words. *Every woman loves a grand romantic gesture.*

The driver glanced up into the rearview mirror. "Chelsea Mar Gallery."

Greg removed his wallet, handed the driver the fare and a tip, grabbed the bouquet, and helped the taxi driver lift his two suitcases from the trunk. The air stung with cold. Rubbing his hands together, he blew on his fingers, hoping to breathe warmth back into his skin. Wheeling his luggage onto the slick sidewalk, he strode toward the gallery, the bouquet of lilies tucked against the top of one of the suitcases.

Glimpsing his reflection in a storefront window, he winced. *I should have stopped at the apartment and dropped off my stuff. I look like an overdressed homeless man with day-old flowers. How unromantic.*

The door of the gallery was open, and he stepped

inside the warm cocoon of the lobby.

A receptionist greeted him. "How may I help you, sir?"

A flutter of butterflies launched from his stomach, and his palms sweated. "I'm here to see Amy Bartholomew, the curator."

As the receptionist flipped through the scheduling book, she frowned. "Do you have an appointment?"

Light laughter bubbled up from the exhibition halls.

Amy. He turned toward the sound.

Abandoning his luggage, he clutched the bouquet of lilies as he wandered through the light and shadows of the gallery, searching for the location of her laughter. Rounding a corner, he stopped, his breath caught in his throat.

A woman with long platinum blonde hair dressed in a black pencil skirt and red heels stood before a podium with her back to him. She bent to arrange a collaboration of nested dolls and saffron eggs with the help of a short, broad man dressed in paint-splattered T-shirt and ripped jeans.

Anger balled up in Greg's chest, and his fists shook until the scent of lilies wafted across the room. Holding his breath, he struggled against the desire to pry the two of them apart. Finally, he found his voice. "Amy."

Turning, she broke away from the exhibit. She widened her sapphire blue eyes and parted her ruby red lips. Glancing from his face to the lilies and back to his face, she lifted her hands to her chest and gasped. "Greg?"

Drinking in the sight of her, he rushed across the

hall, wrapped her in his arms, and swept her off her feet. Twirling, he buried his face against her shoulder, breathing in the sweet scent of the lilies he purchased. Tears shook his chest. When he finally released her, he handed her the bouquet and knelt down on one knee. "I know I've already proposed, but I'm asking you again. Will you marry me today at one o'clock in city hall? We can still have the big wedding in September, but I'm not falling asleep tonight without you as my wife."

Biting her lip, she glanced over her shoulder.

The man touched her upper arm and nodded. "I'll be at the studio," he whispered.

Staring, she remained silent until his footsteps disappeared. Gripping the bouquet against her chest, she turned her attention to Greg. "I received your messages."

Why did you not respond? He frowned. "Which ones?"

"All of them." She turned on her heels and paced. Pollen drifted from the lilies like fragrant fairy dust. "I didn't think you'd actually come back. After how you responded when I asked you to come to opening night, I didn't think you really wanted to be together anymore." Stopping, she shook the bouquet. "Everything always revolved around you. For years, I held onto a dead relationship. Even your mother suggested I let you go."

His mother's words coming from Amy's mouth stung twice as badly as the first time he heard her say them. "I'm sorry." Fear and dread raced through his blood, and beads of sweat dotted his forehead. Standing, he rushed to her side. "I can't let you go. Please, marry me. Today."

"That man who stood beside me just moments ago is Robert McKenzie." She crossed her arms and lowered her gaze. "I'm seeing him romantically."

Grief and disappointment plunged through him, her words like bullets. "Since when?"

She lifted her gaze. "Opening night. We've become inseparable."

Gazing into her sincere blue eyes, he collapsed inside. Of course, she was dating McKenzie. He was here while Greg wasn't.

"I hate you." After dropping the bouquet at her feet, she slapped his freshly shaven cheek. "Why did you come back?"

He lurched to the side, startled. Blood curdled away from every extremity, leaving him cold. He remembered Maddy punching his arm that first day they met, telling him he was a scoundrel for cheating on his fiancée. "Should I cancel the wedding?"

Stepping back, she shook her head. "Let me talk to McKenzie first."

Why did she need to consult her lover? He curled his shoulders to his chest, his gaze falling on the scattered lilies. Maddy said every woman appreciated a grand romantic gesture. Wasn't his return to New York big enough? He pushed back his shoulders and lifted his chin. He would not be defeated in the war for Amy's affection. "I can't compete with the thrill of new love. My love is old and worn out and thin like that tattered blanket you still sleep with at home." He inhaled. "I came back because I love you forever, and I'm never leaving again."

With the tips of her warm fingers, she rubbed the

raw cheek she previously slapped. "I love you, too, but love is not enough. I need someone who will help me raise a family, because plenty of children need a home, and, more than anything, I want to provide a home for one of them."

When he gazed into the misty tears in her blue eyes, he thought of Maddy and how much pain Darren caused her by calling her fat. He caused the same pain in Amy by not having children. "Let's adopt. I worked for a great attorney who might know someone who can fast track the process." He cupped her face with his hands. In the next two hours, she would choose either one man or the other. With a tight knot in his stomach, he hoped she would choose him. Opening his mouth, he poured his heart into her with a kiss.

She responded by wrapping her arms around his neck and ramming her breasts against him, receiving his deep and silent kisses.

When his lips finally left her mouth, he wove his fingers through her soft hair and closed his eyes, breathing the fragrance of her fruity perfume, hoping for one more chance to never say goodbye again.

Chapter 24

In the middle of a customer's call, Maddy's cell phone lit up on her desk. She grabbed the phone and stared at the caller ID.

The General.

She glanced at the clock against the wall. Why was he calling at eleven-thirty when his wedding was scheduled for one o'clock? After placing the customer's call on mute, she answered the cell phone. "What happened?"

"My hunch was right. She's seeing that artist, McKenzie." He choked on a sob. "She's not sure if she wants to marry me or not. I'll know in the next half hour."

What woman doesn't fall for the grand romantic gesture?

On the other line, the customer droned on and on, complaining.

"Hold on a second. I have to respond to this customer." She lowered the cell phone and took the caller off mute. "Have you tried logging out of your account and restarting your browser?"

"I don't see how restarting my browser will help me access the menu bar," the customer said.

"The problem is your browser," Maddy explained. "When you restart the browser, you accept the changes from the update, which allows our program to also accept the changes. Let me know when you're logged back into your account, okay?" After placing the caller on mute, she grabbed her cell phone. "Are you there?"

"Yeah, I'm here." He sniffled. "I shouldn't be calling you at work. You're busy."

"And you're falling apart." She shook her head and sighed. "I'm sorry she didn't respond the way you wanted. She must have fallen hard for this guy."

"When I walked into the gallery, they were together."

Anger bristled up her back. How dare she? But then Maddy remembered how she met Greg, who was also looking for someone else. How dare he feel upset because he caught Amy cheating when he cheated the whole time he lived in Georgia? "What will you do?"

He sighed. "Go to my apartment. Call my mother and let her know I'm back. Wait for Amy's response."

Tightness restricted her lungs. She coughed. "Are you staying in New York?"

"We'll see."

The air deflated from her lungs. *Why would he return? I have nothing. No place to live and no stable job.* In her other ear, she listened to the customer. "Greg, I need to help this customer. May I call you after work?"

"What about Darren? Aren't you picking him up at the airport?"

"No, I'm meeting him at home. I'll call you during my commute, okay?"

"Okay."

After she ended her call with the General, she felt a

sense of foreboding inch across her scalp. Why was she wrong about Amy? Didn't she know anything about women? Or was she so different she couldn't see straight?

"I've logged back into my account," the customer said. "Everything's running okay."

She jostled her attention to the caller. "Is there anything else I can help you with?"

"No, ma'am."

She glanced at the clock. Six minutes and thirty-two seconds. "Thank you for calling PerfectFit.com where romantic dreams come true." As soon as she logged out of the queue, she stood and trudged into the kitchen for a drink of water. Leaning against the sink, she folded her arms over her chest. Less than thirty minutes from now, Greg would know whether he would become a married man. She bit her lower lip to stop her mouth from trembling. She could still taste his minty toothpaste on her tongue. Why did he have to kiss her? Why did he have to go back to New York? Why did he have to change everything? Closing her eyes, she breathed in deeply, filling her lungs with oxygen, struggling to find a moment of peace.

****

Greg unlocked the door of his apartment and stepped inside the room of light. He rifled through his suitcase and removed the camera. Time to document what remained of the life he left, only to return. Focusing the lens, he snapped photographs of the naked beige walls. No pictures, no paintings. The carpet, once a luscious pile of snow white, was replaced with blonde laminate flooring. The air smelled sweet from the scent of candles. The austere furniture was strategically arranged. In the kitchen, a comparative market analysis from a local real estate agent lay on the counter. With one hand, he flipped through the photographs and pie charts of recent neighborhood sales and heaved a sigh.

What happened to his home?

In the bedroom, he sat on the edge of the perfectly made bed and ran his hand over the satin comforter. Over the years, the blood red color faded to a muted blush. After returning the gifts from family and friends after the first failed wedding attempt, he purchased the comforter.

Tears filled his eyes.

He lifted the camera. "Here's a self portrait of the artist as a broken man." Aiming the lens at his face, he pressed the shutter release button. He snapped one photograph after another until tears blurred his vision.

Setting aside the camera, he laid on the mattress. With his head on the pillow, he folded his hands on his chest and stared at the ceiling. What shape would his life have taken if he stayed in Georgia? Would he have been any happier? Would he have given his relationship with Maddy a chance?

Alone, clouds of depression scuttled across his interior landscape, casting shadows of doubt and gloom throughout his mind. *My father was right. I'm better off dead. No one loves a cripple*. He grabbed the satin comforter in his fist, remembering to breathe. *One thousand one, one thousand two...* Rolling onto his side, he grabbed his phone and called his mother.

She picked up on the second ring. "Hello?"

"It's me." He fell onto his back and stared at the

ceiling. "I've returned to New York to marry Amy."

"What about that other man?"

He closed his eyes. "You mean McKenzie?"

"She told me after Easter. She brought him to meet her family." She coughed. "I told you to let her go."

"I can't." He exhaled. "I love her. And I want to marry her. Today." Glancing at the clock on the nightstand, he calculated the time. "If you leave now, you'll arrive at city hall in time to witness our one o'clock wedding."

"What about McKenzie?"

He ran fingers through his hair. What if she chose McKenzie instead of him? "She's telling him goodbye. She'll be back in an hour."

"Is that what she told you?"

Bile lurched into his throat. How dare she parrot his dead father? He shifted on the bed and thought of Maddy. A surge of confidence powered through him. If she was here, she would encourage him to the finish line. "I must have faith."

She scoffed. "You're a fool. I'm not wasting my time for a wedding that probably won't happen."

"I don't blame you, Mom. But I'm not a fool. She will choose me."

"Call me *after* you're married. Then I will believe you."

Sadness roiled like storm clouds through him. He swallowed through the tightness in his throat. Thinking of his chronic infidelity, Amy's dalliance with McKenzie, and his mother's stubborn resistance, he circled back to his father. The thunder and lightning of anger he kept bottled inside for thirty years shattered into awareness. Tears pricked his eyes. He struggled to sit and swing his hips over the side of the bed. Gazing at his slacks, he could not tell which leg was which, although he knew. "Mom, I can't keep holding onto the past. We're all broken. Maybe not everyone is as visibly broken as I am, but none of us is perfect. Amy's not perfect. You aren't perfect. And Dad wasn't perfect." He paused, catching his breath. "I cannot win a war against my family. I have to forgive every single one of us. We're doing the best we can."

"He loved you."

Nodding, the storm clouds dispersed and a ray of hope shined through him. "I believe you. In his own twisted way, I'm sure he cared."

A long moment of silence stretched between them.

"Do you still want me to come to your wedding?"

He smiled. "Of course, I do."

"Then I'll be there. See you and Amy at one o'clock."

After the call ended, he stood and paced across the soft carpet. Picking up an old framed photograph of himself and Amy at the senior prom, he caressed the outline of their bodies with his index finger. They were young and naïve, just teenagers, pretending to know more than they could possibly conceive. When he lifted his hand, a faint impression of his fingerprint smeared against the glass.

A half hour later, the lock in the front door clicked. Heels clip-clopped against the laminate flooring.

Sinking at the edge of the bed, he waited with his heartbeat stuttering against his ribs.

Amy drifted into the room, her shoes muffled by

the thick carpet. Sitting beside him, she brushed away stray hairs from his forehead and smiled. "I spoke with McKenzie."

"And?"

She deepened her smile. "I choose you."

Relief washed over him. Exhaling, he gathered her into his arms and shifted his weight until she tumbled onto the mattress beside him. Rolling around, he chuckled until joyous tears streamed down his cheeks.

Giggling, Amy wrestled out of his arms and glanced at the clock on the nightstand. She tugged his hand. "Let's go. We don't want to be late for our wedding."

"I have one more surprise." He nuzzled close for a kiss. "My mother is meeting us there."

She frowned. "You talked?"

Nodding, he stroked her cheek. "Yes, I did. I don't know how she feels about everything, but she's coming to support us."

Amy bowed her head and sighed. "Does she forgive me for cheating?"

A pang of empathy squeezed his chest. He lifted the curtain of hair over her shoulder and tilted her chin until she met his gaze. "You aren't marrying her. You're marrying me. *I* forgive you."

Tears clouded her blue eyes. "You're a saint."

Shaking his head, he cupped her face with his hands. "No, I'm just human." Should he tell her about the woman he almost strangled in Atlanta? Trembling, he swallowed his fear. "I've struggled with being faithful, too, but I've worked on my flaws, and I'm committed to being everything you need me to be, now and forever."

For a long moment, Amy gaped in silence. Finally, she tilted her head. "How many times did you cheat?" She tightened her lips into a straight line.

He glanced away. Churning twisted his stomach. Should he have died with the truth? Lifting his chin, he met her harsh gaze. "None of that matters."

"Anyone I would know?"

Flinching at the shrill tone of her voice, he shook his head. *I should have kept quiet and lived with the lie.* "Listen, Amy. I'm a different man. Maddy changed how I think of women, including you."

She raised her eyebrows. "You had sex with Maddy?"

The exasperation in her voice and the startled look in her eyes pierced his concentration. He nervously laughed, hoping he didn't betray the longing and desire he fought against when he thought about the opportunity to start over with someone new. "No, Maddy's my friend. She helped me see how deeply I love you and how stupid I've been for running away." He smiled. The strength and power of their friendship burned in his chest. "I'll always be thankful for her help. With your permission, I'd like to keep her as a friend." He touched her face, rubbing his thumb against her moist cheek. "I'm not leaving again. I promise to be faithful. What more do you want?"

She shook her head. "I...don't...know."

Standing, he offered his hand. "Do you still want to marry me?"

She curled her fingers over his palm and rose. "Of course, I do."

Squeezing her hand, he coached his thoughts. *No matter what happens, remember to say, "I do."*
****

In the middle of the Clifton Crunch, Maddy called the General. The phone rang and rang until it clicked over to voicemail. "Just checking to see how you're doing," she said. "Please let me know you're all right."

Clutching the steering wheel, she thought about her own problems, from the changes at work to Darren's arrival at home. She glanced at the Pig-N-Chik, hungering for a platter of pulled pork. Would she ever learn to control her cravings? Or would she always fight against her emotions?

Fifteen minutes later, she drove into the parking lot and turned off the ignition. Slipping out of the car, she squinted at the drops of rain that pelted against her forehead. She hobbled into the lobby. Her thighs still ached from the Sunday run. After ducking into the elevator, she leaned against the wall and closed her eyes during the ascent. When the elevator jerked to a stop, she opened her eyes, lurched down the hallway to her apartment, and turned the key in the door.

Bright fluorescent lights greeted her. Darren stood from the couch and smiled. His broad brown body filled the room. "Hey, Beautiful."

She stopped and stared. *He didn't call me Porky.* Softness molded against her shoulders. *He called me beautiful. Greg called me beautiful. I am beautiful.* She set her purse on the coffee table. "How was your flight?"

Wrapping his arms around her waist, he tugged her into a hug. "Long and boring." He kissed her mouth. "I missed you."

Why did you keep leaving? Hardness tightened her chest. She wriggled out of his embrace. Greg's voice echoed in her head. *Give him a chance. He might surprise you.* Her grand romantic gesture failed with Amy. Why would Greg's advice work for her? She sank into the sofa cushions and studied her hands. "Our relationship isn't working. It hasn't worked for a while." She twisted off the ring. "I don't want to get married. I want to move out."

With wide eyes, he stared at the ring. "Did Greg put you up to this maneuver?"

She raised her eyebrows and clenched her hands into fists. "Greg has nothing to do with our relationship."

"Oh, yeah?" He stepped back, expanding his arms to encompass the room. "Things were fine between us before he entered your life. Now you complain about everything."

With shaking hands, she placed the ring on the coffee table next to her purse. With her elbows propped on her knees, she cupped the sides of her head with her hands and stared at a speck of lint on the carpet. She must have missed that piece of lint from the last time she vacuumed. Did Darren see the speck? Or did he no longer care whether the apartment was clean?

Her cell phone rang from inside her purse. She braced her spine, expecting a call from the General. If she answered, Darren would think Greg was more important. She didn't want to leave Darren with that impression, regardless of the truth. In this moment, she wanted to focus only on Darren.

"Is he calling?" Darren rummaged through her purse. "Why don't you take his call?" He shook the cell phone in his fist before he swiped the screen and answered, "Hello?"

She widened her gaze, her heartbeat drumming in her chest. For a moment, she wanted to seize the phone, but she sat paralyzed by Darren's unprecedented action.

"Yes, she's here." He extended his arm with the phone. "It's a woman."

A woman? She studied the softness in Darren's face. What woman would be calling her? She held the phone against her ear. "This is Maddy."

A burst of giggles erupted. "It's Amy. Greg's wife."

Wife? She trembled. He's married. Dark clouds closed around her thoughts. Why was his wife calling her?

"I wanted to thank you for helping Greg return home. He says he's a different man because of you and your friendship," she said. "We're sending you a picture from the wedding. You must visit with your family. I want to meet all of them."

"You're welcome." A ray of gratitude broke through the clouds of depression. *I'm happy for you, but I'm sad for me.* "Congratulations on your marriage. I heard you waited a long time." A delightful sigh filled the phone line.

"Thirty years."

She glanced up at Darren who stood beside her, listening. "Well, I guess there's some truth to the saying, 'Better late than never.' " She forced a smile. Why was she speaking with Amy and not the General?

Didn't he know she needed to hear his voice reassure her everything would turn out all right? "I'll talk to Darren and let you know when we can visit. Again, congratulations. Tell Greg I said hello."

"Why don't you talk to him?"

A moment of muffled shuffling crackled over the line before his deep voice boomed. "Hey, Maddy, can you believe I did it? I'm married." He lowered his voice. "Can you talk?"

She glanced up at Darren then down at her feet. "Darren's back, so I can't be on the phone much longer."

"Remember to stay strong. Don't let him bully you. State what you need and what you want, and let go of the results, okay?" He exhaled. "Remember I'm here. Call or text anytime."

"Okay, I will." Tightness squeezed her chest. Even though he was married, he was still here as her friend. She exhaled. She finally had a friend, someone outside her family, who could love and support her through any challenge. "Congratulations. We'll visit soon. Goodbye." After ending the call, she clasped the phone between her knees. *He's married. He chose her. She chose him.* She stared at her engagement ring on the coffee table. *Darren chose me. Do I choose him?*

Kneeling, Darren met her gaze. "I'm sorry. I didn't know."

Shaking her head, she tensed her jaw. "How could you? You're always jealous and protective."

The phone beeped with a message.

Turning the phone over in her hands, she studied the picture from Greg's wedding. Amy wore the frothy white gown that was two sizes too small for Maddy's short, stout frame. She blinked, and her vision blurred. After setting the phone next to her engagement ring on the coffee table, she rubbed her eyes.

Darren scooted beside her on the sofa and held her. He brushed the hair from her forehead. "What can I do to make you stay?"

Lifting her face, she soaked in the concern in his black eyes. His question sparked an opportunity. *State what you need and what you want*, Greg said. Her advice worked with Amy. Maybe his advice would work with Darren. She gulped. "I need a friend and a partner, someone who will accept the challenge to grow alongside me." She sniffed, wiping her nose with the back of a hand. "Greg helped me lose weight and feel good about myself. He's married now, and both he and his wife want us to come to New York for a visit. They invited the whole family."

"I'm sorry I was jealous." Grabbing her hand, he squeezed her fingers. "I assumed you were romantically involved with Greg." He kissed the back of her hand. "I can help you lose weight. I can be your workout partner."

Be patient. Give him time. Don't let your anger blindside you. Greg's words raced through her mind. *Give him a second chance. Let him surprise you.*

Plucking the ring off the coffee table, Darren slid the gold band on the third finger of her left hand. "What time is boot camp?"

She stared at the diamond, a symbol of commitment. Anger and disappointment loosened in her chest. She breathed in deeply. When she exhaled, she felt the burden of the last few months leave her body. She smiled. "We have to leave at five-thirty to make the six o'clock class."

Wrinkling his forehead, he groaned. "That's early."

Jabbing his side with her elbow, she winked. "Only four more weeks."

Mumbling, he nuzzled her neck with his nose.

She giggled, feeling the clouds of darkness disperse and the rays of hope shine within her. With Darren's help, she would get through boot camp. She would get through anything.

Epilogue

Eighteen months later
Atlanta, Georgia

Maddy followed soon-to-be five-year-old Collin into the dining room. Tires crunched in the gravel driveway.

Lifting the lace curtain, Collin peered outside.

A rental car drove up to the front door and parked.

Suddenly, Maddy felt her palms moisten and her heartbeat stutter in her chest. A tall, thin man with gray-streaked hair and brown eyes slipped out of the driver's side. He smiled and waved.

"They're here." Collin spun from the window and bolted toward the foyer.

Trailing after him, Maddy laughed. Even after three months of morning sickness, the churn of nausea surprised her. Unlocking the door, she gazed at Greg as he unloaded two suitcases from the rental car's trunk. Amy—a rail-thin blonde wearing a smart dress, pearl necklace, and heels—and Toby—a nine-year-old Asian boy dressed in a T-shirt, jeans, and sneakers—flanked either side of him as he walked up the steps.

"Here, let me help." Maddy grabbed the nearest suitcase.

Greg narrowed his gaze. "Shouldn't you be taking

it easy?"

"I'm not sick." She laughed, swinging the suitcase in her chiseled arm. "I'm pregnant."

Amy offered a quick hug. "Congratulations."

"Thanks." Maddy nodded toward Toby, who Greg and Amy adopted six months ago. "How've you been, big guy?"

"Fine, thank you, and you?" He tucked his arms against his body and smiled.

Toby was the perfect image of politeness, much like his adopted mom, Amy.

"I'm doing well. I survived twelve weeks of morning sickness."

Collin grabbed Toby's slender hand and tugged him up the staircase. "Let me show you my army trucks. I'm hoping to get more for my birthday tomorrow."

"Do you have any sketch pads?" Toby asked. "I like to draw."

"No, but my sister does."

Maddy flashed a smile. "Looks like they've become friends."

Footsteps shuffled against the marble floors. "Greg. Amy." Chris opened his arms. "Glad you could make it for Collin's birthday party tomorrow." He waved toward the suitcases. "Remy, take those suitcases to their rooms. Why don't we go into the parlor for a drink?"

Peering through the wall-to-ceiling windows, Amy clutched the pearls at her neck. "The whole world looks on fire with all these fall colors." She spun toward Greg and shook a finger. "I told you to bring your camera."

Greg flinched. "Sorry, I just didn't think I'd have time to take a few shots."

From the kitchen, Jane strode with a purposeful step followed by Remy who carried a platter full of glasses of iced sweet tea. She handed one to Greg and another to Amy. Hooking her hand in the crook of Amy's elbow, she nudged her aside. "You and I can go outside for a tour of the garden."

"Perfect." Amy beamed.

Standing side by side, Jane and Amy looked like sisters. Maddy winced. No matter how much weight she lost, she would never be model-thin like them. Sure, she looked better than the last time she saw Greg and his family during a visit to New York. Over the past year-and-a-half, she lost fat and gained muscle. Every ounce of her screamed fit and fabulous, but inside, she still sometimes felt like Fatty Maddy. Maybe she always would.

As soon as the women disappeared, Remy placed the empty platter in the kitchen before helping Chris with the suitcases.

Alone, Greg wrapped an arm around Maddy's shoulders and kissed the top of her head. "Where's Darren?"

"Here I am." He strolled across the foyer with a bright smile. "I helped Johanna with the cake." He extended his arm to shake Greg's hand. "Welcome back to Georgia. How was the flight?"

"Not bad." Greg released Maddy and shook Darren's hand. "Congratulations on the pregnancy."

Darren flashed a smile. "Maddy's been a trooper. She worked out through morning sickness. The doctor says she'll have to give up power lifting until the baby's born, but she can continue jogging."

Lifting his eyebrows, Greg turned toward her. "Do you want to get up early for a run? We can go to Lullwater Preserve and watch the sunrise."

A smile brightened her face. She turned toward Darren. "Would you like to join us?"

"Nah." He shook his head. "I prefer sleeping in."

Glancing around, Greg pinched together his eyebrows. "Where's Peter?"

"Don't worry. He'll be here tomorrow." Darren waved toward the parlor. "Let's have a seat and catch up."

After sinking against the hard back of a Colonial-style sofa, Greg set his untouched glass of iced sweet tea on a coaster and clasped his hands between his thighs. He pointed toward a photograph of Maddy's and Darren's wedding in Kauai last fall. "Isn't your anniversary coming up?"

Catching a glimpse of the photo, Maddy nodded. She liked the simple white dress she wore against the bronze of her skin. "In two weeks, we'll be married for one year."

Greg chuckled, shaking his head. "Time goes by too quickly, doesn't it?"

"Any snacks?" Darren offered a plate full of cheese and crackers.

"No, thanks." Greg lifted his hand.

Maddy frowned. "He doesn't eat cheese. He's vegan."

"Oh, sorry." Darren slapped his forehead. "I'll get a bowl of fruit."

As soon as Darren left, Maddy sidled closer on the sofa. "Are you ready for your next exhibit?"

He shrugged. "I've been too busy proofing legal briefs to find the time to go on photo shoots. Once I earn enough, we can buy a house in Connecticut without selling the apartment in New York, and I can slow down and just focus on my art." He pointed toward her. "How's the job search?"

"Awful." She grimaced. "Since PerfectFit.com closed its office in Atlanta, I've been stuck with only management offers in the retail sector."

Darren returned with a bowl of fruit.

She beamed. "I might stay home until the baby's born."

"I make enough for her to be a housewife." Darren sat on the other side of Maddy. "I accepted a promotion to regional sales manager. I don't have to travel very often." He patted Maddy's knee. "Works for both of us, doesn't it?"

She nodded. After the first year of being alone with Darren, she craved some space. Now, with his new job opportunity limiting travel to six times a year, a balance restored in the teeter-totter of their relationship. "He gets to see the world, and I get to see him."

"Good." Bowing his head, Greg stared at the carpet. "Everything's worked the best for all of us."

"Hey, General." Collin stood in the doorway, clutching an Army action figure. "Will you play war?"

For a long moment, he froze.

Maddy bit her lower lip. She knew Greg still struggled with PTSD, even though he learned how to deal with his anxiety without retreating from the ones he loved. His adopted son didn't care for war games, preferring the solitary pleasures of drawing and reading. But his friendship with Collin demanded a different kind of presence.

Standing, Greg slapped his thighs. "Okay, I'll play." He grabbed Collin's hand.

Maddy smiled and turned toward Darren. "Do you think he'll be the same way with our child?"

Darren lifted his eyebrows. "What do you mean?"

"Willing to get out of his comfort zone."

Tugging her into his arms, Darren laughed. "Oh, baby, don't you know by now he only tries so hard because of your friendship?"

She sighed, relaxing into Darren's warm embrace. *Just like I only run because of his.*

****

The next morning, Greg drove the rental car to Lullwater Preserve.

Maddy sat beside him, warming her hands next to the vents. "Everything is so quiet this early."

Nodding, Greg studied the faint gray streak of light against the horizon. "The best time to run." With a sidelong glance, he grinned and patted her knee. "The whole world is ours."

She giggled, cupping her fingers over his hand. "I've missed you."

Turning into the parking lot, he sighed. "I've missed you more." He tugged his hand free and maneuvered into a space beside the entrance. After opening the door, he stepped out into the brisk morning air. Breathing in, he filled his lungs with the scent of sweet licorice and decaying leaves.

Joining him, she placed her hands on the warm hood and stretched out her calves. Heavy moisture hung in the air. "Smells like rain, doesn't it?"

He nodded and leaned over into a side stretch. The muscles between his ribs ached. "If I signed up for the New York Marathon, would you run?"

"Hell, no." She scoffed. "You're lucky I can run a 5K without stopping once."

"Really?" He arched an eyebrow. "Well, I'd like to see."

She stood and broadened her stance. "I'll show you."

Scanning the length of her body, he nodded. "You're solid."

Frowning, she jabbed his side. "When will you say I'm slim?"

"Never." He chuckled. "You're big-boned like Peter. You'll never be slim."

"But I'll always be strong." She winked.

Wrapping his arms around her waist, he lifted her into the air and twirled her around once before setting her down. "I'm stronger than you now."

"Wow." She tossed back her head and widened her eyes. "Have you been lifting weights?"

Curling a bicep, he grinned. "Bench presses."

Honks and squawks ripped through the silence.

Tilting his head, he squinted at a flock of migrating ducks flying through the predawn light. As soon as the ducks disappeared, he offered his hand. "Shall we?"

She glanced into the cavernous opening beneath a canopy of white oaks, poplars, sweet gums, pines, hickories, and beeches. Slipping her hand into his, she nodded. "Let's go."

He jogged down the path, his footsteps keeping pace with hers. The crisp fall air squeezed into his lungs, and tiny clouds expelled from his open mouth. The stomp-clomp of his slapping foot and running blade sliced the atmosphere, waking woodpeckers and white-tailed deer on the hills surrounding the path.

Between huffs and puffs, she released his hand. "I want you to photograph the progress of my pregnancy."

Glancing sideways, he arched an eyebrow. "What do you mean?"

"Taking photos of my naked belly as the baby grows."

He flushed, thinking of her smooth skin stretched tight against the growing fetus. "Why choose me? I'm a landscape photographer."

"You're the *best* photographer I know." She pouted. "You're the only one I trust."

For a long moment, he considered the work from a professional point-of-view. He could expand his portfolio and maybe garner more regular business from other moms-to-be in New York, which would allow him to buy that house in Connecticut. The potential for profit and pleasure flowed through him. "Sure."

After exhaling, she grinned. "Too bad you didn't bring your camera, or we could start taking pictures today after Collin's birthday party."

"Ah, one more reason to come back and visit." Ducking beneath a low branch, he held out his hand where the road forked. "Follow me."

Clutching his fingers, she ran beside him into the gulley. "Do you ever think about what would have happened if you stayed in Georgia and I broke up with Darren?"

Tightness seized his lower back. Over the months, his attraction to Maddy subsided, replaced by a deep and everlasting caring. When she mentioned "What ifs," he ricocheted back into the tug of war of love and lust he thought he conquered once and for all. He arched his eyebrow. "Really, Strong?" A tingle of pleasure rippled through his arm and warmed his body, and he instinctively released her hand and increased the distance between them. "We resolved that issue long ago. We work perfectly the way we are."

"You're right." She nodded. "We do."

"Aren't you happy?" He loved the way her skin glowed.

"Of course, I am." She broadened her smile. "I'm married. I'm pregnant. I'm here with my best friend." She lifted her arms. "What more could I want?"

Tension uncoiled from his lower back. In the eighteen months since he left Georgia, he married Amy, resumed an old hobby, and adopted a child from Korea. The urge to escape flitted occasionally through his thoughts but never settled deep in his bones, forcing him to run. The contentment arising from a rooted life branched out into all areas, giving him a peace he thought he would never find. "I've never been happier." After he brushed sweat from his forehead with the back of his hand, he frowned. "I only wish I bonded with Toby the way I've bonded with Collin."

She lifted her eyebrows. "Amy seems to have bonded with Toby."

Laughter escaped his mouth. "They're a lot alike:

creative, thoughtful, and supportive." He ran along the dirt path in silence. A smattering of orange and gold leaves drifted to the ground where his foot crushed musty spores into the moist air. In the distance, the suspension bridge loomed above the gurgling South Fork Peachtree Creek.

"You're creative, too." She stopped as soon as she approached the ledge. "You should teach Toby how to take photographs."

"Sounds good." Why hadn't he thought of the idea? Jogging in place, he waved. "Go ahead."

Nodding, she jaunted across the narrow bridge. On the other side, she waited.

He bounced as nimbly as a gymnast across the thin wooden planks.

Turning, she powered up the hill. About a hundred yards away, the remains of a stone tower stood amongst the trees like a sentinel. She ducked into the small entrance. Leaning against the cold, rough graffiti covered stones, she gazed up through the portal into the faint pink blush of sunrise. Panting, she exhaled tiny clouds.

As soon as he entered the tower, he collapsed against the opposite wall. "I don't think I'll be running a marathon anytime soon."

She chuckled. "I'm in better shape than you."

With her flushed cheeks and vivid blue eyes, she looked like a blonde Amazonian angel. An itch twitched his fingers. Amy was right—he should have packed his camera. Excitement zipped through him when he thought of capturing Maddy's progressing pregnancy on film. He lurched from the wall and placed his hands on her shoulders. "I'm glad we stayed friends."

She tipped back her head and smiled. "Me, too."

Acknowledgements

Thanks again to Leanne Morgena and The Wild Rose Press for believing in me and in this story.

This book began as a funny chronicle of a woman's weight-loss journey and ended as a sweet tribute to friendship. I started writing Maddy's story in the summer of 2017. By October, wildfires blazed through Sonoma County. With the threat of spreading flames, mandatory evacuations forced broken families into shared homes. Tensions escalated as people jockeyed for privacy and space, loyalties suddenly divided and united in strange collaborations, forcing one to rethink the definition of family and home, having and not having, abundance and loss.

A week later, amidst the heart of the chaos, I escaped to Atlanta, Georgia, for a work seminar. Upon returning to the ruins of my city, a new character emerged. He wasn't your typical hero—strong, confident, and masculine. He was someone as broken and damaged as the main character. Writing each scene from their respective points-of-view, their parallel stories collided, and love bloomed.

Thank you, Doug Greenberg, for inspiring the creation of Greg. Your friendship has not only changed the trajectory of my story but also my life.

Many thanks to the anonymous U.S. Army Lieutenant of the Cold War who shared his experiences living with PTSD. Your stories added color to what otherwise would have been a black-and-white portrait of a wounded hero. Any errors regarding PTSD, military life, and combat are solely mine.

Thank you, Renee Hoffman, for encouraging me to tell the story I needed to tell while also keeping in mind the market. Your faith in me keeps me going. You are the light in my soul.

Thanks to Ed Turpin for sharing hundreds of stories of technical support calls he fielded before he started his own business. Continual gratitude extends to him for maintaining my website and offering professional and personal advice. Your more than thirty years of loving support are greatly appreciated.

Thanks also to Leanne Refvik who helped choose the title. I appreciate your passionate caring and honest feedback.

Most importantly, special thanks to Kevin Gross. You are the heartbeat that underlies everything I am and everything I do. You are my hero, and I love you forever.

A word about the author...

Angela Lam, formerly Angela Lam Turpin, is an American writer. She is the author of five novels, a short story collection, and a memoir.

Visit her at:

http://www.angelalamturpin.com

Another Title by this Author
The Divorce Planner

Thank you for purchasing
this publication of The Wild Rose Press, Inc.

For questions or more information
contact us at
info@thewildrosepress.com.

The Wild Rose Press, Inc.
www.thewildrosepress.com